A HERO'S PASSAGE

A HERO'S PASSAGE

J. D. LITTLE

Identifiers:
LCCN: 2022918121
ISBN: 979-8-218-08147-8 (paperback)
ISBN: 979-8-218-08148-5 (hardback)
ISBN: 979-8-218-08149-2 (eBook)

Available in paperback, hardback, e-book, and audiobook

For Sherri: You always believed I could.

CONTENTS

All the Darkness in the world cannot
extinguish the light of a single candle.

-- St. Francis of Assisi

PROLOGUE

The pain was in his chest. He had been aware of it for some time as it grew, forcing its way into his dreams. He knew it would get worse. It always did. He fought to ignore it, to hang on and hide as far away as possible. But then he knew he couldn't escape it, as the pain found its way into his dream, turning it dark. His fears grew harder to dispel until they finally overwhelmed him.

He opened his eyes to the darkness and found himself back in his bedroom. It was pitch black. *Must still be the middle of the night.* He laid still, his eyes opened wide, staring up at the slightly lighter patch that marked the featureless ceiling above him. His mind was racing like his heart.

This wasn't the first time this had happened. A few months ago, he had awoken several times in the night, gripped with the fear that his heart might explode at any moment. He had gone to the doctor. They had run all the tests, put him on a treadmill, given him an ultrasound—he had even worn a heart monitor for twenty-four hours—but they had found nothing. His heart was fine.

"Go home. Relax and stop worrying," the doctor had told him. It was just stress. His fears were driving him over the edge.

After that the attacks had stopped until now.

His heart skipped a beat. He jerked upright in the bed. It had never done that before. His mind reeled as the pain grew sharper. He propped up a pillow, leaned back against it, and closed his eyes, trying to force his heart to slow down. *It couldn't be good that it was racing like this! How many beats is a heart good for in a lifetime?* And then it skipped again.

"Shit!"

He hopped out of bed. The fear was so intense, it was like a wall surrounding him, pressing in on all sides, crushing him. He couldn't just lie there any longer.

The dog moved, and he patted her head. "It's okay, girl," he lied.

He opened the bedroom door and moved out into the living room, where a small lamp was shining in the far corner. The welcoming patch of light seemed to call, *come to me!* Instead, he picked up a blanket and pulled it tightly around himself. He was freezing, so cold that his teeth were chattering.

He glanced down at his chair, but though his legs were shaking and weak, he couldn't simply sit. He had to keep moving. He started to pace; he always paced anytime he needed to think or was a tad nervous. He plodded on through the living room, past the couch, and into the kitchen, all the way to the far wall. Then he turned and reversed the path back to the starting point. His mind absorbed in thought, oblivious to his surroundings. *Were the doctors wrong?*

The pain grew stronger, almost overwhelming. It was centered in his chest like a sharp knife cutting deep into his vitals. His hands started to shake. He was still cold, even with the blanket pulled around him. His whole body was shaking now.

This must be it—the End.

Should I call someone? Could they even get here in time? And if I'm wrong? If it's just another panic attack, I would be so embarrassed, the little boy yelling wolf.

But what if I'm not wrong? Maybe it's too late already? Am I about to die? Pass through that final veil and learn the answer, to what lies beyond! Will I meet God?

Was He even real?

Or were the others, right? The atheists and all the rest. Was this life really all there was? No God, no heaven, no hell. Nothing but this mortal coil? Was everything you witnessed, everything you did, everything you ever thought or dreamed of, gone in a puff, like a wisp of smoke in the wind? Was it as if you never existed, the moment your brain stopped functioning?

What was the point of life then?

You were born, you lived, you learned, you loved. All gone in a flash! You might as well not be. And, what of all those tales about changing the hero by showing him what life would have been without him? It didn't matter; nothing did in the end! Good or bad, happy or sad. Nothing we did would ever mean anything if it just vanished. Are our lives more than mere words on a page? Are we no different from a squirrel crushed under the wheels of a passing vehicle?

But if that was true, why struggle? If, in the end, none of it matters, then why fight? Just give in and accept whatever fate has in store for you.

But they weren't right! They just couldn't be.

He had always believed in God, and now he clung to that belief. He felt deep down he had a soul, and it would live on after death.

Besides, he had proof of a sort—if you could call it that. He had seen it, the wispy image of Tina standing beside the bed in California, days after they had laid her to rest in Arkansas. He had known instantly who she was, standing there in the dark, and why she was there. They had been very close growing up, and her murder had hit him hard. But when he saw her beside the bed, he knew she was there to show him it was all right. It was as if she was saying, "You can relax, let it go. I'm in a better place now, and no one will ever hurt me again."

So, if Tina's spirit had been there that night in the darkness, there had to be life after death. It was the only explanation that made any sense. And if Tina still existed after death, he would too. He believed that with all his being. He had to, for it was all he had left.

The pain flared, his knees grew weak, and he collapsed into the easy chair. He pulled the blanket tighter. Cold—he was so cold.

"God, help me, please!" he whispered.

I know you have no reason to; I've never given you one, not in all my life. I've always meant to put you first, but there was always something else—the kids, the game, the job that somehow got there before you. I felt you in the pit of my stomach each time I looked at a beggar on the street corner, but then, the light would change, and I would go on with my life, the beggar's plight forgotten.

No, I don't deserve your help, your grace, but still, please be kind when I stand before you. See that I am but an imperfect man, made in your image, a pale copy of the original full of fears and doubts, with a thousand questions and no patience to wait for the answers. I know you understand that I only see a hint of your vision. I've struggled with my desires and refused to submit to your will or to accept your plans for me, though I know they are far beyond anything I have ever dreamed of for myself.

But all that was useless now, as he sat waiting for death to claim him. It was all such a waste—his life, his dreams, all the things he could have done, if only.

The light in the corner seemed to grow brighter, or was it that the world around the lamp grew darker? All the darkness in the world, focused in one point. His eyes locked on the lamp. He felt the dog jump up into his lap, drawing closer as if to comfort him. He heard her whining in fear. He wanted to comfort her but didn't have the strength.

A door opened somewhere. A hand touched his, and warmth flowed into him for a moment before the cold reclaimed him.

"Oh, my God! What's wrong?" a familiar voice called out from the dark. A set of eyes, dark brown and full of tears, came into focus before him. He could see the fear in them.

Surely the Lord is my salvation. I will trust and not be afraid. The Lord Himself is my strength and my defense. He has become my salvation.

"Yes, something is wrong with my father," another deeper voice said from beyond the light, the fear plain as it faltered.

I am the resurrection and the life. Whoever believes in me, though he dies, yet shall he live.

The trembling faded away. The light grew brighter still, the world dying around it. Maybe the brightness was the reason tears flowed across his cheeks, but maybe not. Suddenly, the cold was gone as the light flowed into him. The pain disappeared. He felt warm and at peace as the light claimed him and all that he was.

My Lord, I am ready.

PART ONE

A NEW LIFE

CHAPTER ONE
DENIAL

The light was hard in his face, shining straight down from above, but the world remained black all around him. His head felt like it was splitting in two, the pain radiating out from the back, but that didn't seem right. He seemed to remember the tightness and the pain being in his chest.

He tried to move, and though it seemed impossible, the pain swelled even higher, and he collapsed back into his cocoon of darkness.

He remained still, hoping for the pain to fade and his vision to return. Slowly, his eyes began to adjust to the sharp contrast between the light above and the darkness below. As they did, the world finally came back into focus, but it wasn't the world he had expected. Instead of his comfortable living room, he found himself sprawled on a cold floor surrounded by huge wooden crates stacked high above him.

He craned his neck and tried to make sense of what he was seeing, but he quickly grew drained and surrendered again to the pain. His head thumped against the deck. The strange world around him exploded into a million pieces, forcing him to close his eyes to shut out the pain.

Where was he? How had he gotten here? He tried to remember what had happened and struggled to concentrate on his last memories, but nothing came. His mind was empty; his memories gone.

Fighting panic, he jerked open his eyes, and the world around him spun out of control. Then gradually, one of the nearby crates wavered into focus. He blinked hard several times, and a series of shapes stenciled in black finally stopped moving. He tried focusing his attention on them and slowly realized they were letters or numbers and decided they must mean something. Still, it was impossible to dredge anything up from his pain-wracked brain.

I should know this, he thought. He was sure they were words, simple ones even, yet he couldn't decipher them. It was as though a fog had rolled in, blanketing everything that had once been crystal clear.

Then, as if someone flipped a switch, his mind snapped into gear, and he easily read the label.

American Red Cross, Medical Instruments
Destination: Liverpool, England
Gross weight: 1,252 pounds

Why in God's name was he in a warehouse? He had been lying in bed when the pain started. He recalled the light flaring in the living room. It had seemed to be reaching out for him as if to claim him. Now, somehow, he was here. Wherever here was.

He tried sitting up. The pain flared again, almost forcing him back down into the darkness. He slowly slogged his way up through the pain, and finally, it receded to a tolerable level. He then tried to examine his surroundings, but his head began throbbing. It felt like it was about to burst, and he clamped his hands around his head, trying to hold the pending explosion at bay.

The pain gradually receded.

Finally, he recovered enough to start looking around again. He immediately noticed the floor was metal, as were the walls. And while he knew most warehouses had metal walls, he'd never heard of metal floors.

Blinking into the light above, he saw it wasn't a light at all. Instead, it was a large square opening in the ceiling with the clear blue sky beyond.

What kind of warehouse has a hole cut in the roof?

"But maybe this isn't a warehouse after all?" he mumbled aloud.

His eyes picked out a few cumulus clouds drifting leisurely across the sky. It was a beautiful day. The opening was at least thirty feet above his head. *That's awfully high.* Then he noticed a second deck about two-thirds the way up. *A deck? Why do I keep thinking of it as a deck instead of a floor? Decks are on ships.*

More importantly, why was he lying in the middle of the deck in pain? What could explain that? None of this made any sense. The last thing he remembered was sitting with his daughter-in-law—doing what? Damn, he couldn't remember!

What the hell is going on? Did I have a stroke? he wondered. "It could be a stroke." *But in a warehouse? Why am I in a warehouse? And how did I get here?* He recalled looking for something. *That can't be. I don't even belong here. How could I be looking for something? Maybe it's just a bad dream?*

That's it. He was dreaming. He was now talking aloud to keep himself calm. "Pinch yourself and wake up." He tried it. "Ouch." He shook his head, and another wave of pain engulfed him. "Crap! Don't move your damn head," he scolded himself.

This was no dream. That pain was too real.

He suddenly remembered seeing fear in a pair of brown eyes. That was real, too. Nothing was making any sense. *Start with the basics*, he told himself. *If this is real, how did I get here? But more importantly, how do I get out of here?* He suddenly realized he couldn't see any windows or doors.

With a growing sense of fear, he reached out for the nearest object, the crate marked Red Cross, and using it as a crutch, he levered his way to his feet. His head once more felt like a toy top, spinning around, and all he could do was hold on. He knew if he let go, he would splat against the steel walls.

Bit by bit, the spinning slowed, and the world steadied. He once again felt the bedrock beneath his feet, or maybe that was the wrong term. He could feel the ground moving and realized with a start that he might be on a ship!

Looking around, he noticed a pattern in the walls. They were flat panels, not corrugated, like most warehouses, and they overlapped with lines of rivets holding them together. It looked exactly like the Titanic in those old movies.

They don't build them like that anymore, he thought. "I've got to get out of here," he whispered.

He finally spotted a ladder over on the far side of the compartment. If there were no windows or doors on this level, he would just have to try another. He started moving toward the ladder—or at least that was the idea—though he only managed to get a few steps past the Red Cross crate before he had to stop. He leaned hard against another pallet his eyes refusing to focus, the world once more spinning out of control.

"Just breathe. Slowly now, one, two, three," he counted, forcing himself to relax. His vision eventually cleared, and a pool of bright red came into focus on the floor at his feet. That couldn't be blood! Could it?

"Oh, my God," he croaked, and his right hand flew to the back of his head. "Ouch!" He pulled his hand away, and it was covered with the same red color. "Damn." No wonder he felt like shit. It was a miracle losing that much blood hadn't killed him. He chuckled softly. It sounded different from how he remembered his laugh, lower-pitched. It had to be the acoustics.

"Now for that ladder." Even his voice sounded a little odd, now that he thought about it.

Pushing himself off the pallet, he staggered toward the base of the ladder. He came up hard against it, bumping his head as he did so. He was starting to get a little better at this moving around—well at least he didn't almost pass out this time.

Leaning back, he looked up the twenty feet or so to the deck above. Could he climb that far without losing his balance? Doing that would put him right back down here, maybe with a broken neck, this time.

Was that it? Yes, it had to be. It explained his headache, the blood, the back of his head. He had fallen from up there. *Damn! That's a long way down.*

He tried to remember falling, but it was still a complete blank. It felt as though it had happened to someone else. Everything from sitting in his living room until he woke up here had vanished. How long ago was that? An hour or a year? He had no idea. Why was he here on a ship and not in a hospital? The only thing he could remember was those big brown eyes filled with fear. Who was she? It seemed he should know her, but he couldn't even remember her name—much less his own, for that matter!

He panicked as he realized he didn't know who he was.

He searched his memories. It felt like he was a child running wild in a library, but the shelves were all empty. All the books were gone. His entire life wiped clean like the blackboard in a classroom at the end of the day.

All he could remember was that woman's eyes and the pain. Oh, God, that pain, shooting out from his heart. It felt like an elephant was standing on his chest, but that was wrong. The pain was in his head, not his chest. He suddenly felt the impact, the lance of white-hot pain exploding through the back of his head.

He moaned, a long low sound filling the compartment around him and reaching to the open air above. "Is anyone up there?" he cried. "I need some help. Please, help me." God, please let there be somebody up there!

"Someone, help me, please," he shouted as loud as he could. But no one answered. No one was about. Where in the hell was he? Where could all the people be?

"I guess I'll just have to do it myself." He was having a full-blown conversation with himself. He'd heard that was a sign you were losing it. "Well, who wouldn't be?" Yup, he was losing it.

He grabbed the rung of the ladder just above his head and took his first step up. *One step at a time*, he thought to himself. He started coaching himself. *Take it easy. All you have to do is just take one step at a time.*

He climbed a second rung and glanced down at the deck below. It was working. He took another step and then another.

Too fast! A wave of vertigo hit him. His left hand slipped off the ladder, his arm beginning to windmill as he fought to keep his balance. Then, just as quickly, the dizziness vanished, his strength returned, and he grabbed hold of the rung again, steadying himself. He pulled himself tight against the ladder, hugging it to his chest, his heart racing.

Closing his eyes, he thanked God for small favors.

He reminded himself to go slowly.

Keeping his eyes level, he climbed one more step, giving himself a break afterward. Yes, that was what he needed, a pause between each step, time to recover from the effort, and for the spinning to slow down a little before he attempted the next rung.

Even with those precautions, he began to grow worried, for, after each step, it took him a little longer to recover. Longer for the spinning to slow and for his strength to return. *How many more steps are there?* He didn't dare look to see, afraid of losing his grip again and ending up back down on the floor.

Then his eyes cleared the edge, and he peered out over the upper deck. *Thank God!* He wrestled himself up and over that edge and onto the deck, where he laid still for a moment to catch his breath.

Standing, he turned to face the compartment and slowly studied it from this new angle. It was vast and nearly empty, unlike the deck below. He guessed it was at least fifty feet in each direction with steel walls on all four sides. He realized this was the 'tween deck," called that because it was between the deep hold below and the main deck above. From here, he could see that the lower level was almost full of wooden crates arranged in neat stacks rising to just short of the underside of the deck on which he stood. A few narrow passages had been left to allow for some movement between the rows of cargo. He was in a hold, the crates were cargo, but don't they ship freight in steel containers? So why all the wooden boxes?

He noted that the level he was on was only half as tall as the lower one, but it had the same large hatch overhead. Only a few crates had been stacked and braced on this level, and he somehow knew that was why the hatches were still open. There was more cargo coming.

Then twenty feet away to his left, he saw what he was searching for—a hatchway. It was the standard naval type, metal with latches (or dogs, in Navy parlance) in all four corners and a knee-knocker below. Knee-knocker, now that was a naval term. Where had he learned that one? Not too many would know what it was, but of course, anyone who ever caught their shin on one would never forget it. He had to be on a ship. But how had he gotten here? And how had he ended up at the bottom of a cargo hold? *Hell, it had been years since—since what? Since he—* Damn it! He almost had it! Shit! It was gone again. Everything was blank once more. The fog thick as pea soup.

But still, for some reason, this place and everything around him seemed familiar. As if he had been here before, and yet, he was also sure he didn't belong here. How could that be? Familiar and not? As though he was two people.

He took a deep breath, tried to steady his nerves, and pushed off the rail, swerving his way across the deck in the general direction of the watertight door. After a couple of course corrections along the way, he grabbed one of the dogs and pulled himself up against the cold metal door. He then knocked each of the four dogs off, one after another, and pulled the heavy door open. It squealed in protest on hinges long overdue for a meeting with a grease gun. Stepping up and over the knee-knocker, he entered a dimly lit passageway. A single low-voltage bulb burned inside a wire safety cage high on the bulkhead at the far end. Two more watertight doors, one on each side, opened into the passageway, and a set of stairs (or in seaman's parlance a ladder or companionway) directly under the dim light led up to the deck above.

He worked his way down the passageway, leaning hard against the bulkhead for the necessary support. It seemed he was defaulting to nautical language—deck instead of floor and overhead, bulkhead, and ladder instead of ceiling, walls, and stairs. Only a seaman would do that, right? Yet he wasn't a seaman, was he? He was still drawing a blank.

At the end of the passageway, he glanced up before he started climbing the ladder, one rung at a time. It was hard going; the ladder was very steep, but at least it wasn't straight up and down like the first one.

He eventually reached the top and found another landing, this time with standard doors—no dogs or knee-knockers. Both were locked, and he had no choice but to continue on down the passageway. He knew he was growing weaker with each step. If he didn't find some help soon, he wasn't sure how much farther he could get on his own. *Will anyone find me down here if I pass out?*

It took a couple of minutes before he recovered enough from climbing the ladder to continue. He had to find someone. Like a drunk, he staggered on toward the light that filled the end of the passageway. Somewhere he heard voices and music. He could swear it was Harry James' trumpet, but he couldn't tell where it was coming from. The sounds just seemed everywhere and nowhere all at once.

It wasn't any help. There was nothing he could do but keep going.

At the end of the passageway, he stepped out into bright sunshine. He was right! It was a ship. He took in his surroundings. A single mast stood tall in the center of the deck. It was a well deck, surrounded by superstructures fore and aft and four-foot-high bulwarks port and starboard. It was also obvious he was at the stern of the ship due to the general layout of the area. A pair of large hatches were cut into the deck, one before the mast and the other aft of it. Both stood open wide to the blue sky above. Several booms were latched to the mast, and they were poised above the open holds, held in tension by heavy steel wire wrapped around numerous pulleys. Each boom was anchored at one end to a deadeye near the top of the mast and at the other end to one of the four large winches which sat in a circle around the base of the mast.

The ship was berthed bow in, starboard (or right) side to the pier. A two-story warehouse stood parallel to the vessel in the center of the pier, and several sets of railroad tracks ran along the dock between the warehouse and the ship. The warehouse was lined with large overhead doors, most of which stood open, revealing neat rows of crates and sacks staged within, ready for loading onto either a ship or a train.

The well deck and the pier were empty without a soul in sight. Nothing moved. Was it a ghost town as well?

No, that was wrong. There were birds—hundreds of them— in constant motion. Flocks of seagulls, crows, and blackbirds wheeled in formations against the blue sky, some diving into the chop of the harbor, others sunning themselves, eating, or jostling with each other for a better position to watch the never-ending show playing out all around them. At the fantail, a red flag with a Union Jack in the upper right-hand corner drifted in the light breeze, a Red Duster, the flag of a British merchant ship. Why would he be on a British ship?

Then a tugboat puffed past, heading upriver. *How do I know it's going upriver?* The current. He could see the water flowing in the opposite direction. The tug was fighting the current, beating its way upriver, past the docks.

He crossed the deck to the outside bulwark, and as he did so, the view of the harbor opened before him. He stopped dead in his tracks and stared at the scene before him.

"Oh, my God," he said in a barely audible whisper.

He knew this place! It could be nowhere else but New York. He had seen it in a thousand photographs and hundreds of movies—enough to recognize it instantly, even though he had never been here in person. He could see the Brooklyn Bridge and the Empire State building beyond in the distance, then he noticed Battery Park and lower Manhattan across the dirty flood that was the East River, and off to his left, out in the middle of the bay, the Statue of Liberty. She stood unmoving in all her green glory as a menagerie of ships slowly steamed by.

He had seen this visual previously, but it still seemed wrong, like so many of the other things he had come across since waking up below. While he shouldn't be anywhere near New York City—after all, he lived in Texas—where did that come from—something about this place wasn't right. It wasn't complete; a lot of the buildings seemed to be missing. And the boats were all old-fashioned with smoke pouring black from their tall, thin stacks. It was as if he were watching a movie of New York from the 1930s or maybe the 1940s. But of course, that couldn't be. Could it?

"Mister Ross, there you are," roared a voice from behind him. He turned around and found a mountain of a man standing in the same hatchway from which he had recently emerged.

"Mister Ross, are you okay?" the mountain asked, concern appearing on his face as he peered across the deck at the other man.

"Are you talking to me?"

"Aye, sir," the mountain replied as he started across the deck. "No one else around."

"But my name's not Ross."

"That's not funny, Mister Ross." The mountain stopped in front of him.

"Not trying to be. But I'm not Ross. My name is—" What was his name? He tried again to remember. "What is my name?" He looked up at the mountain. "And who are you?"

A sudden wave of dizziness washed over him, and only the quick reaction of the mountain saved him from hitting the deck face first.

"Bloody hell, Mister Ross! What did you do to yourself?" the mountain exclaimed as he noticed the mat of blood-soaked hair on the back of Mister Ross' head.

The mountain then glanced back over his shoulder and roared, "Red! Get your ass out here, on the double."

"Keep your shirt on, boss. I'm coming," called another vaguely familiar voice in a thick Irish brogue. A moment later, a leprechaun with tree trunks for arms stepped through the hatchway, his short, cropped red hair catching the sun. He took one glance at the scene before him, and his manner instantly changed. He became all business, crossing the deck in a flash to help the injured man.

"What happened?"

"Don't know. Just found him like this," the mountain replied. "Help me get him to sickbay, will you?"

Red nodded. He grabbed the man on the side opposite the mountain, and they started forward. The mountain glanced at Red as he asked, "How did you hurt yourself, Mister Ross?"

"Not my name," the injured man managed in a whisper.

"What was that?" Red asked.

The mountain shook his head. "He's all messed up. Says his name is not Ross."

"I don't doubt it. It's a wonder he can talk at all. Must have banged his head but good, what with all this blood."

"Do you remember how you got hurt?" The mountain tried again.

Shaking his head, he thought, *they still believe I'm this Mister Ross, whoever he is, but I know better.* While he couldn't remember who he was, at this moment, he knew it wasn't Mister Ross because Mister Ross obliviously belonged here, and he didn't. But he had no strength left to fight. So, he just let them carry him across the well deck to the starboard side ladder, up one deck, then forward past the engineer's berthing, the stack and number three hatch, and on into the starboard passageway in the forward house. By now, he was past wondering how he knew all that. Maybe they were right after all, about him being this Mister Ross.

The mountain opened a door on the port side of the passageway and flicked on an overhead light within. Moving sideways, the three men entered the compartment, and the mountain and Red helped him on to the lone bunk, which ran fore and aft against the inside bulkhead. He felt himself sink into the crisp white sheets spread upon the thin mattress, but even that poor excuse for a bed was a godsend to him.

"There you go, sir. Just lay there and take it easy. We'll get the captain down here in a jiffy," the mountain said.

Leaving Red to finish getting the injured man settled in, the mountain stepped out into the passageway. "Sing, you in here?" he roared.

A second later, a short, heavy-set, Chinese man in his early fifties dressed in dungarees and a white top popped around the corner. "I'm here, Mister Bailey," he said with a quick bow.

"Now, how many times do I have to tell you to cut out that garbage? This here is a ship in His Majesty's Merchant Navy, and I'm just one of the worker bees. Save all that shit for the officers."

There they go again! His Majesty's? It's been Her Majesty's since 1951, or was it '52?

"Yes, Mister Bailey. I forgot," the Chinese steward said, and he almost bowed again before catching himself, then glanced sheepishly at Bailey.

"Shit, Chinaman," Bailey said, shaking his head, "I give up. Never make a proper seaman out of you."

"No, Mister Bailey," Sing replied with another bow.

"To hell with it. Get the captain. Tell him, Mister Ross is hurt bad."

The steward then looked at the injured man for the first time. His eyes opened wide as he took in the blood, the pale complexion, and the vacant expression. "Yes, yes, I go quick," he said with a bob of his head. He disappeared before Bailey could react.

"I told you, I'm not Mister Ross," the injured man said as he struggled to stand up.

"Just relax, Mister Ross," Red chimed in from beside the bed as he tried to hold the man down, but the injured man refused to give in this time.

Rising to his full height, he spelled it out. "I'm not this Mister Ross. I'm not sure who I am, but I know I'm not Mister Ross."

Then he stopped, all the fight gone in an instant as his eyes locked on the reflection in the mirror above the sink on the opposite bulkhead. The change was so sudden and complete that both Bailey and Red took an involuntary step back, shocked by the transformation. They glanced at each other and then at the injured man as he continued to stare, unblinking, at the image in the mirror.

He slowly stepped away from the bed, only catching himself from crumbling onto the deck with a hand to Bailey's shoulder. He hobbled on by, his eyes never leaving the mirror. Finally, he stopped directly in front of the sink, both his hands hooked on the rim for support.

This can't be! It just can't be. The universe was suddenly adrift, and the world flipped upside down. Nothing was as it should be—not even the face in the mirror!

CHAPTER TWO

ANGER

The man in the mirror was younger, maybe in his mid-thirties, with a lighter but still solid build, a man who worked for a living. His nose was bent, probably broken at some point. The hair was lighter, almost sandy, the eyes gray instead of his regular brown, the lips fuller, and he was clean-shaven. In all, it was a strong face, handsome by some standards, but it was not his face.

"This isn't right."

"What isn't, Mister Ross?" Red asked.

"That's not me!" he cried, pointing at the face in the mirror. But the lips were moving, and his words were coming out of that mouth. "It's got to be a dream. A dream, that's it. I'm dreaming. This is all a bad dream."

"Mister Ross?" Bailey looked a little spooked, "Are you alright?"

"Hell, no, I'm not all right. I don't know who I am, where I am, and now it seems I'm not even me anymore."

Red took a step back.

"Mister Ross, you're scaring the help," Bailey whispered.

"Good, I like the company."

He continued to stare at the image in the mirror, studying it. "You called me, Mister Ross. Who is Mister Ross?"

"Not funny, sir."

"I'm not trying to be. Who is Mister Ross? What does he do?"

"You're the chief officer, sir."

"Chief officer." So, he was the ship's senior deck officer, second in command below the captain. "Me."

"Right, sir. You came on board a couple of weeks ago in Charleston after our Mister Stokes broke his leg."

"It does seem we are having a run of bad luck with chief officers lately, doesn't it?" chimed in a new voice from beyond the doorway.

He dragged his attention away from the mirror and turned to meet the newcomer, an older man, fiftyish with gray hair and a slight slouch in the shoulders, wearing a faded blue jacket with four tarnished gold rings on each sleeve. He also noticed the curl in the top stripe, the standard British mark of a deck officer. This was the captain, the man the steward was sent after. One look into those eyes, and you knew you were in good hands; he was the very picture of a ship's captain, one with many years of experience.

Suddenly it all made sense—the accents, the executive curl, the Red Duster at the fantail. This was a British merchant ship. Things were starting to fall in line! But still, what was he doing here, and why did he have a different face?

Then a new thought occurred to him, "But why am I here," he began, "an American, aboard a British ship?"

"Afraid, there aren't too many qualified British first mates lying around in Charleston just waiting for some fool to break his leg." the captain answered. "But you know that already."

"Maybe not. Seems he's a little confused right now, Captain. Busted his head wide open, he did," Bailey supplied.

"Did he, now?" The captain replied as he slipped into the compartment for a closer look. "How in the hell are you even on your feet?" he asked as the amount of damage registered. "Sit down before you collapse," the captain ordered as he slipped an arm around the injured man and helped him back onto the rack. Grateful for the help, the injured man collapsed on to the bed without a fight as his head began spinning once more.

"Bailey, get the kit out. Red, you get me some wet towels. I need to clean him up first."

"Aye, aye, sir," they both answered and hopped to.

With the wet towels, the captain proceeded to clean the wound. It took three good-sized ones to remove most of the blood and allow the captain to examine the injury at last.

"Busted the skin wide open. Bailey, get a needle and some thread ready. I'm going to have to sew this up, but there doesn't seem to be any damage to the skull. Good thing you have a hard head." Then glancing toward Red, he said, "Here, take the keys and get some iodine out. I'll need to kill the germs first."

Red took the proffered keys and opened a metal cabinet on the forward bulkhead. "Where would it be?" he inquired in barely recognizable English.

"Top shelf, port side."

"Aye." He handed the glass bottle of dark liquid to the captain, who poured half the contents onto a clean towel and started to coat the back of the injured man's head.

"And get me a pair of scissors. Got to remove some of this hair, too. Afraid it will spoil your good looks for a while, Frank." The captain instinctively used the man's given name to help him relax.

This is all wrong. I can't be this Mister Ross, but these people do seem familiar. Could I be wrong? That would make sense; after all, I am in his body. And if I am in his body . . . But what of my memories? I remember another face and another place—a whole other life. Suddenly, a pair of frightened eyes flashed before him for a moment. It was so real it took his breath away.

Seeing his reaction, the captain said, "Sorry, Frank. I've got nothing for the pain. You will just have a screw up your courage and take it like a man."

My name is Frank?

Frank nodded, and the captain took it as permission and began to sew the back of Frank's head together with no more concern than he would have had if it had been an old torn shirt he was mending. Each time the needle bit into Frank's scalp, it felt like a hot lance shot through his head, but somehow, he suppressed the desire to scream the top of his head off. It would be kind of counterproductive anyway since the captain would just have to sew it back on. The other men silently marveled at his fortitude.

Bailey, for one, had to admit to himself that the Yank was a little tougher than he had judged him in these last few weeks. Yes, he knew his job, but for anyone to just sit there, with a small twitch in his cheek being the only sign that he was having the back of his head sown together, was a performance few could manage.

A dozen times the captain passed the needle through one side and out the other, producing a neat little row of tight zigzags, all shipshape and Bristol fashion.

"There. All done," the captain said, dropping the bloody needle and its remaining thread onto the steel tray Red had placed beside Frank.

"What now?" Red asked.

"Well," the captain searched his mind trying to remember if he had missed anything from the first aid instructions, he had read years ago. "Please, get Mister Ross some aspirin. And then help him to his cabin. Sleep is always the best medicine in the long run. Be right as rain in the morning." The captain tapped Frank on the back before he exited the compartment. "Don't worry about anything else right now, Frank," he ordered. "Just go get some sleep."

"Aye, sir," Frank responded automatically.

"Bailey, you go get Mister Stratton. Tell him I want to see him right away in my cabin," the captain finished as he walked away down the corridor.

"Right, sir," Bailey called after the captain, then turned back into the room. "Red, after you get Mister Ross all settled in, get back aft. About time to turn to, and I guarantee the rest of those goldbricking apes are just messing around waiting for someone to show up and tell them what to do like they never loaded a ship before."

Red acknowledged the order as he reached into the still open medicine cabinet and picked up a bottle half full of aspirin. "Should I lock this back up, boss?"

"What do you think? And don't you go helping yourself to anything either."

"Who me?" Red panned as he closed the door and slipped the lock back into place.

"Red! Stop clowning and get a move on," Bailey ordered from beyond the doorway, already on his way to find Mister Stratton.

Red moved over to the bed. "Here we go, sir." He helped Frank to his feet. "Get you right to bed, we will."

As Frank reached his feet, his head began to spin again, ready to take flight. The pain was a constant throb now, and he closed his eyes, trying to suppress it.

"Could you please get me some water so I can take that aspirin now? My head is killing me."

"Right. No problem, sir." Red glanced over his shoulder longingly at the retreating bosun. Then, easing Mister Ross back down, he marched over to the sink to get the water.

As Frank's eyes followed Red, something caught his attention. An old calendar hung on the bulkhead next to the medicine cabinet. He had seen it earlier but had paid no attention to it. It was a simple calendar of the type put out in the thousands as advertisements by businesses all around the world; this one was for a ship's chandler in Plymouth, England. Its best feature was a poor-quality painting of a sailboat caught in the wind racing across an open bay, blue skies behind it. But it wasn't any of that which had captured and held Frank's attention. No, it was the date printed in large type right below the sailboat. April 1941.

"Is that right?" Frank asked, pointing at it.

Red glanced at the calendar. "No," he said, reaching up and tearing the next couple of pages off. "I guess no one has been in here in a while. There you go. June 11th."

"The year. Is the year, right?"

"Mister Ross, how hard did you hit your head?"

"Just answer the damn question," Frank demanded.

"Of course, it's right. Nineteen forty-one," Red replied.

Nineteen forty-one! It's nineteen forty-one? How in the hell is it nineteen forty-one? This has got to be a dream. Nineteen forty-one. I wasn't even born in forty-one.

Red took hold of Frank's elbow. "Now, come on, Mister Ross, let's take our pills and go to bed."

He jerked away. "No! You don't understand. This isn't right. I don't belong here."

"A little late for that, Mister Ross. We sail in a few hours."

"I don't mean that. I mean, I don't belong in forty-one," Frank said, pleading with the seaman. *Someone has got to believe me!*

"Okay, I'll play along. When do you belong? I've always been partial to old Napoleon me-self. Square riggers and all. Men were men then, and women were women, if you know what I mean, sir."

"No! Not the past. The future."

"Great, always liked Buck Rogers. Be great to sleep through this war and wake up five hundred years in the future."

"War? What war?"

"You know the war. Against Hitler and the Nazis."

"Of course, World War II. June of forty-one. France has fallen. The U.S. is still neutral. Have the Germans attacked Russia yet?"

"Attacked Russia? Why would they? Hitler signed a treaty with old Joe and carved up Poland between them. It's what started this whole damn thing in the first place."

"Yes, that was just a—" Frank stopped and glanced at Red. *He's humoring me. Doesn't believe a word of it. Would I believe me in his place?*

Frank crossed back to the sink, hands on the rim once more, his eyes studying the face in the mirror. "That's not me." But it was. The proof was staring back at him. The calendar, the people, the face; it couldn't be right. "Maybe it's all a dream? And I'll wake up in the morning, and it will all be gone." He turned back to the room. "But what if it is real? Just imagine? A chance to live in nineteen-forty-one, to be a part of it. Wouldn't that be something?"

"Right, Mister Ross. My old man, he talked about the Great War. The trenches, the machine guns mowing the men down, those mustard gas attacks. More like a nightmare if you ask me. Hoped it would skip a generation or two this time around. So much for wishing."

Frank looked at Red, for the first time, at all the details in this compartment, all the other ones he had been in so far. It was too much. He had a sinking feeling in the pit of his stomach. There was way too much detail; this couldn't be a dream. Can't be. How could his mind create all this in a flash? That was what a dream was, right? A flash in his brain, over in a few seconds.

He turned back to the sink, turned the water on, and began to douse his head with handful after handful. *Wake up. Please wake up, damn it!*

Red retreated a couple of paces, wondering if it was catching.

The water was cold, refreshing, but it didn't wake him up. It didn't end the dream. He was still here.

"Mister Ross, do you need some help?" Red offered, unsure of himself.

Frank stopped dumping the water on the back of his head. It wasn't helping; the wound was throbbing again.

"The aspirin."

"What?"

"The pills," he pointed at the bottle in Red's hand.

"Oh, yeah. The dope. Here, you go."

Frank took the bottle and fished a couple out and then on second thought, added a couple more, "This is quite a doozy," he explained to the seaman, who simply smiled.

"I don't doubt it, sir."

Red nodded his head as Frank popped the pills into his mouth and washed them down with a cupful of water.

He turned the faucet off. "Maybe you can help me to my cabin now?"

"Sure thing, Mister Ross." Red took him by the arm, and the two made their way out of the sickbay. Red stopped long enough to pull the door closed behind them, and then he resumed his place under Frank's arm as he helped him to his cabin.

Frank tried to relax; there was no sense fighting it. Dream or not, he was clearly in nineteen forty-one. The people, the ship, the world beyond—it all seemed real. How it had happened, he didn't have the slightest idea. It didn't really matter how; it only mattered that it had and that it explained everything he had encountered since waking up down in that hold. Everything but the most important question of all—why?

Why had someone or something dropped him into this body, an American seaman, an officer, on a British tramp steamer in the early days of World War II? They might as well paint a target on his back. The Germans were sinking these ships left and right. They had nearly starved the British right out of the war.

"What is a Yank doing on a British ship?"

"They said it was 'cause you volunteered."

"Good for me."

"Not so far." Red laughed. "Here we go. Chief Officer's cabin." He opened the wooden door. Inside was a single berth running fore and aft with drawers under it. Against the bulkhead just inside the door was a basin with a mirror above. A wardrobe and desk occupied the opposite wall, and a single open porthole, positioned above the bed, looked out on the sunny day beyond. It was small but lived in, comfortable.

"You just lay down here and take it easy, Mister Ross."

Red helped him up into the rack and pulled a blanket up over him. He then backed away, still not sure it wasn't catching. "You need anything else? I have to get back to work, or the bosun will skin me alive."

"No. I'm good for now. You can go."

Red started out of the cabin, then stopped. Pointing at the light switch, he asked, "Off or on?"

"Off, I guess."

"Sure thing." Red flicked the light off and closed the door behind him. Frank listened to his retreating footsteps, clicking quickly along the passageway.

"It's not right," he said to himself. "Not fair, either." The pills were starting to work; the pain was a dull ache now. All his strength was gone. "I guess busting your head open is exhausting work." Or was that because of his having changed bodies? His eyelids were heavier than a load of bricks. His head rolled to the side.

He noticed a black and white photograph in a gold frame on the desk. The man whose face he had seen in the mirror was in the photo with two women, obviously related to him, one middle-aged, the other very young, both in stylish dresses, still the standard garment for women in forty-one. He had always preferred women in dresses.

The Frank Ross in the picture was wearing a new jacket with a single stripe. He was a third officer, just got his ticket, still lean and hungry. Who was Frank Ross? Who were the two women, his mother and a sister, perhaps? Or a girlfriend? Damn, he hadn't thought of that before. Did the real Frank Ross have someone important he was leaving behind?

Nothing he could do about it. He couldn't even write a letter telling them what had happened. He didn't know what address to mail it to. *I'm sorry, ladies!*

Once more, his mind came back to the critical questions. Was this a dream, or was it real? And why was he here?

His eyelids were getting too heavy, and their weight forced Frank to close them.

• • •

Fog, the pea-soup kind, so thick he couldn't see his hand in front of his face. He stepped forward, his hands out in front of him, feeling for obstructions. *Not again!* This waking up in different places was getting old. The last thing he remembered was falling asleep in his rack aboard the ship.

No, that's not right! That was only a dream. So, this place is real, but where the hell was he? It seemed he had been here before, had met somebody here. But he couldn't remember who. A voice echoed in his head, repeating words with no real meaning to him. Fear filled his mind and threatened to turn his stomach to mush.

He couldn't see a damn thing except for the fog, and it seemed not only to block his vision but to muffle sounds as well, for he could no longer hear his footsteps. He heard nothing at all. The air was still and heavy, weighing in on him from all sides. Nothing moved, not even his feet now, for it suddenly seemed he was standing in cement, unable to move.

The fog seemed alive somehow, a presence, waiting for something, but what?

A slight breeze caressed his face. He turned toward it. Something was there, in the fog, a shadow, an area slightly darker than the rest. It seemed to move, or was it just the fog shifting in the breeze?

He stepped toward the shadow. For some reason, it didn't seem strange that a moment ago, he couldn't move an inch, and now he was nearly running after a mere shadow. His fear was gone as he concentrated on chasing the shadow. It moved faster and faster; he finally broke into a run, but no matter how fast he ran, he couldn't keep up with it.

Suddenly, it was gone.

He stopped, his chest heaving as he tried to catch his breath. Looking all around, his hands stretched out before him as he searched the murky depths. Where was it? It couldn't just vanish. He felt all alone. It seemed his hands, his arms, then even his body was fading away just as the shadow had, into nothingness. He felt himself becoming a part of the mist.

Then in the blink of an eye, he was solid again. The fog began to thin, and his field of vision spread out in all directions. In an instant, he could see farther than ever before, maybe to the edge of forever, but it was all empty. There was nothing as far as he could see.

Then the gray brightened to white, and the ground and the sky became indistinct. He turned in a slow circle, his eyes searching for something. But what? He felt someone was coming.

Where was he? What was this place? He hadn't ever seen anything like this before. *No, that's wrong. I have been here.* He abruptly remembered his daughter-in-law's eyes and the fear within. Then a scream pierced the ether, and the fog closed in around him once more. It pressed in on him. He couldn't breathe. The mist was crushing him. His heart stopped.

Then, he was in the hold, staring up at the blue sky.

He had been here, in this place between worlds, but someone else was here with him then.

Suddenly, a man was standing beside him. He turned to face him. The man was young, dressed in dungarees with a blue jacket and an officer's cap. That face; he had seen it before.

The man smiled for only a second.

"Where am I?" he asked the man.

"Not important. We only have a moment."

"What's going on?" He continued to press.

"You mustn't fail. I did. And now they all die. I failed, but they will pay the price."

He stared into the man's gray eyes. "I don't understand. Who will pay?"

"Now it's your turn to set it right. You must succeed where I failed. You have to set it straight."

"I don't know what you're talking about." He pleaded with the man.

"Yes, you do. The memories are there. Just reach out to them. The calling must be answered."

Then he was all alone, again. He spun around, searching for the man, but he had vanished in a flash. The fog came rushing back, closing in all around him. He reached out, running through the mist. He stopped; his hands were fading away in front of him. Then all of him was fading into the mist.

● ● ●

He jerked awake and found himself sitting up in his rack onboard the *Polites*. The *Polites*. *Where did that come from?* But that's right, the ship's name. The *Polites*, the S.S. *Polites*. Homeport Liverpool. No, not S.S. she wasn't a steamer; those were diesel engines humming away below. The *Polites* was a motor ship, an M.S. or M.V. as they will be called. But again, how in the hell did he know that?

He looked around. The sun was still shining in through the porthole, but the change in its angle showed he had been asleep for hours. Then he felt the motion of the ship. They were underway. Heavily laden as she was, the ship was rolling slowly in the onshore tide. They were just outside the New York narrows heading out to sea.

He tried to get up, but a hand on his shoulder stopped him.

"No, you don't. Not after a blow like that. You need to stay in bed for at least a day," said a woman's voice.

He turned his head, and the pain lanced right through him.

"See, I told you," the voice said. "Now, just lay back and take it easy."

He did as he was ordered, giving into the woman's authority. And as he did so, she came into his field of vision. Light brown hair was pulled back into a bun on the back of her head. Young, early twenties, he'd say. Beautiful. She took his breath away, or maybe it was the new wave of pain cutting through him at that moment. No, it was her face, the face of an angel, all in white. She smiled at him.

"My name is Helen Morris. Your Captain Egan asked if I would look in on you." It was then that he realized her clothing was a nurse's uniform, with blue and white stripes, and complete right down to the cap perched on top of her head. Right, he remembered the manifest listed ten American Red Cross nurses as passengers for transport to England.

"Welcome aboard. I'm glad to meet you. I guess my name is Frank Ross," he managed, despite the pain.

CHAPTER THREE
BARGAINING

"You guess your name is Frank Ross?" she inquired with her right eyebrow arched. It was a lovely eyebrow.

"I'm not really sure about anything right now."

"Is that since you hit your head, or have you been unsure about things for a while?"

"I don't know. I can't remember anything before waking up in that hold. At least, not clearly."

"Okay, that happens with concussions sometimes," she stated. "Nothing time won't fix."

"But how much time?" He gazed up into her green eyes.

"Can't tell. Sometimes it's only hours; other times, it can take days or weeks. Why? Are you in a hurry?"

"It would seem that way."

"Not to worry. Your Captain Egan seems to be the understanding type. I'm sure he knows how serious a head wound can be. He also said, if need be, they can get a replacement for you in Halifax. So, don't worry, Doctor's orders."

"That's nice, but they can't," he said, trying to sit up again.

"No, you don't." She pushed him down with surprising strength. "You may see yourself as the indispensable man, but tonight you're down for the count. Just lie there and let me finish checking you out." She then slowly examined his wound with her long delicate fingers. Here and there, she cleaned away some dried blood before moving on to the next set of stitches.

"Your captain would make a fine doctor. He did a great job on you, all nice and tight with good spacing. Yes, it should heal with just a small scar."

She crossed to the basin and began washing her hands. "You're lucky. A blow like that could have killed you. Would have for most people."

For a moment, Frank was happy just to lie there watching her scrubbing her hands, her long fingers entwining with each other as the soap slowly disappeared down the drain. He loved women with long fingers.

"What was that?" he asked.

She turned back to him, "You were lucky. You could have died in a fall like that."

"Yup, good old Frank Ross. Can't hurt him. His head is as hard as a bowling ball," he answered, studying the overhead, remembering the face in the fog. And the cryptic words, "Now they all die." What did that mean? Did it include this beautiful creature? Of course, it did. All means all. Everyone on this ship was going to die. But how? And even more importantly, what was he supposed to do about it?

She finished washing her hands and returned to his bedside. "Here, take these. They will help you sleep. The best thing for you right now." She held out two yellow tablets and a glass of water.

"Listen, you look like a good sort. Don't ask me how I know, but you have to get off this ship. If you don't, you're going to die."

"Well, thank you for the information. But what do you say we go ahead and take our pills now and worry about that later?"

"I know it sounds crazy. I know I have just had a head injury, and the last thing you want to do is listen to a crazy man, but I know what I'm saying is true." He gazed up into those green eyes again, pleading for her to believe him.

"I am sure you believe it, but even if I did, there's nothing I can do about it. I'm just a passenger on this ship under orders to proceed to England. It seems my employers think I'm needed there. Besides, I'm sure Captain Egan is doing all he can to make sure we get to Liverpool safely. Now, please?" She held out the pills and the glass again.

She didn't believe him. Why should she? He was just a crazy guy spouting a bunch of crazy words. "Okay." He reached up and took the pills, swallowing them with a swig of water. She smiled at him with her perfect white teeth.

"Good," she said, emptying the rest of the water into the sink. "I'll be back to check on you later. I'll bring you something to eat, too. Now, get some sleep." She then snapped the light off and exited the cabin without a backward glance.

"Really impressed her," he mumbled to himself. "The angel of my dreams couldn't wait to get out of here. Get away from the crazy man." He shook his head, and the pain swamped everything for a moment.

"What did you expect?" he continued as the pain subsided. "Going on like a mindless fool with that wild, implausible story. What did she expect? I did just fall twenty feet right onto my head."

No, I didn't. He did—the real Frank Ross. I stepped in after that, but I am stuck using what's left of his mind.

How in God's name did he fall? Those safety lines were all in place, even afterward. How did he fall over them? Was it an accident? Or a… "Wish I could remember what happened." *Didn't he say all the memories were there? I just had to.* "What was it he said?" He couldn't remember. Damn it, this not being able to remember was getting old quick.

His eyelids were growing heavy, and he didn't have the strength to fight it. He surrendered to it as he laid there watching the sun's dying light move slowly back and forth across the cabin door in time with the ship's slow, steady roll.

• • •

A slow, steady beep-beep-beep cut in through the pain. His body hurt all over, but especially in his chest. It felt like somebody had played drums with a baseball bat on his ribcage. That was wrong. It was his head that hurt, not his chest. He tried to move, but his limbs refused to respond. He tried to speak, but something was in the way. Something was stuffed down his throat. Then he heard voices. They sounded far away, moving around like fireflies floating in the ether, coming in close and then fading out. Or maybe someone was just playing with the volume, up and down, up and down. In and out, close then far away. First, they were to his left and then to his right. He just wished they would stay in one place. All this moving around was playing havoc with his stomach. If they didn't stop soon, someone would have a mess to clean up.

He tried to concentrate on just one voice, focusing on the sounds, struggling to match them to words and the words to meanings. It sounded foreign, but he knew it wasn't. He simply had to work a little harder—force himself to concentrate—to comprehend. He tried to pick out a single word since it seemed sentences were beyond him.

"Stroke."

There. A single word. Stroke. *What was a stroke?* He should know that.

"Coma."

Another word. *That's kind of like sleeping, right?*

"Days."

The words were coming faster now.

"Weeks even."

What does it mean?

"He might never wake up."

A whole sentence. *Are they're talking about me?* "I'm here. I'm awake. Just look down."

Did I say that out loud?

"I think he said something!"

"No, it's just his brain misfiring. He is under heavy sedation. Trust me; he can't be awake."

"Maybe not, but look."

Then the pain flared again, along with the light.

"My God, help him," a woman's voice cried.

• • •

What the hell was that?

He opened his eyes, but it was pitch black, and he couldn't see a damn thing. Where was he? A moment ago, he had been in a hospital, and someone was talking about him.

Was that it? He had had a stroke. Yes, that would explain things. He had a stroke and was in a coma. And all this is just a dream. It was his damaged mind trying to make sense out of what was going on around him. Maybe it was the drugs helping to fix the damage or perhaps just finding a way around it, a way back to the real world. But if that was right, how long would he be like this—alone and lost in the dark?

But was he alone? He heard sounds somewhere in the distance, voices, music, the steady rhythm of the ship's engines, the twin diesels, the heart of the beast, buried deep in the hull. No, he wasn't alone. He was back on the *Polites* in nineteen forty-one.

Night had fallen, and the sun was long gone. As his eyes adjusted to the darkness, the details of his cabin emerged from the gloom—the desk with the chair before it, the basin beyond, and the outline of the door to the passageway. Only a very faint halo of light made it past the seal around the door. They must have secured the passageway's overhead lights. Night lighting only, a few red bulbs, one at each end of the corridor. The U-boats were out there, lurking in the dark, waiting for their next victim.

Above him, he watched the blackout curtains swaying with the ship's roll, but they were still wide open. No one had entered his room. They were not in the war zone yet, so there was no real need to close them. Beyond, he could see the sky, and the stars were out in all their profusion. It wasn't bright enough for the moon to be up yet. So, it was not yet midnight. How did he know moonrise was at midnight? Another of those facts, just popping into his head.

Suddenly, part of the sky disappeared, the stars blotted out as though something or someone was standing there in the way. He gazed at the darkness. A head; it was a head. Someone was looking in, staring down at him. They moved on. And so, did he, to his feet and out the door in a flash.

He ran around the corner to the weather door on the athwartships passageway. Grabbing the lever, he jerked it up, swung the heavy door open, and rushed out onto the open deck beyond. He let the door swing loose behind him. He didn't have time to secure it.

Standing still, he could feel the light breeze created by the ship's motion. He could see the dark bulk of the nearby shore, here and there lit by the lights of a beach house. They were still just offshore. That would be Long Island, well east of New York City. They would shadow the south coast all night at twelve knots.

Stop it! It was disconcerting how his mind was providing all these little details. Details—his damaged mind had to be working overtime to come up with all this. Unless, no, this was just a dream. No way it could be anything but a dream. He was in a coma, lying in a hospital bed, trying to recover from a massive stroke. After all, he was just a middle-aged accountant with four grown sons. Their names were—well, just because he couldn't remember their names didn't mean this was real. There was no way he was on a British tramp steamer sailing off the coast of Long Island in the summer of nineteen forty-one.

Movement, to his left, down the deck, near the smokestack. He ran aft toward it.

Stopping short, he pulled up beside the port winch in the lee of the towering stack. He held his breath, listening, his eyes probing the surrounding darkness.

He was sure something had moved near here, but none of his senses could detect a presence now.

They must have moved on, but no one went down the port side; he would have seen them. They must have moved across the ship to the other side.

He slipped silently past the hatchway for the number three hold to stand beside the starboard winch.

Again, he stood still, listening, and waiting, his eyes probing for any sign of someone out there. The wind was stronger on this side, much stronger. The background sounds were louder, which made it harder to hear. He was afraid he might miss it. Then he felt something. Somebody was there, in the darkness, behind the winch, pressed flat against the bulkhead. He held his breath, afraid to look, afraid even that would give away the fact that he knew they were there.

Then, he heard a sound, heavy breathing; someone was trying to control it, fighting to remain silent. He felt like he could just reach out and touch—

The weather door immediately forward burst open, and three women stepped out into the patch of light on the deck accompanied by a man in uniform. The two gold rings on the sleeves sparkled in the bright light.

Frank turned to face the newcomers, and in that instant, he knew he had messed up.

The other man bolted out of the shadow, bowled him out of the way, and scampered off aft.

Frank caught himself against the safety lines and instantly bolted after the fleeing shadow.

"Mister Ross," Helen's voice called out from behind him.

The fleeing shape disappeared down the ladder to the after well deck, and Frank followed only seconds behind. On aft, he ran past the number four and five hatches.

Then his quarry made a mistake. He slipped up the ladder onto the fantail, the tail end of the ship. There was only one way off—back down the ladder, the bottom of which Frank now guarded.

Smiling to himself, he climbed the steps one at a time, his eyes peeled, searching the murky space before him. The shadow had gone to ground, and the fantail seemed deserted. This wasn't going to be easy! While the fantail was a small area, it contained any number of hiding places, lots of dark voids. Still, if he kept on his toes, it was only a matter of time before he cornered the shadow and discover who was so determined to keep his identity hidden.

Gradually, Frank worked his way aft past several pieces of equipment, a ventilator, and the workboat secure in its davits, until he reached the steering engine with its small wheel. From here, the ship could be piloted if the steering chains broke or the bridge was otherwise damaged.

He still had seen no sign of the man he knew was here, somewhere. He had seen him climb that ladder, and no one had left the deck since. Then he heard a movement behind him. *Damn it; I must have walked right past him.*

Frank spun, not sure what he would do.

"There you are, Mister Ross," Helen said, standing at the top of the ladder.

At that moment, he heard a swish and tried to duck but wasn't quite fast enough, and something heavy connected with the side of his head. Stars exploded in front of his eyes, and his legs collapsed beneath him.

"Mister Ross," the girl screamed.

He hit the deck hard, his head bouncing off the nearby bulkhead. For a moment, things began to fade out, and then she was beside him.

"Are you all right?"

He pushed her away, knowing the shadow would be making his escape. As he fought to his feet, he saw the phantom quickly vanish down the ladder, back onto the well deck. He tried to follow, not willing to give up the chase, but his strength failed him, and he pitched forward onto his face once more.

"Just lie still, Mister Ross. I'll get someone to help."

"No, I can still catch him."

"Catch who?" she asked.

"The shadow."

"Does the shadow know?"

"What?" he asked, looking up at her.

"You know. The shadow knows."

He continued to stare at her with a blank expression. She sighed. "You know. What evil lurks in the hearts of men?" She paused, and when he showed no recognition, said, "The radio show. The Shadow."

"No, the man I was chasing. I had him cornered. Then he hit me. See?" He grabbed her hand and put it to the knot on his head.

"Yes, I feel it, but you hit your head when you fell."

"But you must have seen him. He ran right past you."

"Sorry. I didn't see anyone but you."

CHAPTER FOUR
DEPRESSION

A knock jolted him awake. Sitting up, he looked around. *Where am I?* Nothing looked familiar. He was in a room not much bigger than a shoebox, sitting on a built-in bed with a small round window in the wall right above it. To one side, a wardrobe sat beside a sink and a mirror, and on the opposite wall was a small roll-top desk with a chair strapped down between the legs. A lone bulb burned in a socket above the mirror, casting strange shadows around the room. *How did I get here?*

The knock sounded again. Then the day before came flooding back into his addled brain. The events played out in his mind, beginning with waking up at the bottom of number five hold, then the captain sewing him up, the nurse Helen checking in on him, then chasing the shadow up on to the fantail, the hit to the head, and finally, the girl helping him back to his cabin. He particularly remembered the look of pity on her face as she helped him into his rack.

The Shadow knows. Of course, he knew about the old radio show. It was a big hit in the thirties. With the eerie music and the deep voice reciting the line, the Shadow knows what evil lurks in the hearts of men. Yes, one hell of an impression he had made.

Only the shadow knows. *Great, I'm glad he does because I sure as hell don't! No, that's not right, either. I know. I'm supposed to save them because he, the real Frank Ross, failed. He failed, and it cost him his life, his head cracked open like a melon, down there at the bottom of number five.*

The question was, how did he end up down there? Did he just fall? That didn't seem likely, a first mate, with years of experience, just slipped and fell over the safety lines? While in port? He didn't believe it. The real Frank Ross didn't just fall. He couldn't have. But if he didn't fall how did he end up down there? Was he pushed? And if he was, by whom? The Shadow? Not the radio character, of course, his shadow, the one he chased last night. They had a fight, a struggle, and the real Frank Ross went over the safety lines, hit the deck, busted his head open, and bled to death.

But why?

Why were they fighting down there? Why was Frank down there in the first place? Alone? It was noon, lunchtime. All the rest of the crew had knocked off, were off eating or relaxing somewhere else. So, why was the real Frank down there alone? What was so damn important? Was that it? Was he looking for something, and for some reason, didn't want anyone to see him? Or was it that he saw something or someone down there and followed them into the hold? Only the Shadow knows.

Now, for some unknown reason, God has stuck me in Frank's body, thereby, giving everyone a second chance: for Frank Ross to save the ship, for these people to live, and for me. He gave me a second chance to matter—a chance to do something meaningful, to change the world, to have my great adventure, and maybe—an image of the girl floated before his eyes for a moment—perhaps even a little romance.

The knock sounded for the third time.

"Yes," he answered, his mind still fixed on the girl.

The doorknob jingled as someone tried to open it. "Just a minute," he said as he remembered locking the door after the girl left, afraid of uninvited guests. He struggled out of the rack, his body one unending ache, and hobbled across to the door. Once there, he had to grab his head to stop it from falling off his shoulders and rolling under the desk. He would never find it if it did.

Then the knock came again, only this time, it was louder, more insistent.

"Okay, okay," he managed as he flipped the catch off. "Come in."

The wooden door swung open, revealing one of the mess boys. A young man of maybe seventeen, he was tall and as thin as a reed, dressed in black trousers and a recently pressed short white jacket. He held a tray full of food and a pot of coffee before him.

"I got your breakfast here, Mister Ross," he said with a strong British accent.

Frank's nose caught the smell of the food, and he suddenly realized how hungry he was. How long had it been since he ate? "Great, I could eat a bear."

"No bear. Just eggs and bangers," the boy replied in all earnestness.

Frank smiled. "That'll do."

The boy entered the cabin and crossed to the desk, where he set the tray down and began laying out the items as if he were setting the table in a grand ball-room. He had brought everything Frank could need for his morning repast. Frank helped by pulling the chair out of the way. He sat down as he watched the boy go through his presentation. Finally finished with the food, the boy sat the tray aside and moved to the bed, where he undogged the porthole, lifted the hatch open, and latched it to the overhead catch. He then pushed the glass open to let in a fresh sea breeze.

Instantly, the smell of the open sea filled the room, and the light of the new day flooded in.

"Much better," the boy said, turning to look down at Frank. "It was getting a little stuffy in here. Beg pardon, sir."

"No, problem. What's your name?"

For a moment, a look of surprise crossed the boy's face. "Mister Ross, I've been serving you for two weeks now."

"I'm sorry. I should know, but I hit my head yesterday. Twice, actually."

The boy's face shifted back to a smile, "That's right. The captain said you hurt yourself, and you might forget some things. My name is Freddie. Freddie Kimball."

"Okay, Freddie. Thanks for the food." Rising, he pushed the chair over to the desk. "It looks good, and it smells even better." He leaned forward and took a deep breath, savoring the intense aromas.

"I'll have to tell the guys. They'll get a kick out of it. No one's ever complimented cook's food before," the boy laughed.

Just then, the ship took a sharp roll to starboard, and Frank almost lost his balance. It was only Freddie's quick move to his side, grabbing his elbow as he did, that saved Frank from ending up in a heap on the deck.

"Guess my legs are still a little wobbly."

"It's okay. I understand," Freddie offered. And with a little help from the boy, Frank slid back into the chair before the next roll. Then he scooted it back into position, and without any ado, began digging into the food.

"I'll leave you to it, then. But I'll be back later for the dishes." Freddie started for the door. "Oh, after your meal, the captain asked if you could join him on the bridge? If you're up to it, of course."

"Sure, tell the captain, I'll be there," Frank responded between bites of runny eggs.

• • •

Half an hour later, after finishing the eggs and bangers (sausages to Americans), and a quick visit to the officers' water closet (or WC) to shower and shave, Frank climbed the two interior ladders to the bridge. He was past being surprised by the minutiae he knew—like where the WC was and even what it was. He was even starting to get used to the new face staring back at him from every mirror he saw. This couldn't be a dream. There was no way a damaged mind could create such a detailed world. And people it with the variety of characters he had run into so far—Freddie, Bailey, Red, the captain, Helen, and even a second engineer named Angus, whom he had met in the WC. Who would have guessed? A Scot as an engineer? Never in a million years! Well, maybe that one his damaged mind could have managed.

But if this wasn't a dream, then it had to be real. Not even considering how such a thing could happen and simply concentrating on the ramifications if it was real was enough to tax his poor aching head. Just imagine, he was on a British ship, a tramp steamer, headed for England in the summer of nineteen forty-one at the height of the Battle of the Atlantic with scores of German U-boats waiting in their infamous wolf packs to attack and sink any ship flying the Red Duster (just like the one on this ship) that dared to enter the war zone. That alone was enough to scare anyone, but that line—"and now they all die"—hung over him like a hammer, ready to deliver the final blow, splitting his head in two.

Then there was the shadow, that mysterious someone. Did they actually kill the real Frank Ross? The more he thought about it, the easier it was to believe. Why else would they now be stalking him if they didn't? At this rate, he might not even live long enough to worry about the U-boats.

At the top of the second ladder, he stepped out onto the brightly lit bridge. It was another glorious summer day, the temperature in the seventies, the weather decks bathed in sunlight. There were only a few scattered clouds dotting the expansive blue sky. A fresh wind, mostly generated by the ship's forward motion, boiled in through the open doors on either side of the wooden wheelhouse.

The captain, in a pair of dungarees and a faded blue shirt, his cap pushed back high on his head, was studying a chart spread across a table set hard against the aft bulkhead in the starboard corner. A short ape of a man stood at the wheel, front and center, his feet braced against the ship's constant roll, his eyes locked on the binnacle before him. Off to port, Red was talking with the third mate, Mister Eddy.

"Ah, there you are," the captain began.

"Yes, sir. Freddie told me you wanted to see me."

"Aye, that I did. To see how you are feeling."

"Better."

"No more shadows?" the captain asked.

"So, she told you." He should have known.

"Not on her own. But Mister Brown told me they stepped out on the deck last night just in time to see you running like a mad man off toward the stern. Luckily, she went after you. Told me you hit your head again. Do you plan on making a habit of that?"

"There she is. Three points off the port bow, Captain," Mister Eddy called from the open doorway. The captain picked up a pair of binoculars from the chart table and strode over to the forward windows. He zeroed in on the location the mate had specified, thirty-two points around the compass, eight to each quarter, so not quite halfway between the bow and the port quarter.

"Well, Mister Ross?" he asked, still trying to spot the object in question.

"No, sir."

"And the shadows?"

"Gone, sir." Frank knew no one on board would believe any part of what he thought was really going on. Even he had trouble believing it. No, they would just write him off. They already thought he was half crazy. What did the captain just say? *Running off like a mad man.* They probably would lock him up in his cabin until they reached Halifax and then have him bundled off to the closest available loony bin. And they would then all die, without a doubt. "Wasn't much myself last night." *What an understatement!*

"Understandable after that fall you took. The nurse told me you were lucky it didn't kill you."

How true.

"I got it, Mister Eddy. Almost four points."

"Yes, sir. We're coming up on it quickly."

"Very well. When it is on the beam, come left thirty degrees."

"Aye, aye, sir," the mate replied.

"Here, you want a look?" The captain held out the binoculars. Frank, feeling a tad odd, took them. Pressing them to his eyes, he began looking out in the general direction the captain had been. He readjusted the focus, and an empty sea came into clear view.

"A little farther to the left," the captain suggested.

Frank panned left until a bright red and white blob popped into view. He stopped, fine-tuned the focus again, and read the word 'Nantucket' painted in giant white letters on the side of a ship. Of course, the Nantucket lightship! The last navigational aid an outbound ship would see on the way to Europe. Set here, forty miles southeast of its namesake island to mark the southern edge of the Nantucket shoals and the beginning of Georges Bank. They would come left now, north-northeast, to cut across the open sea to catch the southeast corner of Nova Scotia, then follow the coast north into Halifax.

Damn! It was disconcerting the way facts, figures, and details were just popping into his consciousness, and it was happening more the longer he stayed. *Maybe I am Frank Ross? No, it's just as the real Frank said. The memories are all there, locked away in his addled brain. Just relax and they will come. Wasn't that a line from some old movie?* It seemed easier not to fight. The knowledge and memories were there, in his head, but when he tried to force it, he came up with nothing. *Don't think about it. Just react.*

"You got it?" the captain inquired.

"The lightship."

"Right! On course and on time," the captain stated as he noticed Frank smoothly swaying with the slow roll of the ship. "Seems you're no worse for the wear. Think you can return to duty?" Frank lowered the glasses, fighting to keep the fear in his gut off his face. The captain glanced at his watch. "Your section is up again in six hours. You ready for it?"

My God! Me, officer of the deck! "I'm not sure?"

"No better time for it. In six hours, we'll be in the middle of nowhere. Wouldn't be surprised if you didn't have a single sighting during the entire watch. No one and nothing to run into."

Frank continued to stare straight ahead, afraid to look anywhere, sure they would see through him.

"I'll, of course, stay on deck with you for a while, in case you need it."

Frank stood still, his mind racing, trying to remember the stuff he needed to remember. His mind once again a total blank. *Relax!* He glanced over at the third mate, the current officer of the deck. He looked young, barely old enough to shave, but he seemed at ease, even with several ships in sight.

"Come on, man. You're starting to scare me." The captain turned to face him. "No U-boats in these waters. Be out in the deep before they show up."

U-boats? He thinks I'm afraid of the Germans. "No, Captain. That's not it. I'm . . . well, I'm having trouble remembering things." *Only a little white lie.*

The captain visibly relaxed. "I would think that is normal with an injury like yours. I'm sure the best thing is to get back to using it. Push it. Don't let the damage set in permanent like."

"I'm just not sure, sir," Frank said, turning to face the captain. "I might forget something and get us into trouble. Maybe get someone hurt."

"Nonsense. I told you; I will be around. It's my arse on the line. Besides, I've been training junior officers for thirty years. You don't think I'm stupid enough to leave you on your own until I know you can handle things? I'm smart enough to know a head wound could play with your ability to handle the job. But we won't know the truth till you try it. And I can't afford to carry a useless chief officer into the war zone, can I?"

Oh!

"Of course, Captain. I wasn't thinking about that." The captain was right. In the war zone, he would need all his officers, and he could probably find a good English chief officer or at least a Canadian to replace Frank in Halifax. "You're right, sir. I'll be here."

"Good. Now that's settled, I've been wondering why."

"Why?"

"Yes. Why were you down in number five all by yourself in the first place? That deep hold was loaded in Baltimore. And you checked it out the night before. You signed the loading plan. Something you missed?"

"I don't know, Captain. I have no memories of the accident itself. Nothing until I woke up down there."

"Captain, we're abeam the lightship."

"Very well, come left to zero-five-five degrees."

"Aye, aye, sir."

"Well, if anything comes to you, I would love to hear it."

● ● ●

Frank sat alone in his cabin, in the only chair, his feet braced against the wooden desk to stop his constant rolling across the linoleum tiles. The Atlantic rollers had grown more pronounced since the turn to the northeast a few hours ago, and they were now hitting the ship broad on the beam, setting up a steady roll back and forth—not quite strong enough to disrupt life on the ship but definitely enough to make moving around a bit more interesting, at least for the next few hours until they moved off Georges Bank. Then as the sea deepened, the size of the rollers would recede, their energy dissipated in the growing depths.

From where he sat, he could watch the horizon through his porthole as it rode up and down with the ship's movement. With each new wave, the line separating the deep, almost purple of the sea from the pale washed-out blue of the late afternoon sky rose and fell across his rounded portal on the world. He noted the blue sky was broken here and there with the white of a few stray cumulus clouds—flat bottoms, puffy looking, altitude less than six thousand feet, fair weather, a good sign. It was another of those endless little facts he now knew without knowing how he knew them. It was a constant reminder of his situation, which brought him back to the source of his present mood. The captain, in all his brilliance, had decided he was ready to return to duty. Couldn't blame him. He had to do the work of two men, after all, until Frank was back.

But only he knew the truth; he wasn't the real Frank. He wasn't the trained seaman that the real Frank was. Yes, he had been in the Navy, as a supply officer, forty years ago. And yes, he had stood bridge watches, but as a junior officer of the deck with a far more experienced officer on the bridge just in case he screwed up. And the captain had been there most of the time, so there was no way for him to endanger the ship and crew. Here, it was different. No one would be looking over his shoulder. Why would they? They all thought he was an experienced, certified deck officer. In fact, by law, to sail as a chief officer, the real Frank had to have his master's ticket, which meant not only was he an experienced seaman, but he was also qualified to be a captain in his own right.

But at this moment, the very thought of having all their lives in his hands was liquefying his intestines. His mind raced over the same thoughts again and again, creating ruts, digging himself in deeper, and making it harder to crawl out of the hole he was digging for himself.

He alone would have responsibly for the ship—a 426-foot long, 6,000 gross ton, metal box carrying sixteen million pounds of freight, and ten female passengers along with a crew of 38 men and traveling at over a thousand feet a minute. It would be entirely in his hands. Just imagine the damage he could do!

It will come to you.

How could he be sure of that? He was a human being, by definition, a flawed and imperfect creature. Add in his Swiss-cheese memory, and it was a perfect recipe for disaster.

It will come to you.

"How can I be sure?" he whispered to himself.

Then, a knock at the door jerked him out of his self-induced trance. Looking around the cabin, he realized it had grown dark. He glanced at his watch. By the glowing hands, he read the time, twenty minutes before four. No, 1600 hours, ship's time. Just a few minutes left before his watch.

The fear gnawed at his guts. He couldn't do it. No matter what the real Frank said. Or the captain, for that matter.

The knock repeated.

"Who is it?" he asked, only now becoming aware of the knocking.

"Helen Morris." the muffled voice said.

He was out of the chair and at the door in a second. Pulling it open, he vaguely heard the chair crashing into the bed behind him. He blinked several times as his eyes adjusted to the light, which haloed her reddish-brown hair. Then the green eyes came into focus along with the red lips and the button nose. All he could manage was to croak, "Hi."

She looked past him into the darkened cabin. "I'm sorry. I didn't realize you were asleep."

"No, I was just—" He stopped and glanced down at the deck. Could he? Did he dare? "Sitting in the dark. Too lazy to get up and turn the lights on." With that, he hit the switch, and white light filled the room.

"Here." He crossed the room and sat the chair back on its rollers. "Come on in. Have a seat."

"Thank you," she said, taking the offered seat. Frank moved into the doorway, standing there with the door open, but his body unconsciously blocking her retreat.

"To what do I owe this visit?" he inquired.

"I was just checking up on you." She blushed as she heard her words. "I mean, I was just going to check on your head. You know the stitches."

"Of course," he replied, trying to ignore the other possible meaning. It was just as her blush implied, an unfortunate turn of words. He glanced away to cover the sudden feeling of disappointment that washed over him. Why disappointment? No reason she would have any feelings for him. After all, he was the crazy man chasing shadows in the dark.

She stood up. "Your turn." She pointed at the chair.

He nodded, stepped past her, and sat down. She closed the door and turned back to him. "Turn your head, please." She stepped up close behind him. He could smell her light scent, Chanel, maybe. Then her fingers were in his hair, opening a gap to examine the wound underneath. She leaned in closer, her breath against his neck. He closed his eyes.

"Yes, it looks fine. The stitches are nice and tight, the wound clean. No sign of infection."

She stepped away, taking a deep breath as she did.

"Just keep it clean, and we should be able to remove the stitches in a week or so. It will leave a nice scar, though."

"Too bad my hair covers it. I've heard women love scars." Frank said, opening his eyes.

Helen turned toward the door as he stood up and returned the chair to its place under the desk. She stopped and looked back at him. His expression pulled at her; he looked so much like a lost puppy. She closed her eyes, her mind awhirl. Her hand fell away from the doorknob.

Turning toward him, she said, "Mister Ross, are you okay? I mean, truly okay?"

"You said everything looked fine."

"No, not the wound. Inside. You look, well, lost."

"That's a word for it."

"It's nothing to be upset about. You took a terrible fall there. It would have addled anybody's—"

"That's it. It's the fall. It scrambled my brains. None of this is real. But then the fall wasn't real either. Not really." He lifted his hand to her cheek, a light caress. "Not even you are real. Such a shame." He turned away and trudged to the edge of the bed. He leaned hard up against the wooden frame as he gazed out the porthole, his eyes locking on the blue water beyond. Slowly, he took a deep breath of the salt-laden air drifting in on the breeze.

Helen stood studying the back of his head, the warmth of his touch still on her cheek. She was concerned for him but not sure what was going on, either inside him or between them. She was aware of the physical attraction she felt, had been since that first moment the night before when she sat watching him sleep. But his actions last night on deck and this scene now left her with serious doubts. At times, he seemed quite normal, and then, suddenly like now, he went off the deep end.

He had settled back into a trance-like state, staring out the porthole at the ever-changing sea.

She made up her mind, crossed the compartment, and stepped up behind him. Then put her hand on his shoulder.

"Mister Ross?" she whispered.

He jumped, surprised by her sudden closeness. As he jerked around, his arm hit her in the chest. She fell away, flailing out with her hands for support. He automatically grabbed for her—and ended up pulling her up hard against himself.

They stood stock-still; their breaths caught in their throats. Two sets of eyes—his gray, hers green—locked. Something passed between them. For a moment, it seemed he was adrift in those green pools, lost forever.

"Sorry," he eventually managed.

"It's okay. I took you by surprise," she whispered as she stepped back, disengaging from his arms, struggling to pull her eyes away.

"Should have known you were there," he mumbled. "It's just... too much. I don't know what to do. Don't even know what to make of it all."

Frank pushed past her, suddenly needing space. He turned sideways to avoid touching her again. She backed up into the corner, her shoulders pressed against the cold metal bulkhead. It gave her something to hold on to.

"What don't you understand? Maybe I can help?" she offered, her hands stretched out, aching to touch him.

He turned back toward her. His eyes searching her face, lost for a moment again in those twin pools.

"No. You would never believe me."

"But why wouldn't I believe?" She took a step toward him.

"Because it's nuts. The whole thing is plain nuts. Finish me off in your mind; it would. You would probably lock me up yourself."

"Maybe it won't sound so bad if you talk about it out loud with someone else?"

He looked down into her trusting face. He needed somebody to talk to. Why not her? He suddenly needed her to believe him.

He dropped onto the bed. "Sit?" he pointed to the chair.

She sat, pulling the chair toward him.

"Now understand, I know this sounds crazy."

"You said that before."

"I know, but I can't say it enough."

She bit her upper lip, "Well?"

"I'm not Frank Ross. The real Frank Ross died at the bottom of that hold yesterday afternoon."

She blinked her eyes, glanced away, searching for something to say. "Okay, then. If you aren't Frank Ross, who are you? Because the captain and the others are sure you are. Frank Ross that is."

"I told you it would sound nuts. But it gets even worse. They think I am Frank Ross because this," he pounded on his chest, "is his body."

"This killed him," he said, touching the back of his head. "And then someone or something, God maybe, put me in here to take over for him."

She covered her mouth with her hand, unable to speak. Then she started to shake her head gently back and forth.

"I told you."

She jumped to her feet. "Yes, you did. But, but how was I to know?"

"How crazy I am?"

Now it was her turn to stare as her eyes locked on the pipes in the overhead. He sat still watching her. Her entire body echoed the conflict raging inside. He wanted to reach up, to ease her torment but instinctively knew that she had to work it out herself.

Finally, she glanced down at him. "So, you're not the real Frank Ross. You are just what? Occupying his lifeless body?"

"Yes."

She laughed, a nervous little laugh. "You're serious?"

He nodded; the look on his face spoke volumes. "You said yourself a fall like that would kill most people. Well, it did. It killed the real Frank Ross."

Her mind was aswirl, thoughts running wild. "My God. You are nuts!" She backed away, starting for the door. He grabbed her arm. She pulled away.

"Please, don't go. Hear me out."

She backed up against the door. She looked up at him, at his face, and into his brown eyes. "You really believe this?" Wait, brown wasn't right. She looked again, and this time she saw gray, just as she remembered. *What's going on here? Could it be?* "Then, if you're not Frank Ross, who are you?" she demanded.

"I don't know. Not for sure."

"Of course, you don't," she said, feeling like a fool.

"No, it's just it's all messed up in here." He tapped his head. "His memories, my memories. It's like someone just poured them all into a bowl and turned the mixer on.

I can't tell where one ends and the next starts. It's bits and pieces. My first car was blue, a seventy-three Nash. I think. Maybe. No, Nash was gone by seventy-three. Frank Ross' first car was a thirty-two Nash; that's it, mine was a Jeep. Then there was the moon shot, the oil embargo, computers, my sister Mabel. No, I don't have a sister." He glanced over at the picture of the two women on the desk. "He had the sister. It's all just a mess. The only thing I remember clearly is my daughter-in-law's eyes staring at me as I—"

Helen crossed the compartment and dropped back into the chair. She stared at him, not yet convinced but totally confused by his rant.

"I know how it sounds, and it would be easy to just write it off as a mad man's delusions."

"Exactly. Why should I believe you? You offer this fantastic story and give me nothing to back it up but your word. I didn't even know you two days ago. And now I'm to trust you?"

"You have to."

"Why? Why do I have to?" she implored.

"Because I need someone to believe me." He stood up and looked out the porthole again. He saw a flock of seagulls wheeling in the distance, and for a moment, wished he was as free as them.

She stared at his back as he stood gazing out the window. Suddenly, she needed to comfort him. He was that lost puppy again. Alone and in a world, he didn't understand and couldn't make any sense of.

"Why would I lie?" he asked, his face still turned away, his words lost in the breeze.

"What?"

"Why would I lie?" he repeated, turning toward her.

"I don't know. There are probably a hundred reasons."

"That's right. This is all one strange attempt to get you into bed."

"It could be. I've heard of some strange types. And who knows? It almost worked." She rose to her feet. They stared at each other.

Then, she turned and again started for the door.

"Okay. He said they all died."

She stopped, her hand on the knob. "Who died?"

"All the people on board this ship."

"Me?"

"You all die."

"Who is he?"

"The real Frank."

She closed her eyes tight. "You almost had me." She jerked the door open and stormed out, almost running over a seaman in the passageway.

The seaman watched her go, his eyes locked on her bottom as it swayed from side to side. "Women," he said under his breath. Then he turned to Frank. "Captain sends his respects and wonders where the hell you are, Mister Ross."

Frank glanced at his watch and grimaced. "Sorry, I lost track of time."

CHAPTER FIVE
ACCEPTANCE

Frank stepped out onto the bridge from the inside ladder, feeling a tad more at ease this time. He stopped and looked around the light-filled compartment. The wheelhouse was a wooden structure added a decade before, enclosing the original open bridge to make watch standing a little less daunting. It was perhaps twenty-feet wide by a dozen feet deep, but despite its generous size, it still seemed a little crowded, due to several large fixtures set around the compartment. The most prominent of which was the ship's wheel, a good four feet across and mounted dead center facing the seven large windows arrayed along the front bulkhead. Red, the current helmsman, stood on a raised platform set directly behind the wheel with his feet set shoulder-width apart and his hands widely spaced upon the wheel. He used the spokes to rotate it back and forth, fighting the ever-changing currents to maintaining the ship's ordered course. His eyes constantly shifted between the view ahead and the compass set inside the binnacle, which sat a couple of feet in front of the wheel.

It was of the old-fashioned type with a metal hood to allow it to be lit at night, and it was balanced by two large iron balls attached to short arms sticking out on either side. The balls, one painted red and the other green like the ship's running lights, were adjustable, allowing for them to be moved about to offset the ship's magnetic field so the compass within would read true. To the helmsman's right sat the engine order telegraph, which allowed the bridge to notify the engine room, five decks below, of any needed changes in speed or direction by moving one or both of the handles, one for each of the *Polites* two propellers. He noticed both were currently set at full speed ahead. He also noticed both doors out to the bridge wings were still latched wide open, allowing the cool sea breeze to blow through the compartment, making it quite pleasant where he stood next to the ladder.

A black curtain, drawn open against the bulkhead, set off a small alcove behind him to the right. It was barely large enough to contain the sizeable flat-top desk that sat pushed against the after bulkhead and a set of cubbyholes which lined the outer wall clear to the overhead, filled with dozens of rolled up charts. One chart, showing the Gulf of Maine from Cape Cod north to Nova Scotia, was spread out on the table, weights in all four corners to hold it flat. A pair of dividers and a compass lay discarded on top of the chart.

"Ah, there you are," the captain said from beyond the door, out on the starboard wing where he and the second officer, Mister Stratton, stood together in the shade of the wheelhouse. "Please, come and join us."

Suppressing a grimace, Frank started for the door. He nodded to Red as he exited out onto the bridge wing.

"Sorry, lost track of time," he said as he joined the captain and second mate.

"Right. Knew it was something like that," the captain replied in a flat tone before changing the subject. "You can go, Mister Stratton. I'll handle the turnover."

"Aye, sir," the younger man said. Nodding to Frank, he beat a hasty retreat through the door back into the wheelhouse and out of the line of fire.

"I know you are still new to my ship, Mister Ross."

"Yes, sir. I know. It won't happen again."

"Make sure it doesn't. I wasn't at all happy with the way they put you aboard in the first place. What with faking an injury and all. Do you realize they didn't even check with me before they did it? They simply showed up with you in tow. It's a complete pile of rubbish, forcing an unknown officer on a ship just as we are about to go into the middle of a war zone. Bad enough to put a Yank on board, but as my chief mate? You understand me, Mister Ross? A mate can make or break a ship quicker than a lousy captain can.

"These men," he said, gesturing toward the seamen in the wheelhouse, "have been given a piss poor lot in life. Rotten food, horrible living conditions, dangerous work away from family and friends for months on end, and a pittance for pay. And now to send them into a war with a ringer as mate. It's too much, you hear me?"

"I'm sorry, Captain. I didn't have a choice either." *That's the understatement of the year!*

"They told me you were one of their best—a spy who knows his way around a ship. Supposed to have his master's ticket. Do you?" Captain Egan stared Frank in the eyes.

"Yes." An image of the certificate on the bulkhead down in his cabin flashed through his mind. Well, at least, the real Frank Ross did.

"Got it out of a Cracker Jack box, did you?"

"No. Earned it after fifteen years at sea." Suddenly, a flood of images of him, standing watch after watch on a variety of ships, played past his mind's eye. He remembered visiting Shanghai, Hong Kong, and Portsmouth, and even transiting through both canals, Panama and Suez.

"A little long in coming, wasn't it? Is that it, a little slow, are we?" The captain asked as he noticed the faraway look filling Frank's face.

"No, sir! I started as a cabin boy." The facts were coming faster; they seemed to be there precisely when he needed them. "Had to learn math from scratch, didn't get that far in school," he replied through clenched teeth. "I crawled up through the hawsepipe," he continued, using the nautical term for someone who started at the bottom and climbed his way up.

"Good. I see you have a little fire in your belly. So, do I need to go over any more of the rules?"

"No."

"What was that?" the captain demanded, rising to his full height, still several inches shorter than the American's six-foot-one frame.

Frank instantly, keying on the captain's posture, snapped to attention. "No, sir! I know the rules, sir."

The captain relaxed back against the railing. "This isn't the Andrew." He used a slang term for the Royal Navy. "But I still expect my officers to act like professionals. Obedience to rules could be the difference between life and death for everyone on board."

"Aye, aye, sir."

"Good. We have an agreement. I will expect you to act like my chief officer and stop messing around at the bottom of number five. Agreed?"

"Yes, sir."

"Now, back to work. We are seventy nautical miles east-southeast of Chatham Light, steering zero-three-zero magnetic. Making turns for twelve knots. Seas are running northeast to southwest at three to four feet. The wind is out of the northwest at force two. All watchstanders have been relieved. The standing orders are posted in the logbook. You are to maintain course and speed. The watch is yours, sir." The captain saluted.

"I have the watch, sir," Frank replied with the standard phrase and returned the salute. *It will come. At least, when I am angry!*

"Very well. I'm going to hang around for a while if you don't mind."

Though it was a statement and not a question, Frank responded, "Of course not, sir. It is your ship."

"I'm glad you realize that," the captain snapped as he passed through the open door.

Frank remained where he was in the lee of the wheelhouse, the wind blowing past him, the deck rolling slowly from side to side. The *Polites* rode the groundswell rolling in off the starboard bow, long and low, driven by some storm far out to the east in the wide-open expanse of the North Atlantic. The warmth of the sun, now low in the west, reached his face only as the ship hit the bottom of its roll to port.

He took a deep breath and slowly released it, followed by a second and then a third. As he continued to breathe in the sweet salt-laden ocean breeze, he felt the tension in his shoulders begin to unwind.

He closed his eyes and willed himself to relax. Slowly, he reopened his eyes, taking in the scene all around him. The deep blue sea here and there topped with a white cap as the light breeze blew off the top of a wave. The lighter blue sky was dotted with lacy white clouds drifting across the vast expanse. He suddenly remembered how big the sky at sea was on a clear day like today, with no trees, or buildings or mountains cluttering the horizon, restricting it only to that space above your head as it was on the land. And at his feet, the ship was always moving, up, down, sideways, alive, riding the waves. She was a beast yoked but still yearning to run free.

He stepped forward to the railing. Covered with a canvas dodger, it cut off the wind below his waist. His hands went to the top rail, and he was lost in the moment, watching the forepeak riding the waves, the spray arcing out fifty feet on each side of the ship, feeling the slight rumble in the deck as each crest broke against the bow. It was a never-ending spectacle as wave after wave came rolling down on the ship.

"All things for the glory of God!" he whispered to himself as his heart skipped a beat, and his spirit took wing. "This. This is what I always wanted but never had the guts to reach for."

He was suddenly at peace. It no longer mattered what came next, for at that moment, he was content, standing there watching the *Polites* riding up and over the combers, one after another. This was worth it.

He looked around the ship. She was a classic three island design like thousands of other freighters built in the first half of the twentieth century, so named for the three raised "islands" built on top of the main deck. At the bow was the forecastle, or the fo'c'sle (pronounced folk-sol) in seaman's jargon, containing the crew's living quarters. Then at the stern came the poop originally used to house the officers because it was where they sailed the ship from, in those days of yore, as the rudder and its controlling tiller were by necessity located there.

Later, after the advent of steam propulsion, the most logical place for the large, bulky engines was low in the hull and amidships, but that created a problem with all the obstructions, the smokestacks, the air intakes, and the paddlewheels, blocking the view from the stern. Thus, the bridge, which was originally a real bridge-like structure running between the two large boxes built on either side of the ship to protect the paddlewheels, was born and with it the amidships house, the third island. And the officers moved forward to be near the bridge and the engines below.

"Mister Ross, I have a fishing boat one point on the port bow," a voice called down from above.

Frank glanced up and saw Jackson, one of the ordinary seamen who had been with the ship for seventeen months on his first voyage away from home. He had earned good marks in the old chief officer's logbook. Damn it! It really was coming back to him, the real Frank's memories, bit by bit just as he needed it. Jackson was up on Monkey Island, the wheelhouse top, a pair of glasses in his right hand as he pointed toward the distant boat with his left.

"Out there," he called.

"How far?" Frank replied as he looked out in the indicated direction.

"Five miles, maybe."

The answer explained why he couldn't make out the boat. *Damn it, forgot about that.* He quickly ducked into the wheelhouse.

"Any spare glasses?" he asked Red.

"In the drawer under the chart table, sir."

"Thanks." Frank crossed to the table and started opening the drawers underneath one at a time. Along with a wide array of objects, dividers, compasses, pens, pencils, blank paper, and old message forms, he found an ancient pair of binoculars down in the fourth drawer. He grabbed them and hurried back out the open door on to the port bridge wing.

At the forward rail, he put the glasses to his eyes, spun the knob, and began focusing on a small blur. Unable to clear the view, he pulled the binoculars away from his eyes and, with a glance, discovered the lenses were coated with a thick layer of gunk. *Great.* He had no choice but to return to the chart table, trying not to look over at the captain who had retired to his favorite spot, the starboard corner of the wheelhouse, hard up against the forward bulkhead.

Next to the chart table was a small cubby where a coffee urn sat on an electric warming plate. Beside the urn was a small sink with a cold-water tap. Frank turned the water on and slipped the binoculars under the flow, rinsing off the lenses front and back, wiping the gunk off with his fingers. *I must remember to search for Frank's pair before the next watch. I'm sure he has some. Most officers do.* Once the gunk was gone, he turned the water off and picked up the grimy towel hanging from a ring set above the sink.

"This is really going to help," he muttered to himself as he wiped the glasses dry and then polished the lenses.

Finished, he replaced the towel and hurried back out onto the bridge wing, again trying, unsuccessfully, to ignore the captain's critical gaze. *What does he expect? I did die yesterday!*

Back at the rail, he finally focused the binoculars on a small fishing trawler, about sixty feet long and just shy of ten thousand yards out. "Good job, Jackson.

But report distances in yards, not miles, and drop the 'maybe.'" His eyes never left the smaller boat. It was flying twin black cones from its mainmast, meaning it was engaged in fishing, with its trawling nets out and thus unable to maneuver. "So, I must."

Quickly, he ran the scenario through his mind. *The trawler's bow is pointed northeast, say zero-four-zero or zero-four-five degrees magnetic, ten or fifteen degrees south of our course—speed, slow, max four knots, probably less. Let's say three; that's one hundred yards a minute, range ten thousand yards. That means he's two thousand yards off my course. At three knots, he'll cover that in twenty minutes. And I'll do the ten thousand in twenty-five. Even with his angle, he'll beat me.*

"Come right, steer course zero-four-five," he called out to Red.

"Coming right to course zero-four-five, aye," Red replied as he spun the wheel to the right.

Let's see; we'll run parallel for, say, fifteen minutes. At three hundred yards a minute—forty-five hundred total—that would give me two miles to spare. Then come left to—not zero-three-zero. I'll be two miles starboard of the current track. I need something a few degrees farther to port to hit the mark.

Frank stepped into the wheelhouse, crossing behind Red to the chart table. "Let's see."

"I'm steady on zero-four-five, sir."

"Very well. Rudder amidships. Maintain course."

"Aye, aye, sir."

Frank picked up the dividers and quickly began to work out the new base course.

"The captain has left the bridge," Red called out from behind him.

Frank turned to look around, and sure enough, Egan was gone. "Well." *Guess he's satisfied.*

Frank went back to the chart, and a moment later said, "Messenger."

"Aye, sir," another seaman responded from the wing.

"Please, notify the captain we will continue on zero-four-five for," he glanced at his watch, "another ten minutes and will then come left to zero-two-eight as a new base course to the navigational mark southeast of Nova Scotia."

"Aye, aye, sir."

• • •

Four hours later, an exuberant Frank left the bridge via the outside ladder on the starboard side. The sun was low in the western sky; the first stars had appeared in the growing dark above. Ralph Stratton, the second officer, was on the port wing with his sextant, shooting stars in an attempt to get a celestial fix on the *Polites'* position. At the same time, the third officer, young Mister Eddy, had the deck for the 2000-2400 (spoken as twenty hundred to twenty-four hundred) watch. Each of the three mates—Frank, Stratton, and Eddy—stood two, four-hour watches each day, with Frank taking the 0400-0800 and 1600-2000 watches, Stratton got the 1200-1600 and 2400-0400 watches, and Eddy had the remaining two, the 0800-1200 and 2000-2400. Eddy, the junior officer, got the better watches because of his inexperience, so if anything happened during his watch, several other officers, including the captain, would be readily available to help him. And Mister Stratton got stuck with the mid-watch because he was experienced enough not to need that support, while the chief officer was senior enough not to have to get up in the middle of the night.

The last four hours had removed any doubts Frank had about his, or more rightly, the real Frank's, ability to meet any challenges of seamanship he should meet on the voyage. The real Frank might have been out of his league against whoever he ran into down in number five, but as a seaman, he was a natural.

And what the real Frank said—"it will be there"—was true. Each and every time he reached for a piece of knowledge, it popped up. It was only when he was trying to dredge up something, he wasn't sure of or something personal that his memory would fail him. Facts were tangible and readily available, but memories, thoughts, and the like were still wisps of smoke—there one moment at the edge of his consciousness and gone the next.

As he descended the ladder, the heat of the day was fading, the dying sun no longer able to warm the skin and would shortly lose even its ability to light the world. Soon it would set, and an almost full moon would take its place. Even now, the leading edge of its round face was visible above the eastern horizon, faint and wavering in the haze.

Frank's stomach growled at the smell of food from the saloon as he continued aft on the upper deck, unwilling quite yet to withdraw from the evening air.

He was in love, totally smitten by the ever-changing sea.

At the after end of the upper deck, he stopped, leaned against the railing, and gazed out across the rippling surface. It had changed color, darkening from a glorious blue velvet in the bright sunshine to an almost gray now, but still, even in its present somber guise, it grabbed his attention and held it.

He remembered sitting spellbound by the sight of the Rockies in Colorado, but even that couldn't compare to this. All his cares had disappeared, drowned in the dark abyss at his feet. How long he stood there, unmoving, oblivious to the world around him, he would never know. The sun had set in the west, and the stars burst out from under the blanket covering the void above with an endless array of shimmering lights, white, blue, red, and more numerous than the grains of sand on every beach he had ever trod. The sea transformed into an ever-shifting mirror, reflecting here and there a small fraction of the incredible show above.

How insignificant man was, he thought, compared to all that God has created! To believe any of us is more than a speck in the grand scheme was the height of foolishness. For each of us is but one of billions of creatures that inhabit for a moment, this speck of dust in a forgotten corner of the universe. Our plans, our hopes, and our desires, our most extraordinary creations, are less than aught to Him. And yet, was he not a living example of man's importance to God? Had God not put him here? For some reason, the Creator of heaven and earth and all therein had deemed him worthy of attention. And if he were worthy, where must man stand in God's eyes?

If God be for us, who shall stand against us?

At that moment, the hatchway below him opened, and three crewmen exited. As one dogged the hatch down, the other two continued aft across the open deck. The third finished with the hatch and quickly rejoined his mates, their conversation never stopping. A moment later, the three disappeared into the after-housing, where Frank knew the petty officers were housed.

He stood looking down at the now deserted deck and remembered his stepping out of that same passageway into the bright sunlight yesterday afternoon. Had it truly only been a day? Not even thirty hours since he had awakened down in the bottom of number five, his head busted open, blood everywhere, who he was and where he was, a mystery to him. And now, here he was a master mariner; he even had a certificate from the United States Maritime Commission to prove it, at least to everyone, short of God, who alone knew the truth.

Master mariner. As chief mate, he had to be one just in case something should happen to the captain, for that would leave him in command. Him, in command? God sure does move in mysterious ways.

But that reminded him of a question, in fact, *the* question. If the real Frank Ross was a master mariner, how in the hell did he end up dead at the bottom of number five? A master mariner falling over the safety lines? In port? The real Frank had said, "I made a mistake, and now they all die." What kind of mistake? Had he gone stupid? Leaned too far out over the safety lines and lost his balance? Or was it somehow connected with his mysterious visitor last night, the shadow? And what was he doing down there in the first place? Was there something down there in number five? Or did he catch someone doing something?

Frank looked around. No one in sight. He hurried down the ladder to the well deck and through the hatch into the amidships' housing. He turned left and found the scuttle in the deck. Then, he spun the wheel and knocked the dogs off, lifted the hatch, and threw it back on its stops.

A glance and down he went, pulling the scuttle closed behind him. On down the ladder and he stepped off onto the 'tween decks of number four. It was only half full. They were to pick up a final batch of cargo in Halifax on the fifteenth. The crates were pushed up against the port and starboard bulkheads, really the inside of the hull, and roped into place to keep them from moving even though there was little chance of that on this leg of the voyage.

In the center of the space, the pass-thru to the lower hold was now closed off with wooden planks laid in two layers, the lower running port to starboard, and the upper fore to aft, with wooden battens used to lock the boards in place. Nothing was at present sitting on the wooden floor, leaving a nice open space for that final shipment.

Frank moved around to the starboard side of the deck, stepping up to the steel door in the aft bulkhead. On this level, dogged hatches in the watertight bulkheads allowed for movement between the various compartments but still preserved the bulkhead's protection against flooding. Down in the lower holds, no such access was allowed. Since Frank wanted to look around at the bottom of number five, the only way in was from directly above. He opened the hatch and stepped through into number five's 'tween deck. Here, the compartment was much the same as in number four with the opening in the deck and the overhead, now both closed with wooden planks locked in place. But unlike number four, this hold was full. The last of the Red Cross equipment had been loaded and secured after his little accident.

Frank, using what little light the handful of safety lamps provided, wished he had thought about finding a flashlight before coming down here. He began to check the labels on the various crates—medical supplies, equipment, syringes, incubators, surgical clothes, various instruments. No drugs. Those would be in with the secured cargo forward on the 'tween decks, under lock and key. There were also tents, cots, and a washing machine. Yes, all the equipment they would need to set up a full-service field hospital. They were bringing everything so they wouldn't have to acquire anything locally. No drain on the English, who had their hands full fighting the Hun. They were even bringing their own food—a couple of months' worth to start, more later, if they needed it. The Brits would be hard-pressed to provide even that necessity. Their food supplies were already being rationed. The Nazis had failed at winning the air war over Britain, and Hitler had called off the invasion. So now, the Kriegsmarine, as the Nazis called their navy, was working overtime to starve them out of the war.

This was a waste of time. None of this stuff was here thirty hours ago. Thus, nothing here could have anything to do with what happened to him. Down below, he had to go to the bottom of number five.

He worked his way across to the port side, where the open access to the lower hold was. He reached out for the ladder but pulled his hand back. Something had moved in the shadows across the way.

"Is someone there?" he called.

No answer. He listened to the ship and her sounds, but only heard the standard background, the stresses of the ocean against the hull, creaks and rattles, the crates grinding against each other, the constant rumble of the main diesels. He could even make out the lighter ta-pocketa-ta-pocketa of the generator, but nothing else.

"Getting a little jumpy," he chided himself. "Need to watch that."

Down the ladder, twenty feet to the bottom of number five, a lot easier going down than it had been coming up thirty hours ago. He stepped off onto the deck, surrounded by the swishing sounds of the ocean moving by just beyond the steel plates of the hull.

The lighting down here was even worse than up above. The amount of traffic on the 'tween decks was far greater, but hardly anyone ever ventured down here while at sea, other than the carpenter sounding the bilges and the chief officer checking on the lashings. Only a couple of safety lamps burned from their tiny cages high up in the overhead, casting eerie shadows made worse by the crates and the steady rolling of the ship. The hold was full now. They had added more cargo after his accident before finally closing the hatch above.

He stood still at the foot of the ladder, one hand on a rung for balance. He was still working on his sea legs, but so far, his stomach had not been a problem, thank God! With his head and all the other stuff he was dealing with, a case of seasickness would have been a little too much to handle.

He slowly gazed around the compartment, searching for something, but what? He had no idea. What had happened to Frank down here? What was he doing? Just his job? Was he checking on the quality of the loading during his lunch break? Or was he looking for something? Or someone? Why would he be down here looking for anything?

Who was the real Frank? He most definitely wasn't only a chief officer. Some things he had said in the dream pointed that way. How much credence do you give a dream? But then the captain did mention they, whoever they were, put him on aboard on purpose. Could he actually have been a spy? He thought he had read somewhere that the British had recruited officers to watch for sabotage attempts on their ships. Was that it? He was on board to watch for a saboteur. Had the real Frank stumbled across one?

Or was he simply a good chief officer and, as such, was down here checking on the cargo, making sure it was being loaded right and properly secured for sea? And he just made a mistake, missed a rung on the ladder, got too close to the edge, stepped in something, maybe oil, and simply fell to his death? Thousands do it every day. Why not the real Frank? Merely because he was a seaman, that didn't exempt him from the consequences of stupid mistakes.

But then who was that peeking into his cabin last night? It could have been just someone passing by on the weather deck. But why would they run away? Who wouldn't, with a madman, his head covered in bandages, chasing them? Or maybe, they were up to no good? The crew wasn't supposed to be wandering around outside officers' country.

Damn, his head hurt! He was letting his imagination get carried away. Ghosts, spies—what did he think he would find down here? A bomb, maybe?

"A bomb. You have to get a hold of yourself!"

How foolish could you be?

Shaking his head, he started back up the ladder. "Really, a bomb."

CHAPTER SIX

ARRIVAL

He saw the three nurses as he stepped off the ladder from the boat deck. Dressed in their standard blue and white uniforms, the women were quietly talking as they leaned over the railing watching the waves glide by.

"Good morning, ladies," he said as he drifted by them on his way to the saloon. Thanks to his foray down into number five last night, he had missed dinner, and the only thing he had managed to find was a sandwich of cold cuts and hard bread that Sing, the steward, had whipped up for him. Now, twelve hours later, he was starving. He swore he could even smell bacon cooking.

"Oh, Mister Ross," one of the nurses called out.

With a silent groan, he turned back with a smile pasted on his face. "Yes?" He had no desire to waste time with that bacon calling, but common courtesy and his employer, the Bolt Steam Navigation Company, or more commonly the Bolt Line, required him to answer her.

"What can I do for you?"

A slightly overweight girl with blonde hair and bright red lips, who seemed familiar somehow, stepped forward. "While we were in the saloon, we heard we were off the coast of Nova Scotia, but we can't see anything."

"That's right, we are. But I'm afraid we're still twenty-six miles out," he glanced at Helen, who stood with her eyes glued to the deck, refusing to meet his glance. *Still not sure how to respond to my little tirade, I guess.*

"Twenty-six miles." The third girl, a pretty little brunette, pouted. "You can't see that far."

"Actually, you can, from up there," Frank pointed at the crow's nest high above their heads.

"We can't go up there."

"No, I'm afraid you can't, but you will be able to see the land from down here after we turn in toward the coast later this afternoon. Should be sometime around five o'clock."

"Oh, shoot!" the brunette said. "We were hoping to be the first to see Canada."

Frank glanced over at Helen. "Well, if you three don't mind, I hear breakfast calling me." He started to turn away.

"Mister Ross?" Helen ventured. "There is something I would like to discuss..." she glanced at her two companions; a look passed among them.

"Oh, yes," the brunette got the hint, "We need to get to breakfast too, Potts."

"Might as well, since there is nothing to see," the blonde pouted. She started toward the nearby hatchway; his eyes followed the sway of her ample hips as she moved by him. Then, a shiver ran through him as the feeling hit him that somehow it was inappropriate, kind of like he was staring at his own mother's bottom.

Where in the hell did that come from? He asked himself as he quickly looked away.

After a last sly smile, the brunette followed her, her rail-thin body a lot less memorable than the blonde's delicious curves. *Yuck*, for some reason, Frank just couldn't shake the feeling that he knew the blonde from somewhere.

"Thanks, Marion," Helen said, touching the brunette's hand as she passed.

Frank glanced at the departing women, sure now that all that beautiful bacon would be gone before he got there, again. With a shrug, he turned back to Helen, still standing quietly by the railing. He waited for her to begin, his only movement a slow sway in time with the ship.

When the others were well out of earshot, he whispered, "Potts?"

"Yes, Phyllis Potts."

There was something familiar about that name; just like the woman, maybe the real Frank had met her before, or he had read it on the manifest, but again, his memory failed him.

"We need to talk," Helen said in a serious tone.

"Have you told the captain yet?"

"No, I've been praying."

"Praying? Praying for what?"

"Guidance! Who else can I talk to?" She turned away from him, staring out across the blue expanse. "I mean, you tell me you aren't the real Frank Ross. That you are someone different, a man from what? The future? That the real Frank Ross is dead, and you are just occupying his body." She glanced back at him over her shoulder.

"I didn't know how much of that you caught," he admitted.

"Most of it, I'm afraid. I sat up all night with it running over and over through my mind. What did you mean by the moon shot? No, don't answer that."

She stepped over close to him, and the wind brought him an overpowering blast of her scent, Chanel, he was sure of it now. It was suddenly all around him, filling his head and clouding his senses. He glanced down into those two green pools of hers, staring up at him, glistening in the sunlight. "Then you believe me?" he asked.

"No! I don't. Would anybody? I mean, would you believe it if I told you that story? That I'm a dispossessed spirit from the future sent by God to save the world. It's a classic. Egomaniac with delusions of grandeur."

"I didn't say the world. I'm not that important," he joked. "Just this little ship." He looked at her, his need for her to believe in him plainly written on his face. "And the people aboard her." He turned away; those eyes were too much. Leaning back against the railing, he continued. "That's enough for me."

"Okay, strike the delusions of grandeur, but still, in my place, what would you do?" she asked, turmoil boiling in her eyes.

"I would have gone to the captain the moment you left me last night. I thought you would have."

"Maybe I should. Are you dangerous? Are you going to wake up in the middle of the night and kill us all?"

"Can't you tell? Look at me, seriously." He grabbed her arms and pulled her around to face him. "What is your gut telling you?"

"That you're a good man, a very confused one, but one who wants to do the right thing. And that's the problem. You want so badly to be the hero, but what if you're wrong?" She pulled away and started after her companions.

"So, what are you going to do?" he called after her.

She looked back, "Keep praying and hoping for an answer." She glanced up at the bridge. "But at the first sign that you are a danger to yourself or this ship, I will tell the captain." She disappeared into the athwartships passageway.

"Great," Frank looked up at the sky as he started to wander off aft, his breakfast completely forgotten. "Another pair of eyes watching me. Like I didn't have enough already!"

· · ·

Six hours later, the *Polites* changed course, coming about to north-northwest for the two-hour run into Halifax harbor.

On the new heading, the seas were now on her starboard quarter, running up on her from astern, and with her speed faster than the waves, the ship settled down to her passengers' great relief. The weather remained good, with visibility clear to the horizon. Traffic in and out of the port was light. All ships bound across the Atlantic were being gathered into convoys due to the danger the U-boats presented. Thus, instead of ships sailing in and out on their individual schedules, they now sailed in groups, creating periods of heavy traffic, when one of the eastbound convoys, either a fast HX or a slow SC (though eleven knots was fast only compared to seven) sailed for England. A lot of the inbound traffic was also arriving in groups. One of the westbound ON convoys returning to this east coast port—which was how the city was now being referred to in all the outgoing news reports, as if the Germans couldn't figure out which city they were talking about. After all, the Allies had used Halifax the same way during the last war.

At 1600 hours, Frank once more took the watch, but this time he wasn't reluctant to do so. He was in his element now, quite at ease and confident in his—or more correctly, the real Frank's—abilities. The captain was on the bridge when he arrived, and they had already slowed to half speed for the transit into the inner harbor past the city itself.

Fifteen minutes later, they slowed again as the pilot boat approached. "Boats" Bailey and his crew were busy on the forward well deck setting up a Jacob's ladder for the pilot's short climb up over the bulwark. The pilot turned out to be an ancient man who would have normally long ago put the sea behind him. He had in fact retired years ago but returned when the Pilot's Association called for help to ease the workload.

With a little help from Boats, the pilot managed the climb and landed on his own two feet on the well deck where Frank, now freed of his watch on the bridge by the captain and second officer Stratton, officially greeted him.

"Welcome aboard, Captain." Frank saluted as he delivered the standard honorific.

"Here are my credentials," the Canadian stated as he acknowledged the salute and held out a package wrapped in an oilskin pouch to protect the contents.

Frank took the proffered papers, and glancing at them, replied, "Captain Collins, sir. Everything looks in order."

"You're a Yank, aren't you?"

"Afraid so. The first mate broke his leg in Charleston," he offered.

"Oh." The old man nodded. "Fitting in, are we?"

"A few problems in translation, I'm afraid."

"I wouldn't doubt it," Captain Collins replied with a smile. "Lead on."

Frank led the way up the three sets of ladders before arriving on the starboard bridge wing. "Captain Egan, may I introduce Captain Collins of Dartmouth."

"Welcome aboard," Egan said as the two shook hands. "This is my navigator, Mister Stratton."

"A pleasure, sir." Collins nodded to Stratton, who stood just inside the wheelhouse near the chart table.

Collins took a glance down to verify the pilot boat was underway and returning to the station landing, where it would await the next ship.

"Well, sir," he began, "do I drive?"

"Be my guest," Egan replied.

"Helmsman, come right to three-three-five, and let's have turns for six knots."

Frank started back down the way he had come, for his station during all maneuvers into and out of port was on the fo'c'sle head with the bosun and his crew. They had to be ready to drop one of the anchors, at a second's notice, to stop the *Polites* from running aground or hitting something like another ship, or a pier, or even a bridge, in case a steering or engineering casualty should occur. All of which would make for a bad day.

From his vantage point, Frank watched as they approached the city, which was well protected by several layers of defenses. First up was the submarine net. They slowed to the point of just stemming the tide as they waited for the net tenders, a pair of armed trawlers, fishing boats with one small deck gun mounted in their bows, to open the net, each pulling an end back the opposite way, toward the York Redoubt on the mainland to port, and McNab Island, to starboard. As the gap between the two trawlers began to open, Frank felt the vibrations in the deck grow as the pilot called up more revolutions, and the *Polites* started inching her way on up the channel.

He waved at the deck crew on the trawler to port as they slid through the growing gap. Then as they passed her, he noticed a disturbance suddenly erupted in the water at the trawler's stern as her engine reversed, and she began to back down, closing the gate, barring the entrance to the harbor once more.

He also spotted at least a half dozen sets of binoculars on the trawler, all searching the water around the net, looking for any signs that a German sub was trying to use this opportunity to slip past the net into the inner harbor. The British had already lost a battleship to a German U-boat that got loose in Scapa Flow.

A little while later, the ship sailed past Pleasant Point Park at the tip of the Halifax Peninsula, and then the city itself appeared ahead. It was nothing in size compared to New York, for barely a hundred thousand people called this place home even after the recent population explosion.

The harbor was dotted along both sides with several smaller communities, the most important, Dartmouth, laid directly across the river from Halifax. The *Polites* had to slow to a near crawl for a few minutes at the mouth of the inner harbor to allow a ferry to cross between the two cities.

Right after that, she passed the Royal Canadian Navy's dockyard with its two towering cranes sitting on jetties running out into the harbor. Directly behind the dockyard on a low hill was the ancient citadel, first built in the late-eighteenth century to protect the harbor, which was far more valuable than the small town that then existed, against an attack by the Americans, who were in rebellion against King George III. Frank even glimpsed the old clock tower built by the Duke of York in 1803.

The city's piers were full of ships, and he saw hundreds of people crawling all over them like ants. He counted at least a dozen Royal Navy and Royal Canadian Navy ships, a six-inch cruiser, a few slick destroyers, but mostly those new Flower-class corvettes, even a few with the new, improved fo'c'sle.

But the *Polites* wasn't headed for one of the city's busy piers. No, they were to join an eastbound convoy sailing in two days, so they continued deeper into the harbor to where the rest of their companions were at anchor in Bedford Basin, a large expanse of water beyond the narrow channel just above the city. As they left the congestion of the inner harbor behind, Frank and Bailey began to prepare for anchoring.

With the large number of ships involved—over forty tankers, freighters, and transports were to sail with them—they would have to anchor fore and aft to keep the *Polites* from swinging in the wind, an event that could quickly bring them into contact with one of the other ships.

Mister Eddy, the third officer, was in charge on the fantail with another batch of seamen to handle the ship's stern anchor, which Bailey and his crew had rigged earlier in preparation.

It was an impressive sight as they entered Bedford Basin. Three dozen ships of all sizes and types were anchored fore and aft, in no order that Frank could discern, though maybe the Airedales could from up above, as he noted several planes slowly circling the area. The city's air defenses out on patrol.

Just past the headland, they put on a little left rudder to clear a tanker, then a mile farther on, and the ship went starboard before gliding another two cable lengths after the rumble of the diesels died away. A pair of harbor tugs then spun her about in her length, so she now pointed back the way she had come, ready to retrace her path back out into the Atlantic on Monday morning.

As the ship finished coming about, her bow now pointing toward the headland, Frank felt the engines shut down completely—all except for the generator's ta-pocketa-ta-pocketa. At anchor, the *Polites* would need to continue to produce electricity for herself. A moment later, the current caught her, and she started to drift sideways toward the Narrows.

"Let go forward," the captain bellowed through his megaphone from the bridge wing.

Frank glanced around the fo'c'sle, checking to make sure all the men were safely away from the anchor and its chain, then he nodded his approval, and Bailey swung the sledgehammer knocking the chocks off, and the anchor fell away, free and clear. The water was fifteen fathoms deep below the keel, and the bosun had set up twenty-five fathoms of chain, well over a hundred feet, on the line, and it ran fast and loud. In less than fifteen seconds, it had played out, and the main anchor came to rest deep in the thick muck at the bottom of Bedford Basin, a mile off the oil terminal.

No sooner had the forward chain finished its run than Frank heard the captain bellow again, "Let go aft." A couple of seconds later, the roar of the after chain reached him, and the *Polites,* like all the other ships in the basin, was safely anchored fore and aft.

CHAPTER SEVEN
ON THE TOWN

Frank felt like the Good Humor man, for his employer, the Bolt Line, in standard naval fashion, specified an all-white uniform for its officers during the summer months. So, here he was riding the Barrington Street trolley on his way into downtown Halifax dressed in all white: shoes, pants, shirt, and to top it off, perched on his head an officer's cap with a white cover. Even his undergarments were all white (not to mention a little weird, what with the snaps). The only color he was wearing was the black hardboards on his shoulders, complete with the three gold stripes of a chief officer. In his case, the boards each bore a fouled anchor, set in the American fashion above the stripes instead of the executive curl that the British officers used. He laughed to himself. He had everything but the ice cream and the little silver bell.

Glancing around the trolley, he felt oddly out of place even though several other sailors, all in white like him, were also board. Standing out like this was so out of the norm for him. He preferred to blend in. Ordinarily, he wouldn't have worn his uniform, but Halifax was a war zone, and standing orders required him to remain in uniform at all times. At least he wasn't wearing those shorts like the Brits did; that might have been a deal-breaker, even though this would be his only opportunity to see Halifax; tomorrow he had duty, and the next day they were scheduled to sail for England.

But still, even with the Good Humor outfit, he was chomping at the bit. Just imagine—an opportunity to visit a city that hadn't existed in almost a century. What student of history wouldn't give his eye teeth to step back in time and witness this for themselves?

So, here he was on an electric-powered tram car he with a mix of sailors, dockyard laborers, and office workers, on a short journey back into history.

Barrington Street ran parallel with the waterfront for a mile with residential Halifax on the right, and the Royal Canadian Navy's dockyard on the left, then it took a slight turn to the right, leaving the harbor and the smell of dead fish behind. Up ahead, he could see the slowly approaching downtown, where the small one- and two-story houses surrounded by neatly tended lawns gave way to a dozen blocks of tightly packed red brick buildings three and four stories high. A wide variety of small shops—a butcher, a shoe store, women's fashions, a haberdasher, and a radio shop—inched past as the tram worked its way up the street. In the distance, he could see two separate theater marquees advertising their current features, and suddenly the idea of watching a classic movie in glorious black and white in a real movie palace sounded like the perfect way to spend a few hours. He couldn't quite make out the titles yet, but they were getting closer by the minute. Just beyond the marquees, he could make out a church steeple marking the end of the compact downtown strip.

As the wildly decorated tram car (all four sides were extorting the populace to buy Canadian Victory Bonds) bumped along, Frank saw an array of vintage automobiles whiz by—a Model T, a V-8 Ford, a Chevrolet, and a Pierce-Arrow, to name only a few. This trip was quickly living up to his expectations; it was a dream come true for a history buff like himself.

As they entered the downtown, suddenly, the sidewalks were full of pedestrians. He noticed a mother with her young daughter, a group of sailors in a tight knot, a gaggle of school kids running through the crowd, and even several soldiers in kilts. Must be a Scottish regiment in town. Damn, those were even worse than the white shorts. His eyes never stopped jumping from one group to the next. He wanted to see everything; this was his one chance to really experience the past. It was like a beautifully produced movie but oh-so-much more because it was real. To these people, this was their lives—like yesterday was and tomorrow will be. They had no idea how this would all work out, whether they would win the war or not, and who would live or die. It was almost too much for him to think about.

The tram drew closer to the center of town, and he could finally make out the words on the marquees. The near one was the Orpheus, but they didn't list their feature on the marquee. So, as the tram slowed to let a couple off, Frank joined them in exiting the car. He almost fell, trying to read the poster while not watching where he was going.

"Easy mate," offered a Jack Tar, identified by his hatband as from the HMCS Ottawa, a Canadian ship.

Funny. I thought they would have dropped the hatbands by now. They would allow a spy to identify the ships in harbor by just reading the names on the sailors' hats.

"Sorry," Frank mumbled, moving away from the tram and stepping up onto the sidewalk. There, he stopped and studied the poster below the now playing banner. 'Women untamed! Dangers Unknown! Men Unafraid! You'll find them all. *South of Suez* with George Brent and Brenda Marshall.' A perfect B-picture, and the marque listed two more showings today! Either would work, but the next one was still more than an hour away.

So, he had a little time to kill. What could he do to waste an hour? Then, his stomach voiced its opinion, growling so loud a passing businessman missed a step.

Smiling at him, Frank said, "I guess I am a little hungry."

"I guess so." The man chuckled. "You could try the Green Lantern. It's one of the best in town," the man suggested, pointing toward the next doorway.

• • •

Frank had made it only as far as the soda counter, right inside the doorway. An open stool and a line of patrons waiting for the hostess' attention had altered his plans a little.

Now, he was busy looking over the short menu the soda jerk had handed him a few minutes earlier. He had already delivered the vanilla Coke Frank ordered when he first arrived, and the poor man had been back twice already to get the rest of his order only to find Frank once more engrossed in watching the steady flow of people past his stool in and out of the restaurant proper through a pair of doors to his left. Each time,

Frank apologized and redoubled his inspection of the menu. He was trying to decide if he wanted to settle for a burger or go for something a little more substantial, but he couldn't quite make up his mind as he glanced down the counter to check on the soda jerk's progress. Thankfully, he was still busy with a couple who had just sat down. It seemed they were trying to decide between a banana split and a chocolate shake, but it wouldn't be long before he would be back again. So, with renewed resolve, Frank put his head down and focused his attention on the menu. It was printed in green on heavy white stock, the restaurant's logo on one side, and the menu on the other.

No, who cares what the menu looks like? Concentrate on the food. You're here for the food. You're hungry, remember?

The standard hamburger included an all-beef patty on a freshly baked bun with your choice of condiments.

"Mister Ross," A woman's voice cut into his inspection of the menu.

Looking up, he found himself gazing into those two green pools again.

"Miss Morris," he replied as he tried to scramble quickly to his feet, only to realize it wasn't her who had called his name. The other two nurses stood beside her again. The familiar one they called Potts was the one who had spoken. "And ladies," he added, trying without success to cover his mistake, but his embarrassment sabotaged that effort by producing a bright red blush, which contrasted nicely with his white uniform.

The other two exchanged a glance as Helen stared at the ground, a blush blooming on her cheeks as well. Suppressing a giggle, Potts continued. "I see you're hungry, too, Mister Ross. Would you care to join us? It would pair us off, two and two." She smiled again, and Helen remained staring at the ground, her blush growing brighter.

"Yes, do," the third girl, Marion, added. "Poor Helen doesn't have a partner."

"Okay, stop it, you two. You're embarrassing poor Mister Ross." Helen finally spoke up, their eyes connecting. The other two women tried to suppress their giggles without much success.

Turning to face Frank, Helen continued, "If you cared to, we would be happy to have you join us. I know these two are poor company, but it still beats eating alone." She glanced sharply at her two friends before pointing at the menu and the half-drunk Coke on the counter behind him.

His old standby reaction, to pull away, instantly kicked in, "No, I wouldn't want to intrude on you."

"Well, if you are sure?" Helen offered again before the three women began to move on, and Frank turned back to his drink. Sitting down, he reached out to pick up the menu. He could see the soda jerk sliding down the counter toward him as the familiar sense of loss washed over him. *What am I doing?* He asked himself. *Exactly what I have always done. Saying no when I desperately want to say yes. What is it they say? Doing the same thing over and over and expecting a different outcome. . . .*

"On second thought," he said, turning back toward the women, "I would love to join you." He tossed a green Canadian one-dollar bill on the counter. "Keep the change," he told the soda jerk as he walked away.

"Make that four," Potts corrected herself.

"This way, please," the hostess mumbled as she started through the double doors after grabbing another menu from under the counter.

• • •

The four of them stepped out onto the street after a fine dinner at the Green Lantern. The businessman was right about it being one of the best.

"Nothing against the cook, but that was a cut above," Potts stated with some enthusiasm. The rest agreed with a hearty laugh.

"You know, it's not—" Frank began.

"Oh, I understand," Potts cut him off. "A rolling deck, no fresh supplies, a very limited budget—it's a miracle he can produce anything that's even edible. Still, you've got to admit that was in a whole different league."

"I wouldn't want the cook's job." Marion voiced their mutual sentiment.

"Well," Helen began, glancing down at the sidewalk. She was unsure about how to approach her next subject. After all, a lady didn't suggest such things in polite society. Why she wasn't sure, but her mother was not one for questions on such matters.

"We were thinking about taking in a picture show. Would you care to accompany us, Mister Ross?" Potts beat her to the punch, a knowing smile on her lips.

"Well, I was thinking of the same thing."

"Great. Then it's settled. You're coming with us." Potts and Marion each took one of his arms and down the street they went, pulling Frank along between them past the Orpheus and the poster for *South of Suez.*

Frank glanced back over his shoulder at the receding marquee. "But?" he began before he noticed Helen trailing along a few feet behind them, and suddenly, all thought of George Brent and Brenda Marshall vanished.

Chances, that's what life is, he realized. A series of chances, each a different choice, and with each decision you make or don't make, life leads you down a different path. Most choices cause only small alterations—you dine in one restaurant or another—but some lead to a one-eighty. Most people drift with the current going where life leads, never fighting it, or even deciding where they really want to go, but a few make their choices, take their chances, and go where they want, or at least die trying. He hadn't—not for the most part. Now and then, he had stepped out on a different path, one he wanted to follow, changing his life forever. His time in the Navy was one of those choices. It had always been a dream, but then he let life lead him down a different path, and he walked away from the Navy.

Soon his choices were of less importance. His life was on autopilot, and he just reacted to everyone's demands—his ex-wife, his children, his job—and went along with what they all expected. He followed the well-worn path, like most people, even when it led him to places he never wanted to go.

But now, God had given him a second chance to walk the path less traveled. This time he would change things and grab all he could for as long as it lasted.

"Where are we going?" he inquired.

"Spain," Potts informed him.

"Spain?"

"Yes, with Tyrone Power," she cooed, a look of pure ecstasy on her face.

"*Blood and Sand* is playing at the Capital," Helen supplied. It wasn't exactly his kind of film, but the company made it well worth the price.

● ● ●

Two and a half hours later, Helen and Frank found themselves alone among the crowd as it spilled out of the fake medieval castle that was the Capitol Theatre into the dark streets of downtown Halifax. Only an occasional streetlight was still burning. None of the business signs you usually see in the center of a major city were lit, for here, in Canada, a war was on, and a curfew was in effect. The Civil Defense officials were continually reminding the populace from what distance a Nazi pilot or a U-boat captain could see a single light. The local council was very serious about the war effort, and they took the threat of an attack to heart, even here, six miles up the channel. Behind the protection of a dozen shore batteries, they were taking steps to minimize the city's exposure as a target. They didn't want a repeat of the 1917 explosion that had wiped out half the town.

Frank and Helen flowed along with the crowd for nearly a block before a desperate Frank took Helen by the arm and barreled his way across the flow into a darkened bakery's doorway. He stood with his back to the crowd, shielding her from the pushing and shoving as the last of the throng filed past.

He slipped his hands into his pockets, his eyes locked on the sign advertising cakes of various sizes on the opposite wall inside the closed shop. He didn't dare look at her, not into those deep green pools. Not again. Her Chanel perfume filled his consciousness.

She stood stark still, unwilling to touch him. She had to remain in control. Where had Potts and Marion got to? They were there a moment ago, right beside her. Then, they were gone in an instant, swept away in a rush; either by plan or by accident, they had abandoned her to him. His presence was like a concrete wall, shielding her, cutting her off from the crowd, leaving her with a sense of drowning. She had to fight; she couldn't afford to lose control. Then, her hands reached out and touched him. A shock ran through them both. She jerked her hands away as if he had burned her.

He forced himself to continue to stare at the sign in the darkened bakery. He simply couldn't let himself look at her. He fought to buy time by focusing on the prices of the cakes—single layer, double layer, anything to keep his mind busy and away from thoughts about her trapped between him and the glass door. Her soft, inviting scent filled his head, and he knew he was fighting a losing battle. Where had all these people come from? He needed room and a little fresh air. Anything to clear his mind! It seemed a thousand people had walked past already. Her warm breath caressed his neck. If these people didn't hurry up and get past him, he wouldn't be responsible for his behavior.

God, help me.

Though he refused to surrender, he couldn't stop himself from glancing down into her eyes. Why was she looking up? He was instantly lost and couldn't look away. Ten thousand men didn't have the strength to look away now. His lips started down toward hers of their own accord.

Then, the pressure of the crowd disappeared, and he fell back out of the doorway, away from her.

The spell was broken.

He took a deep breath. Closing his eyes, he steeled himself, trying to recover his control.

Helen sighed. "I wonder where," she managed.

"What?" he asked, still not strong enough to open his eyes.

She pushed past him out onto the sidewalk. She had to escape the confines of that doorway. He was still much too close.

She looked down the street in the direction the crowd had disappeared. "I was just wondering where

Potts and Marion have gone." She quickly looked the other way. Part of her hoped to see their familiar faces, but part hoped not.

She took another step away.

"I don't see them," he said in a hoarse voice.

She made her mistake then. The quiver in his voice tripped her up, and she glanced up into his gray eyes. In that instant, she was lost.

He held out his hand. She took it, and the warmth flowed up her arm and into her chest. He smiled, and without a sound, they fell into step together. She slid in close beside him, their fingers entwined together, neither of them aware of their surroundings.

● ● ●

They were together, arm and arm, on a bridge. It was a small pedestrian-only affair surrounded by a beautifully landscaped garden in the center of town, Halifax's Public Gardens, a few blocks in from the waterfront and close to the Citadel. The grounds were barely visible in the enveloping darkness. No one else was nearby. He could feel her heart pounding against his chest; his own was racing.

How long they had walked, how they had gotten here, he didn't know. He didn't know how long they had been here either. All he was aware of was Helen. Only the two of them filled the entire world, a world which was merely a few dozen feet across, for that was all he could see and all he cared about. It was all that mattered. The rest could have vanished, and neither of them would have noticed.

He couldn't believe this woman he hadn't known existed two days ago—in fact, they had been born more than half a century apart—had come to mean so much to him. He still wasn't sure if this was real or just a dream. Perhaps it was only the dying embers of his brain firing in its final seconds before the desolation of death claimed him for all eternity. Even if that was true, at least for this moment, she was his, and he was hers, as their bodies pressed hard against each other. Her presence filled him to overflowing, and for as long as she was in his arms, all was right with the world, and nothing else mattered.

She moved for the first time in what seemed like hours. How long had it been? He glanced down at her. Even in the dark, he could find those green pools, for it appeared a light shimmered within her.

She smiled. She couldn't fight it anymore; she didn't want to fight it any longer. She rose to her toes. He was so tall. Her mouth drew close to his.

Then a light snapped on. From somewhere behind it, a voice demanded, "What are you two doing here? Don't you know the gardens closed at sunset?"

They both stared into the light like a pair of deer, blind to all but its glow. Dumbfounded, speechless, they just continued to stare.

"Come on, get a move on. You can't stay here." The light dropped to the ground at their feet, and an old man in a guard's uniform slowly emerged from the darkness. "It's time to head home. Wherever that is." With his free hand, he pointed back past him. "That way to the gate."

"Sorry, we lost track of time." Frank began.

"Anyone can see that, son. But it's time to move on."

"Of course." He took Helen's small hand in his, felt her long fingers wrap around his, and they started in the direction the guard was pointing.

As they passed the old man, he whispered, "It's okay, sonny. I've got lost a time or two myself."

They ambled through the gardens, arm and arm, the older man following a few steps behind, all the way to the gate that he opened for them and then clanged shut behind them.

"Now, you get that girl home before you do something you both will regret," the man called after them.

"Old coot!" Helen whispered under her breath, her frustration plain on her face and in her voice. "We weren't going to do anything like that. He'll have people thinking the wrong thing."

Frank glanced around. "What people?"

She jerked to a stop. "Are you siding with him?"

"Whoa!" he said, holding his hands up. "I surrender."

Helen stopped with her mouth open and stared at him for a long moment. Her anger then vanished in an instant, and she burst out laughing.

Frank lowered his hands, a smile coming to his lips as he watched her fight to regain control.

"I surrender, too," she finally managed over the subsiding giggles. "I don't know what caused that." She gazed up into his eyes. "That's not right. I know exactly what caused it." She grabbed his arm, searching for the right place. "Come on."

She pulled him after her. They walked down the street toward a deep doorway full of shadows. She continued to lead, pulling him into the darkest part. Turning around, her back against the red-painted door, she looked up again into his gray eyes. "Men aren't the only ones who get lost." Her hands went up to his face and pulled him close. He could feel her body against his. My God, she felt good!

"Should we be doing this?" he murmured.

"I don't care," she replied, her scent filling his world.

"I mean, I just don't want to do something you will regret."

"Give it up, Frank. I'm a big girl." She pulled him even closer, her breasts pressed against his chest.

"I can see that," Frank whispered, fighting to keep his hands off her. Somewhere in the back of his mind, a small voice screamed that he wasn't the real Frank Ross, that he was here for a reason, and this wasn't it. He couldn't stay, he had no future, and the last thing he wanted to do was hurt this woman.

He tried to pull away.

"Where are you going?" She pulled him close again with surprising strength and lifted onto her toes. Her mouth moved closer to his. He felt the warmth of her breath and, for an instant, wanted to inhale her.

"No," he murmured. He pulled away again. She dropped on to her heels, flat-footed, her arms out, open, suddenly empty.

"What's wrong now?"

"I can't." He stepped into the light. "It wouldn't be right. I don't know how long I'll be here."

"None of us do!" Her mind was spinning, trying to understand, reeling from the pain of rejection. "I could get killed crossing the street ten minutes from now. Isn't that a damn good reason not to put things off?"

"But I told you, I'm not the real Frank. This is not my body." His voice trailed off.

"You could have fooled me," she moaned in frustration. Then she moved over to where he stood. "Frank, look at me!" she demanded. "It's okay. I'm a grown woman, and I know what I am doing. I also know what you think happened is not real. It's just your mind trying to make sense of bits and pieces of memories all jumbled up and thrown together by your accident. I've seen things like this before. When you fell, you hit with such force that it scrambled your brains. Connections were destroyed, pathways your mind has used for decades were broken. It's trying to relearn, reconnect, and repair itself. Relax, it will take time. It only makes sense that you would have trouble putting everything back together. Your mind can't tell what is real and what is just dreams, so it's treating them all the same, trying to create a narrative that incorporates all of them."

"That makes sense. But I remember a different place, a different time, a different life." A vision of his daughter-in-law's fear-filled eyes popped up again. "I had four sons and a job as an accountant. I remember watching movies about this war. Pearl Harbor, Normandy, the Battle of the Bulge. I'm afraid it can't be only a dream."

"Does it make any sense for it to be real? You died somewhere in the future and awoke in a different body, years in the past? That God sent you here to finish some task the real Frank didn't finish? Or does it seem more likely that you are Frank Ross, an American Merchant Marine officer, who slipped and fell? And that the fall scrambled your brains, and now you have all these mixed-up memories?"

"I guess that does sound more reasonable, doesn't it?"

"Of course, it does." She moved closer. "Besides, do you think I would be falling in love with a crazy man?"

He looked down into her eyes. He was lost again as he gazed into those green pools.

Behind him, a thirty-eight-model black Ford Deluxe sedan rolled up to a quiet stop. The rear door opened, and two men in business suits climbed out.

Helen was just rising on to her toes again when the taller one asked, "Excuse me, are you Chief

Officer Franklin Ross of the motor ship *Polites*?"

CHAPTER EIGHT
SPECIAL PASSENGER

"Who wants to know?" Frank asked, turning toward the men as he stepped in between them and Helen.

"Sergeant Preston, Royal Canadian Mounted Police," the taller one answered as he flashed his badge.

"What can we do for you, Sergeant?" Frank relaxed a little but remained wary.

"Your captain has requested that you join him downtown. We are here to transport you."

"Oh." Frank glanced over his shoulder at Helen. "I can't just leave her."

"My partner will give Miss Morris a ride to the landing and see her safely aboard the harbor launch."

The second man opened the car's rear door. "Yes, Miss Morris, you have nothing to worry about. We'll have you safe and sound aboard the *Polites* in no time at all."

Frank turned to her. "I'm sorry—"

"Of course, you have to go. The war calls." She then smiled at Frank as she stepped past him but avoided the hand he held out toward her and, without another word, climbed into the back of the black Ford, followed immediately by the second officer. Instantly, the car pulled away from the curb. Frank watched it glide silently down the street until it took a left and disappeared around the corner.

"Well?" Frank mumbled, somewhat lost by the rapid turn of events. "I guess we're walking?"

"No. Another car will be along in a minute."

"What's this all about?"

"I don't know. I'm just sent to fetch. The reasons are above my pay grade."

Just then, another black Ford Deluxe rolled to a stop beside them. Preston opened the rear door, "After you, sir."

Whipping his hat off, Frank slid across the rear seat to the far side as Preston climbed in and pulled the door closed behind them. The car was already moving before Frank heard the loud click of the door latch. Two more officers, dressed in the same dark business suits, sat motionless in the front seat.

"You guys all use the same tailor?" Frank asked, trying to ease a sudden case of the jitters, but he got no reply. He tried again. "Okay, then, where are we going? You know that much, at least."

The three men continued to stare straight ahead.

"No rush. I've got all evening."

Preston finally glanced over, "Just sit back and enjoy the ride, Mister Ross. All your questions will be answered when we get there."

"All I wanted to know is where there is."

"You'll know that when we get there."

Frank gave up and sat back, fuming in silence, as the Ford turned away from the waterfront and headed out of downtown. So much for Preston's earlier story. Frank looked over at him. "Not a Boy Scout, were we?"

Preston smiled, "Orders."

The car left the built-up area of the city and passed into a small forest dimly illuminated only by the car's partially shielded headlights. It rounded a bend and pulled to a stop at a little guard shack manned by a pair of Canadian soldiers, evidenced by the Canada tabs on their coat sleeves. The driver flashed his identification and then handed the guard a slip of pink paper, which the guard examined in the beam of his flashlight. Satisfied, he gave it back and saluted. His partner at the signal opened the gate by pushing down on the counterweight.

The Ford continued down the narrow road and immediately started climbing a sharp rise, the engine straining slightly under the load until a solid brick wall emerged from the darkness. They immediately rolled through a small portal in the wall, and as they emerged out into a courtyard surrounded by a brick parapet, Frank realized he was in the old citadel, Fort George.

First erected in 1749, the same year the city was established, the fort had been built and rebuilt, repaired, and expanded with each new threat from first the natives, then the French, then the Americans, twice, and now for the second time, the Germans. Fort George had sat silently on top of Citadel Hill, protecting Halifax for almost two centuries without firing a shot. During the last war, the Canadians used it to house individuals of "doubtful" background—in other words, German immigrants and those who had spoken out in support of the enemy. There was no Bill of Rights here, north of the border. Of course, even south of it, in the right circumstances, even the Americans would violate them, as the Japanese Americans were to learn to their dismay in the coming year. So far, in this war, the fort had only served for storage and additional office space.

The car rolled to a stop before a large entrance leading back into the outer wall. A soldier stepped up to the Ford and opened Frank's door. A second, this one with the twin pips of a first lieutenant, appeared behind the first. "Please come with me, Mister Ross."

Frank looked at Preston. "Good night, Mister Ross. This is as far as we go. They'll take care of you from here."

Frank squared his shoulders and climbed out of the car. The lieutenant spun military fashion, on his heels and marched off toward the entrance without another word. Behind him, the soldier closed the door, and the black Ford rolled silently off into the night.

Frank glanced at the soldier who instantly snapped to attention and delivered a British style salute, palm out, the hand even vibrated at the end. *Show off!* The soldier held the salute, waiting for Frank to respond. He glanced down at the white-topped cap in his hand and smiled. *Okay, two can play!* He slipped the cap onto his head, turned to face the soldier, and returned the salute, mariner-style—palm down, fingers curled near the brim, sloppy as all hell. The soldier dropped his salute and turned away in a huff. *Shouldn't have done that.*

"Mister Ross, they *are* waiting," the lieutenant called from just outside the portal.

"Who?" Frank demanded. All this cloak and dagger crap was starting to get old, and he wanted some answers.

The lieutenant refused to play and simply extended his hand toward the portal.

"I know! You're not at liberty to say."

"Exactly."

"Okay then, lead on," Frank said with a forced smile.

The lieutenant spun on his heels again and marched into the corridor. *I bet he practices that in front of a mirror*, Frank thought as he followed several steps behind down a dimly lit passageway. The corridor's walls were of whitewashed bricks, which continued up into a vaulted arch high over his head. His footsteps on the concrete echoed back to him from the dim recesses of the corridor, and somewhere in the distance, he heard water dripping, which explained the overpowering smell of mildew.

They turned a corner, and the lieutenant stopped before a heavy wooden door. He knocked. Twice. The door slowly swung open on silent hinges, and a Royal Navy Commander poked his head out.

"Ah! They finally found you, did they?"

"Excuse me?"

"Excuse you. Do you know how long you have kept us waiting?" the Commander asked.

"I'm sorry, but I didn't know I was expected."

"You're joking, right? It's that odd sense of humor you Americans have."

"No, I'm not joking. I came as soon as that Mountie found me. I was told they needed me for a meeting downtown. Something to do with the convoy, I assumed. But this doesn't seem to be downtown. Beyond that, I have no idea what this is all about."

"Of course, you don't. We haven't told you yet. But they told you in New York to be here at fifteen hundred hours," an American voice announced from inside the room.

Frank turned to face the new speaker. An older man with gray hair and a solid build sat with his feet up on a large wooden desk. He slowly put his feet down, one at a time, and then stood up.

"And you are?" Frank demanded. An American was the last person he had expected to meet here in the bowels of a fort in Canada.

"What in God's name is wrong with you, Ross? Hit your head or something?" the man asked.

"Yes, as a matter of fact, I did." He lifted his cap so the bandages were visible.

"My God, what happened?"

"I guess I fell."

"You guess?" the commander inquired.

"Yes. All I remember is waking up at the bottom of number five a couple of days ago in New York."

"Number five. What the hell is number five?" the American stormed.

"Number five hold. The one furthest aft. I must have been checking up after they loaded cargo in New York. Somehow, I slipped and fell. Busted my head open. There was blood everywhere."

"You slipped?" the American asked. "Since you can't remember what happened, we can't just assume that. This isn't good at all."

"You have a knack for stating the obvious, Donovan," the commander lamented, running his fingers through his blond hair as he paced the room.

"And what happened to all that classic 'stiff upper lip' and 'damn the torpedoes' you Brits are famous for, Commander Fleming?" Donovan asked with a hint of a smile on his lips. Being of Irish descent, he always liked to mess with his British associates.

"Jokes! Donovan? This fool of yours," Fleming said, stopping in front of Frank, "is either a sad sack, slipping all over the place, or the Nazis are far better informed about our operations than we thought. And thanks to his lack of memory, we don't know which it is. In fact, he doesn't even remember he's working for us. Besides, 'damn the torpedoes' was a Yank. 'Every man will do his duty' is our slogan."

"Working for you?" Frank repeated.

"Yes, Mister Ross. You work for me on loan to British Intelligence," the American said.

"And you are?"

"You're kidding, right?"

Frank slowly shook his head.

"Bill Donovan."

"Wild Bill!"

"Never liked that name. Nothing I ever do isn't completely planned out beforehand. I guess you remember me now?"

"I know about you. You work for Roosevelt."

"Yep, that I do. And my presence here should give you an idea of how important this is."

"Its success or failure might just decide the course of the war," Commander Fleming stated, staring at Frank from across the room.

"I doubt that, but it could make things a lot harder if you fail," Donovan said as he retook his seat. "Sit." He pointed at a chair in front of the desk.

"How can I be that important? I'm just a Merchant Marine officer. I'm not even the captain." He was not about to tell them who he really was. That would only get him locked up as a security threat. "Right?"

"Yes, you are," Fleming answered. "But you have been working for over a year now for the BSC, SIS's operation here in America. One of the hundreds—Americans, British, and Canadians—monitoring the waterfront and all the ships heading for England. Looking for signs of Nazi activities, watching over important shipments, keeping an eye out for cargo going to the other side."

"Okay, I've heard of that."

"Good," Donovan stated.

"What does this have to do with me?"

"I give up," Fleming said, turning away.

"This is a little different. A special project." Donovan began after giving Fleming the evil eye.

"Are we still going ahead with this fool?" Fleming dropped into an empty chair with a thud.

"Do we have a choice? He'll be here in a few hours. And the longer he sits here, the more likely the Nazi will find out."

"If they don't already know."

"In that case, the longer he sits, the more time they'll have to arrange a nice reception for him."

"Damned if we do—"

"Exactly!" Donovan turned to Frank. "Tomorrow, your captain and navigator will attend the convoy meeting. You are to stay aboard. Keep your eyes peeled. The Nazis may have something planned, maybe if they don't already have somebody aboard, you can stop them." Fleming laughed. Donovan ignored him. "It'll be their last chance. Then, tomorrow night at midnight, you will have a barge come alongside with a last-minute load. There is room in number four on the 'tween decks, I believe, to stow it."

"How would you know that?" Frank asked.

"Intelligence." Fleming snorted, pointing back and forth between himself and Donovan. "That's what we do. Besides, you set it up that way."

"Me?"

"Yes, the loading plan?" Fleming suggested before turning away with a huff.

Donovan gave Fleming another look before picking up a large brown envelope from the desk, "You will deliver this to Captain Egan just before the barge arrives. It will explain everything to him."

"Everything he needs to know, at least," Fleming added.

Donovan continued as though Fleming hadn't interrupted, "You will handle the stowing of the cargo, and the surrounding area will be secured and guarded at all times. Use the naval gunners aboard. Will give them something to do besides playing with that useless relic they call a gun."

Fleming continued the tag team. "You will also receive an additional passenger. He is a very special passenger. You have an open cabin on the upper deck beside the captain. You will put him in there, and he will remain in the cabin—no wandering about. Even his meals are to be delivered to him. And no socializing with the other passengers, the officers, and especially not the crew."

"Your job is to see that this passenger and that cargo reach England at all costs," Donovan finished.

"Do you understand, Mister Ross?" Fleming demanded.

"Yes, sir." What had he got himself into?

● ● ●

Frank watched the motorboat as it worked its way across the open water toward the landing. He could see a dozen other boats heading in the same direction, one from each of the ships around the anchorage, each with two passengers. Every ship in what would become convoy HX-133 was sending its captain and navigator to the mid-morning meeting with the convoy's commodore and escort commander.

There, they would receive copies of the sailing orders, along with instructions on station keeping, signaling, and, most importantly, what to do if the convoy should come under attack. It was those rules and instructions that would play a large role in whether the *Polites,* her crew, and her passengers would survive the next several weeks, whether she would successfully run the gauntlet of U-boats waiting out there somewhere in the middle of the Atlantic.

"Good morning," Helen said, approaching him from behind.

As Frank turned to face her, a smile broke across his face, driven by memories of the night before. Dressed in her nurse's uniform with baby blue stripes and red crosses on the left breast and sleeve, she was once again distant, sterile, and efficient, except her face was radiant. At the sight of it, his heart swelled with hope—hope his mind instantly crushed with the weight of reality.

"Before you say anything," she began, "I want to apologize for the way I behaved last night. It was just that—"

"No! You have nothing to apologize for. I'm the one who needs to ask for forgiveness. I'm sorry. I let myself get carried away," Frank spouted before she could finish her thought. He couldn't afford to let her finish; his heart wouldn't survive it—no matter what she was about to say. "It was beneath my position and the trust my employer has placed in me. I didn't intend to take advantage of you. I'm afraid that some of my rough edges are still showing. Please, accept my apology and know that nothing like that will ever happen again. Now, if you will excuse me, duty calls."

Frank turned and walked away without a single glance back. He couldn't allow her reaction to sway his determination. He had spent the night tossing and turning in his rack after he had returned to the landing with Sergeant Preston, going over what he now knew. First, the meeting with Colonel Donovan and Commander Fleming had convinced him that this wasn't a dream. He was here in June of 1941 aboard this ship for a purpose. Frank Ross had a mission, an especially important one, and both the British and the American governments were counting on him. He was here to fight the Nazis and to make a difference, as he had always dreamed. This was his chance, and he wasn't going to let his feelings for Helen interfere with that. His mission was way too important.

Moreover, if he wasn't the real Frank Ross, he couldn't bear to hurt her by getting involved only to disappear when he had finished doing whatever he had been put here to do. He may be here now, but that didn't mean he would stay for long, and he just couldn't hurt her that way. Better a little pain now instead of heartbreak later.

Finally, he made it around the corner and paused for a deep breath before slipping down the ladder to the after well deck on his way to check on the 'tween deck in the number four hold. He had a mission, and he intended to succeed.

• • •

Midnight came and went. Everything remained quiet. Nothing stirred out on the peaceful waters of Bedford Basin. The minutes slowly ticked away until the faint peal of dozens of bells echoed across the water to join the *Polites'* single toll to mark the half-hour. The sound rose in a muddled harmony to the ears of two men in black standing together on the starboard bridge wing.

"So, where are they, Mister Ross?" Captain Egan inquired in the silence that followed.

"Not sure, sir. All I know is that the barge was scheduled to come alongside just after midnight. And one bell is after midnight, sir." Frank tried to lighten the mood.

"Yes, and so is eight bells, but I sure as hell have no intention of standing here that long. We must be underway just after sunrise. It's going to be a long day tomorrow. They have forty-nine ships, not counting the escorts, to get out through the narrows and into formation before we can even really get going. We'll be lucky to get it done before sunset."

"I understand, Captain, but I'm sure—"

"Very well, Mister Ross. Another half an hour, and then it's to bed with me."

Twenty-three minutes later, the bosun, Bailey, called up from the main deck. "Something's approaching off to port, sir."

"Well, it looks like your guests have finally arrived, Mister Ross. Let's go meet them."

"Yes, sir."

Frank followed the skipper down three flights to the main deck, where they joined Bailey and two of his seamen. Frank recognized Red, but the other was new to him, a complete blank.

"What's your name?" he asked.

"You don't remember poor George, sir? He's the man who signed you on in Charleston," the bosun answered for the man. "That must have been one hell of a knock on the head you got there, Mister Ross."

Frank glanced over at George again, and this time, the features did strike him as vaguely familiar. Then Bailey and Red began to laugh. Frank turned to stare at the two.

"Sorry, Mister Ross," Bailey said, looking down at the deck, "I couldn't help me-self. George, here, is new. He just signed on from the union hall. Captain wanted a full crew for the crossing."

Frank continued to stare, a fire burning in his eyes. "Funny, but don't let it happen again."

Just then, a barge, towed by a harbor tug, emerged from the darkness into the small area illuminated by the *Polites'* anchor light. The tug deftly altered its course to bring its charge right up alongside the ship with only a slight bump against the hull plates. Its engine revved in reverse for a moment to take her head off, and she slowed to a dead stop right under the light.

A deckhand called up from below, "Ahoy! On deck."

Bailey replied in a low growl, "Keep it down, mate. Don't want to wake the neighbors."

"Catch," the hand called at the same volume as he tossed a line over the gunwale. Bailey caught it, a pained expression on his face. "What can you do?" he asked as he and Red passed it down through the bulwark and then around a nearby bit, securing the line in an instant.

"Heave tight," he called back as they stepped away for safety. The line was quickly pulled taut from below. A moment later, a second line came over forward, where George had positioned himself, and in short order, it, too, was secure and tight.

Bailey watched the whole procedure before stepping up to take a tug on the line to test the job. "Good," he voiced his opinion. George was new and still on probation as far as Bailey was concerned, no matter what his seamen's card said, at least for the first couple of weeks until he proved himself. Looking back at the captain, he continued, "At least, they sent me a man who knows the basics. Can teach the rest. Red, you and George get that ladder over the side."

"Aye, Boats," Red said in his thick accent, already lifting the wooden rungs connected by two manila lines. "Give us a hand here, George."

The new seaman took hold of the ladder from the other side, and then they lifted it up and over the four-foot-high bulwark. Frank noted that the bosun and his men had already secured the upper end of the ladder to the tie-downs built into the bulwark's support structure. They let go of the ladder, and it snaked down the side of the ship. Due to the *Polites'* load, it didn't have far to go, and it landed on the barge with a loud clang.

"Now who's making the noise?" came drifting up from the darkness below.

"Smartass Canuck." Bailey bellowed.

A moment later, a man in his mid-thirties appeared at the top of the bulwark. "Howdy," the American greeted the group on the well deck. "Awfully, glad to be here," he said as he crawled over the gunwale with a little help from Red and landed on the steel deck.

The captain stepped forward, "Welcome aboard, sir. I'm Richard Egan, Master. And this is my chief officer, Frank Ross," he said, pointing to Frank. "He will see to your needs while you are aboard the *Polites*."

The man stuck out his right hand, "Glad to meet you, Captain. I'm Mac."

Shaking the proffered hand, "Just Mac?" Egan inquired.

"Yup, just Mac. Safer that way. Mister Ross," the hand now extended toward Frank.

Taking it, Frank answered, "Welcome aboard, Mac," which earned him a scowl from the captain.

"You American?"

"Afraid so."

"Great! I thought everybody aboard was going to be a limey. Oh, sorry, Captain."

Egan forced a smile. "Quite alright, Yank."

"Touché!" Mac laughed.

"But as you can see, while the *Polites* is a British ship, you will find us a very cosmopolitan group. English, American, Canadian, Chinese, Indian, even a Dutchman or two."

"You learn something new every day."

"We even have ten American nurses aboard," Frank offered.

"Really! Sad to hear that," Mac replied as the corners of his mouth turned up.

"Why?"

"No fraternizing on this trip. I've got my orders. On account of my baby."

"Your baby?"

"Yes, my baby," he said, pointing at a large wooden crate just visible in the pool of light on the barge below. "Can't tell you what it is, of course, but it should help with that nasty little problem of yours. You know, that jerk with the funny mustache."

"That sounds good. We are grateful for any help we can get. Boats, can you get that aboard now?"

"Aye, aye, sir," Bailey replied. "Red, get on the winch. George, up top and free the boom. You two down there get ready. Cargo coming down." The last was directed to the men down below in number four hold.

Then as George threw off the lashings on the thirty-ton boom and Red fired up the heavy winch, ready to handle the lift, Bailey stepped to the port bulwark. "You, on the barge, are you ready?"

"Any time," the voice replied from the darkness.

"Here we go!" Bailey signaled Red, and the winch kicked into gear. The heavy boom, high above their heads, lifted gracefully out of its cradle.

"Captain, you sure we can't turn on the floods? Be a hell of a lot safer with some more light on the deck," Bailey asked over his shoulder.

"No lights," Mac cried from off to the side.

"If you would, please." The captain used his command voice, and no one faulted the American for seeming to shrink a couple of inches in response. "No, Bosun. The powers that be want this hush-hush. The floods would light us up to the whole basin," he explained while glancing over at Mac, his true feelings plain on his face.

"As you say, Captain." Bailey accepted the order.

The boom reached forty-five degrees, and Red stopped the upward motion. Switching smoothly, he swung it out over the side, positioning it right above the crate on the barge below. Once in position, he lowered it to almost perpendicular and finally extended the hook to where it hung just a few feet above the top of the crate. Red then disengaged the winch, locking the boom in place.

"Clear," he called out.

"Go ahead," Bailey yelled down to the men on the barge. In a second, three deckhands were at work, strapping the crate up and attaching it to the hook floating above their heads. Moments later, they finished up and stepped back as the lead man called out, "Lift away!"

Red bellowed, "Clear," and engaged the winch. He released the brake, and the crate lifted into the air, free of the barge. Frank stood watching the skill of the bosun and his crew as the ten-ton crate rose into the night sky, swung in over the bulwark, and disappeared down through the open hatch into number four.

Leaning over the coaming, Bailey took over, directing Red as the crate disappeared from his view. The two men below guided it into the area prepared for it earlier in the day, although the hold had remained sealed until well after dark. To the world, the *Polites* had seemed a ship fully loaded and ready for sea. And in a few hours, they would have the crate secured on the 'tween deck, the hatch cover back in place, and the ship ready for sea, just as she had been at sunset, as though nothing had happened at all.

A few minutes later, with the crate in place below, Bailey let go of the ropes holding the barge and its tug hard up against the side of the ship, letting them proceed on their way to whatever task was next on their agenda. Red and George then started the job of securing the boom and putting the cover back on number four. They began with a set of support beams, which would be followed by two layers of wooden planks laid across each other, and finally, two layers of tarps. The whole mass would then be roped down in place and fitted with a series of battens along the edge of the tarps. They would finally anchor it all in place with a row of wedges hammered in every couple of feet around the outer coaming.

"Ready for sea by zero-four hundred, Bosun. Need to finish well before sunrise. No one is to know we took on extra freight. You understand?" the captain instructed.

"Aye, Captain. We'll be finished."

"Mister Ross, show our guest to his cabin," the captain finished, heading for his bed and as much shut-eye as he could get before the call for sea and anchor detail in the morning. One of the captain's standing orders was to get as much sleep as possible in port, for sleep was always in short supply at sea. By noon tomorrow, the *Polites* would be out past Chebucto Head, pushing her way toward the wide and dark Atlantic.

Frank glanced at his watch and back at the captain as he disappeared up the ladder. *Good for him*, Frank thought. With sea and anchor detail at zero-five hundred per convoy orders and several tasks yet to complete, it wasn't looking like he was going to get much sleep, though.

"Okay, Mac. Let's get you to bed."

PART TWO
CONVOY

CHAPTER NINE
LOST IN THE FOG

Frank opened his eyes.

Not again, he moaned to himself. Once more, he wasn't where he had been, and this shit was getting old! He clearly remembered crawling into his rack on the *Polites* after a particularly grueling watch. While he was still in bed, this wasn't his rack. No, this was a hospital bed, and he was now wearing one of those stupid hospital gowns, the ones with the opening in the back. There was a light blanket spread over him, while a bright light from somewhere above left him isolated in a pool of light surrounded by utter darkness.

How had he gotten here? He vaguely remembered an ambulance and an attendant working over him and then a bunch of doctors swarming around him, but that couldn't be right. He had been on the bridge, standing watch, only an hour ago. How could he have been on the

Polites in the middle of the Atlantic and an ambulance at the same time?

Suddenly realizing his wrist was aching, he glanced down to find an IV taped to his hand with a clear liquid being slowly pumped into him. He tried to move his hand to ease the pain, but it wouldn't move. He tried to speak but found it impossible for his nose and mouth were covered by a mask, held in place by a pair of straps and connected to a couple of tubes running over to a machine sitting beside the bed. *What the hell is going on?* It was clear to him that the machine was breathing for him. He watched as the bellows contracted and felt the air flowing into his lungs, as his chest expanded. Then, as the bellows inflated, he could feel the air being drawn out of his lungs. What the hell had happened to him? An accident, maybe? His head? No, that was on the ship. This one was . . . he was lost. Then, he noticed a steady beep, beep, beep from somewhere above his head.

Calm down! You're not doing yourself any good this way. He started to count slowly. One . . . two . . . three . . . The beeping slowed, and he felt himself grow calmer.

He continued counting, and as he did, the room around him gradually came into focus. Over in the corner, another light drew his attention. Under it, in a chair, curled up, under a blanket, was a woman, fast asleep. He immediately recognized her. *My daughter-in-law.* Those brown eyes popped into his mind again. Then a door slid open, revealing a lighted corridor beyond, and two men stepped into the room.

"Doctor, I need to know. Will he ever wake up?" the tall, thin one asked in a familiar voice.

The older, heavy-set man paused and looked down at the floor. "Well, as you know, he's not really sleeping. He's in a deep coma. And we just don't know. He had a massive heart attack, and his brain was without oxygen for nearly six minutes. In most cases, that means brain death. But in his case, we are still registering some brain activity, though at an extremely low level."

"And?" the younger one prompted.

"He could wake up and be fine, or he could pass tonight. There is just no way for us to know."

Frank sensed movement off to his side and glanced over into those brown eyes. This time they were filled with excitement, and the face was aglow!

"Doctor!" she cried.

But then Frank felt himself being jerked away, as though someone had physically taken ahold of him and was dragging him out of the room. Those brown eyes began to fade away, vanishing into the gathering mist.

"He was awake," the woman exclaimed, her voice already sounding like it was a thousand miles away.

●　●　●

Frank jerked up in bed. He was back on the *Polites*, again. It was dark. He glanced at his wristwatch. It was just after midnight. But that can't be right! It was only three o'clock the last time he glanced at his watch.

The ship shifted as if a wave had hit it. Were they at sea? That can't be. He remembered them sitting at anchor, but as he sat, thinking, trying to remember, he could feel the ship moving, lifting to each wave in time. He even felt the diesels throbbing away down below. Yes, they had to be at sea!

Wait a minute; that's right. They had put to sea today—or was it yesterday? Damn, this waking up in different places wasn't just getting old; it was a real pain in the ass. He kept losing track of where he was and what had or hadn't happened.

It slowly came back to him. They had manned sea and anchor detail at zero-five hundred yesterday. He could remember emerging on deck as the armed cruiser *Wolfe*, the former Canadian Pacific liner *Montcalm,* and the other forty-eight ships of the convoy began coming to life all around them. Then, in a single file with five hundred yards between them, the ships had cleared the harbor and moved out past Chebucto Head.

There in the outer harbor, beyond the submarine net, they had formed up into a standard formation, a box five rows deep and ten columns wide. The commodore's staff had given each ship a unique two-digit number signifying its position—the first digit was the column number and the second the row. Once in position, each vessel was expected to maintain its place, a thousand yards between columns and eight hundred yards behind the row ahead. The *Wolfe* then took up a position forward of the formation, between the fourth and fifth columns, and the convoy began its slow march across the ocean.

This morning, the rest of the convoy's escorts, a destroyer and three corvettes of the Royal Canadian Navy, joined them off the southeastern tip of Newfoundland. Right after that, fog, the pea-soup variety, rolled in, cutting off all sight of the other ships. Now, each had doubled their lookouts and dropped a towing spar over the stern in hopes of avoiding any collisions.

But wait. Hadn't he just been in a hospital bed? Those eyes. He couldn't forget those eyes. Wasn't that the real world? And if it was . . . He glanced around the cabin taking in the details. Familiar and yet. What was this? A dream? Was he actually in this bed or that one? They both couldn't be real, could they? So, which was the real one and which a dream? A moment ago, that hospital had seemed so real, but now it was fading away just like a dream you can't quite remember upon waking.

That had to be the answer. That was the dream because this can't be. How could his damaged mind make up all this? Besides, if he was dreaming, why only this one dream? Wouldn't he be a pirate one time and a circus clown the next? Why would he keep coming back here time after time if it was only a dream? Maybe, it was a nightmare he couldn't escape?

He had lots of questions but no answers— especially to the most important of all.

What do I do? I could refuse to play along. If this isn't real, what does it matter? I could let them all die. If they're not real, it doesn't matter what happens to them. Does it? Hell, I'm dying too. A machine is breathing for me, and that doctor didn't even have the guts to tell my son. What is his name? Damn it! I can't remember! My own son's name. But what if this isn't a dream? Isn't this what I've always wanted? A chance to matter, to be the hero of my own story. To love a woman like Helen and to be loved in return.

He was back in that doorway in Halifax, with Helen trapped against that door, his body pressing close to hers, that perfume filling his senses once more. His fingers reached out in the dark for her. It was almost overwhelming!

Damn it! What the hell? Even if it isn't real, why not play along? This is a thousand times better than any old movie or even those new video games. All you first-person shooters, eat your hearts out! Why not enjoy it for as long as it lasts? Or at least for as long as I last!

He was due on watch at zero-four hundred, but he had things to do first. If he was a secret agent, it was time to start acting like one. *007 to the rescue.* He crawled out of the rack, trying to remember where he put that damn flashlight.

• • •

Frank stepped onto the steel deck at the bottom of number five one more time. It was becoming a habit. He pulled the flashlight from his coat pocket and snapped it on. Instantly, the light illuminated the immediate area.

The crates were just as they had been several days earlier on his last trip down here. That time, he had convinced himself that this was all a wild goose chase, that the real Frank Ross had simply slipped and fallen to the deck, ending his life in a stupid, senseless accident, but now things were different.

Back then, he wasn't sure what was real and what he had imagined. But the events of the last couple of days had revealed that Frank Ross was a spy—or at least a British agent—put on board to keep an eye on things.

And if British Intelligence believed it important enough to put an agent on board, there was a good chance that the real Frank had been down here looking for something. And there was a reasonable chance that his accident was, in fact, no accident.

That being the case, then the threat the real Frank had warned him of could still be down here somewhere in the dark. Was it something he found, something important enough to kill him over? If that was true, then he needed to find it, whatever *it* was, and find it fast.

"But how?" he asked the silent crates.

Where had he been searching? This hold was such a large space; he could be looking for days or weeks and not find it! What had he even been looking for? *Think!* It's supposed to be there, somewhere in his Swiss-cheese mind, but it was impossible to separate his memories from those of the real Frank; they had mixed, blurring one into the next. He couldn't tell where one ended and the other began, or even worse, tell which were his and which were the real Frank's.

Maybe if I stopped and cleared my mind, then it would come. I could try meditation. Clear my mind and let all that other crap go. It certainly couldn't hurt. It might help him order his thoughts, get them straight, let him get a clearer picture of what happened down here. *But how do you meditate?* He had never been into that Eastern mumbo jumbo.

That was it! Eastern mysticism. He remembered seeing a Buddha somewhere on board. Buddhists were into meditation, right? Where had he seen it? It was on a bulkhead beside a rack. No, a bunk! That meant it was a Petty Officer, for all the rest of the crew slept on wire racks.

Then it came to him. Wang Sing, the Steward, was Chinese from Hainan island off the south coast of China. *Of course, he's a Buddhist. Maybe he can help me try to remember what it was the real Frank found down here.*

He glanced at his watch. It was a little past zero-three hundred. It shocked him that he had been down here for almost two hours already. It was time to get ready for his watch.

Before he left, he ran the flashlight all around the compartment. It was like searching for the proverbial needle. Unless he could somehow make sense of his mixed-up memories, he was just wasting his time. He could be looking at it right now and not even know it.

"That's it." He made up his mind. He would see if Sing could teach him some meditation techniques, and maybe he could remember what it was the real Frank found down here.

• • •

On the way to his cabin, Frank peeked into the galley. The second cook, Kuang, was sliding a tray of freshly baked bread out of the oven.

"Morning, Cook," Frank began.

"Ah, morning, Master Ross," Kuang answered, setting the tray down on the prep table.

"That's Mister Ross. Those smell wonderful. Nothing like fresh bread in the morning."

"Yes, favorite part of the job."

"I envy you. Down here, surrounded by these wonderful smells while I am stuck up on the bridge messing with the damn fog," Frank muttered.

"Yes, fog, not good for the convoy."

"No, you got that right. Too many ships, too close together, and none of them can see a damn thing. Somebody's bound to make a mistake if this stuff doesn't lift soon."

"Maybe not good for ships. But good for mess boy."

"How's that?" Frank asked while pouring himself a cup of dark brew from the galley urn.

"He disappear. Kuang no find. Run out of time. Have to do work for two."

"Does he do that often?" Frank queried, the cup hovering near his lips.

"Few times. Not many."

"Well, I will talk to him. Not a good habit to start."

"Thank you. Boy never listens to Kuang. Kuang below him. Only Chinaman."

"That's not right, either." Frank looked at the fresh rolls cooling on the tray. "May I?"

"Help self, please."

"Thank you," Frank picked up the closest one and took a quick bite. "Mmm, that's good. Say, I've been trying to remember what all happened when I fell in New York. It's all a mess," he tapped his head, "in here. I was wondering if some Buddhist mediation techniques might help me straighten it out."

"Could help. But Sing is much better. You talk to him."

"Sure thing. Thank you." He held up the now half-eaten roll as he grabbed a second. "Have to get going, got to go on watch. You have a good day."

Frank exited the galley and moved out on to the after well deck. If anything, the fog was getting thicker. This wasn't any good. The commodore would have to slow the convoy down soon, or he was begging to lose some ships in the fog—or worse, have them pile into one another. But slowing the convoy made it easier to attack; that little extra speed was the reason the authorities had HX and SC type convoys; even four knots was important when you had a Nazi U-boat hunting you.

The only good thing right now was the U-boats weren't this far out from their pens along the French coast—not yet, at least. That wouldn't happen until next year after America entered the war. But of course, you never could tell about a lone wolf. One could be out there right now, lying in wait. If it were, no one would see it, not in this stuff. And it was too early in the war for any of the Canadian ships to have radar, though the British were already starting to equip theirs.

He glanced at his watch; it was three-thirty. "Damn, I need to get going." He bounded up the ladder to the upper deck and forward on the port side, past the engineers' cabins. The morning was a tad cold for June; it must be the latitude. Even early summer was still cold before sunrise when you were this far north.

The dark bulk of the smokestack loomed to his right. He was almost to his cabin.

Let's see. I need my glasses, sextant, might get a chance to shoot the morning stars, though it doesn't look like the fog is going—

A dark shape shifted in the fog beside the winch to his right. It was a man, and he came on at a full run. He had appeared so fast Frank was caught flat-footed. The man hit him dead center, and he was propelled backward, his breath driven out of his lungs. His hands flew up, the coffee mug going one way, while the muffins floated over the railing and disappeared into the fog. Frank came up hard against the safety lines. Pain lanced through him as the top rail dug into the small of his back.

Any doubt about what this was vanished in the next instant as his assailant tried to lift and push him back over the top of the rail, to disappear over the side and into the freezing water below.

Frank grabbed at the man, struggling to lock his arms around him, fighting, hanging on for dear life. He felt himself rolling over the top, balancing on the rail, his feet flailing uselessly in the air. The sound of the sea rose to fill his ears. His heart pounded hard against the inside of his chest. His weight was slowly dragging them both over the railing.

Then, his assailant balked, pulling back at the last second to save himself, twisting free as Frank pitched forward onto the deck. A quick knee to the face threw Frank back against the rail. The man stepped in close, his shadow looming large. He landed a one-two combination, and Frank's world narrowed to a small patch of the dark sky. The assailant reached down, took hold of his shirt, and jerked him to his feet, then delivered a blow to the midriff. Frank doubled over. Another knee to the face, and he collapsed into a pile against the rail.

He knew it was over. He had let his guard down again. This was what happened down in the number five hold. This man, whoever he was, had got the best of the real Frank, and now he's caught me not paying attention.

Frank tried one last time to push himself up off the deck, but another kick connected with the side of his head. He dropped to the deck; the lights dimmed. A familiar voice, from somewhere, told him if he let the lights go out, they would never come back.

Frank pulled his arms up around his head. *Protect your face. One more hit there, and you're a goner.*

The man grabbed his coat and once more jerked him to his feet. *He wants me over that rail and into the water.* Frank tried to push him away, but the move was too slow and only earned him another couple of hard jabs to the ribs. Both blows lifted him off the deck, and Frank fell back hard against the rail once more. He was pinned as another series of blows rained in on him, jerking his body left and right.

"Okay! For God's sake! Just push me over. You don't have to beat me senseless," he slurred against the man's chest. He had failed just like the real Frank, and it was too late to stop it.

The assailant pushed the almost unconscious Frank up against the railing and started to lift him again. He felt himself going over. He could see the dark water swirling below along the side of the ship. It was an excellent way to dispose of a body; even in the middle of the summer, at this latitude, the water would be frigid, just a few degrees above freezing. In his condition, he wouldn't be able to swim for very long. That is if the suction didn't get him first, pulling him down into the screws. Either way, at least, he wouldn't suffer long.

His weight was now helping to pull him over. He was falling, free, his arms swinging around, grasping for something, for anything. Suddenly, his right hand closed around the bottom rung of the railing, locking tight. His body came up hard against the side of the ship, and it felt like he almost ripped his arm out of the socket.

Slam! His face connected with the side of the vessel as he crashed against it a second time, but somehow, he managed to hang on, dangling off the side of the ship. The wind whipped around him, refreshing him as it did.

The assailant, not hearing a splash, realized he hadn't gone in and dropped to his knees. His fingers desperately dug at Frank's poor, abused ones. He began to work on one at a time, digging in under it and pulling it back off the wire, leaving his victim in a progressively worsening position. It was only a matter of moments before Frank would run out of fingers.

He swung his body, reaching up with his left arm trying desperately to grab the rail with his other hand. The assailant batted it away each time he tried.

"Damn, you to hell," he cried through broken lips. Then he realized he was only a few feet away from the cabins. This time, unlike the bottom of number five, maybe he wasn't all alone. Help could be just a few feet away if he could hang on long enough.

"Help!" he screamed once, twice. "Help me!" He screamed again and again.

"What's going on down there?" That was Mister Eddy on the bridge wing.

There was movement on the companionway. Someone was coming. Frank continued to shout at the top of his lungs. In that instant, the attack was over. His assailant faded into the shadows back against the bulkhead as Helen appeared above him at the rail.

"My God," she called as she grabbed for his arm. "Help me! Man over the side."

Frank heard more feet, pounding fore and aft.

"Hold on!" she yelled.

Then several other hands grabbed ahold of him, and Frank felt himself being lifted back over the rail to safety.

CHAPTER TEN
CLEARING

"Well, Mister Ross, are we making a habit of this?" Captain Egan said as he entered the Hospital. "Twice inside a week."

"It does feel that way, sir," Frank answered, sitting on the same unmade bunk as the last time. Standing beside him, Helen was already at work on his many cuts and abrasions.

"Take your shirt off," she ordered.

Egan glanced around the space. Besides himself, the bosun and Red were once more present.

"So, what happened?" Egan cut straight to the heart of the matter.

"Isn't it obvious? Someone tried to kill me—again." Frank responded just as bluntly as he gingerly eased his undershirt up over his head.

"My God," Helen whispered as she surveyed the damage.

"Are you sure? No one saw anything, again."

"Take a good look, Captain. I sure as hell didn't do this to myself."

"Okay. Say I believe you. So, who was it? I'll have Bailey get them down here, this minute."

"I don't know who it was," Frank winced as Helen probed his ribs. "Easy there. I'm already tenderized enough."

"Sorry, I'm being as gentle as I can, but I have to check to see if anything is broken. Other than that nose, of course."

"If the way it hurts is any indication." He managed a smile.

"You were saying?" Egan prompted.

"Yes. He was dressed in black with a hood over his head. I didn't see a thing. He appeared out of nowhere and just started pounding away. After that, I was too busy getting my ass kicked to see anything."

"But surely you have some idea who it was? Was he tall or short? Fat or thin? You had to see something that would help identify him?"

"Not too tall. Shorter than me."

"That's most of the crew." Bailey offered.

"Anything else?" the captain asked, giving Bailey a stern look.

"He was thin. And strong."

"Didn't doubt that," Bailey offered as he and Red exchanged glances.

"Boats!" Egan admonished the bosun.

"Yes, sir."

"Did he say anything?" Egan continued digging.

"Not a word. He was too busy to talk."

"That doesn't help us."

"I know, but I think I may have a way to find him."

"How's that?" Egan inquired.

"I was talking to Kuang just before the attack about using some mediation techniques to help straighten out my memories of that first attack. That may be the reason he tried again."

"How's that?"

"Well, I know he's been following me. He was outside my cabin that first night out of New York."

"The shadow!" Helen cried.

"Right. But when nothing happened the next day, he thought he was safe."

"And he was."

"Yes, but I was just poking around down in number five again."

"And he's no longer feeling safe," Egan finished for him.

"Exactly. He's afraid I'll remember something."

"So, the safest thing for him is to get rid of you. Dump you over the side."

"Right."

"So, what's our next move? Get with Kuang?"

"No, he thinks Sing would be the better teacher. I was going to try to get with him after I got off watch this morning."

"Mister Ross, if you are correct, there could be a bomb aboard this ship. I think that is more important than your standing watch. Boats, be so kind as to inform Mister Eddy that on my orders, he will remain on watch until I can relieve him. It seems our chief officer is at present engaged in other duties."

"Aye, aye, sir."

"Oh! Boats, one more thing." Egan paused for effect. "You keep your mouth shut. I don't want this to get around the ship. It's bad enough the crew thinks the chief officer is a little off-balance, but we sure don't want them worrying about a possible bomb on board."

"Aye, sir," the bosun replied.

"Now, off with you."

As Bailey slipped out the door, the captain turned his eyes on the rest. "I don't have to say that also goes for you three, too. Do I?"

"No, sir," Frank replied as Helen and Red shook their heads.

"Now, Red. Find the steward and have him join us in here."

"Aye, sir."

After Red disappeared, Egan turned to Helen. "Is he going to live?"

"Yes, it's mostly bumps and bruises. The worst of it, besides the broken nose and some sore ribs, is his arm. He nearly pulled it out of the socket."

"Is he fit for duty?"

"Yes. He'll have to wear a sling for a day or two, but he should be okay."

"Very well." He turned to Frank, "I don't think he will try again now that the whole ship is awake. So, I'll leave you in her capable hands. But as soon as you can, get me something we can use—no more guesses. I need facts from now on. I think we are safe for a while. Don't think the bastard plans to sink us with himself aboard, but you can never tell with a fanatic."

"Yes, sir," Frank replied, hoping the captain was right.

● ● ●

As the door closed behind the departing Captain, Helen held up a bandage. "Lift your arms, please."

Frank glanced up at her and slowly raised his arms. "This isn't as easy as you think."

"I can imagine. You look like you've been through hell." She stepped up beside him and placed the end of the bandage in the middle of his chest, "Hold that."

"Which it is? Put my arms up or hold this?" She glared at him. Suppressing a smile, he took hold of the bandage with his elbows up away from his side.

"That wasn't so hard, was it?" she growled as she began to wrap the bandage tightly around his chest. Around and around she went, and as she did, the pressure began easing the pain he was feeling with each breath. After she completed several rounds, he moved his hand out of the way, lifting his arms to give her full access. Then as she reached the end of the ribbon, once more, she ordered him, "Hold this."

He took hold, and she turned away. "You enjoy ordering me around."

Without responding, Helen fished a pair of metal retainers out of a basket in the medicine cabinet. Returning to his side, she finished locking the bandage in place.

"There. You can put your shirt back on," she offered, once more turning away.

He reached for his shirt but stopped with his hand outstretched, his eyes locked on her as she made busy. It was apparent she was avoiding him. He could see her hands trembling. She could feel his eyes boring into her. She couldn't understand why she felt the way she did. He had made it clear he didn't want her. She closed her eyes, just for a moment, and forced herself to relax. Then she returned to her work, preparing to set his broken nose.

Frank picked up his blood-stained undershirt and pulled it slowly over his head. As he pulled it down over the bandage, he let out a low groan.

She jerked around, her eyes full of moisture. Then at the sight of the smile on his face, she blushed and turned her back on him.

"I'd like to thank you," he began.

"Just doing my job," she replied, fighting to regain control.

"No, not this. For what you did out there on the deck. You saved my life."

"No, I didn't." She looked up and instantly realized she had made a mistake!

Unable to look away, she watched as he slowly straightened out his shirt. "But you did. I don't think I could have hung on much longer when you reached me. I was almost at the end of my rope."

"It was nothing. I was only doing what anyone else would," she said, still gazing up into his eyes. It seemed he was moving closer. He could see the turmoil deep in her eyes.

Suddenly, she collapsed into his arms. "Damn you, Frank," she whispered into his chest, tears running down her face. "You don't know what it was like to see you just hanging there. Knowing you could fall at any second."

He squeezed her. "Didn't do it on purpose."

She pushed away with her arms. "Not funny." Frank pulled her close again.

"Sorry. I don't want to hurt you. Just the opposite."

"Is that why you walked away yesterday?"

"Yes. I have a job to do."

"So do I." This time she pulled away, even turning her back on him. She tried to gather her wits as she forced her hands into fists.

"I'm playing a dangerous game here. This proved it. I could end up dead. Almost did. Twice, now."

"We all could. We're on a ship sailing into a war."

"Yes, we could. But this is different. I have someone who is actively looking to kill me for something I don't even remember." He pointed at himself. "Getting involved with me could be very dangerous for you."

"That's for me to decide," she said, turning to face him.

"I just didn't want to hurt you. Even if I win, there is no guarantee I'll hang around."

"I told you before, none of us gets a guarantee. Here in the real world, any of us can be gone in an instant. With no warning."

"I know that. I've run through it all in my mind, again and again. Is it a dream? Or is it real? I don't know, but either way, it doesn't end well for us."

"So, you've decided for both of us?"

He looked away. "I woke up in a hospital this morning. My son was talking to a doctor."

"When was this?" She took a step forward. "While you were sleeping?"

He nodded.

"So, you've decided we are the dream? Why?"

"Honestly? Because I want so much for this to be real."

He pulled her close, staring down at her. She smiled and kissed his neck, her body pressed hard against his. Her scent filled his head. His heart raced. She nibbled on his earlobe. My God! He wanted her so much; it was all he could do to stop himself. Lifting her face to look at him, he saw the green pools shimmering in the light. She was close to tears again.

"I can't." He pushed past her. "Don't you see? It doesn't matter if this is real or not. Either way, it's not right. One way, I'd just be using you; the other, I couldn't help but hurt you. And I won't do that." He stormed out of the compartment.

"But you already have."

• • •

He stood alone at the rail, careless of the danger he might be in. Where was his unknown assailant now? He was likely hiding in the shadows behind him. It was all too much for him. He was out of control.

He wanted her so much.

The feel of her in his arms, her head resting against his chest, was fresh in his mind. He looked down at his hands. He could still feel her, but he couldn't do that to her. He couldn't hurt her, use her to fulfill his desires, and then what? He had no guarantee. How could he? He wasn't even sure he was here, in the past, aboard this ship, fighting the Nazis. It was a dream come true. And that might be exactly what it was—a dream. A dream inside his feverish skull. A product of his imagination produced by his mind, a way to keep itself busy, functioning while his body healed. Or tried to.

If that was true, then why not? If this was just his imagination, then these people weren't real, and who's to care how he treats them? He could take whatever he wanted, what he needed, and to hell with what it cost them.

Suddenly, the hairs on the back of his neck stood up. Someone was coming. He could hear them. He waited, bracing himself for another attack. He was ready this time!

A hand grabbed his shoulder. He spun around, his right hand lashing out.

"Hey!" yelled Red, ducking under the blow. "Take it easy, Mister Ross! It's just me."

"Sorry." Frank suddenly felt foolish.

"I should have warned you I was coming."

"It's okay. Just wound up a little too tight."

"The steward said he would wait for you in his cabin."

"Thanks," Frank answered and started toward the ladder leading down to the main deck. Red stood at the rail, watching him go before shaking his head and heading on aft toward the messroom.

Frank knocked on the door of the steward's cabin. As a senior petty officer, Wang Sing, rated a small but private cabin amidships on the main deck, outboard on the port side. His was the first in a row of cabins housing the ship's whole catering department: Sing, the steward, the cook and his assistant Kuang, and the two cabin boys, Freddie and Jake. Sing was the only one with a private cabin; the others all had to double up.

The door opened to reveal Sing in his white jacket and black pants. Behind him, the small room was a mirror of the Chinese steward, spotless. The few items visible were orderly and arranged. The bed military perfect; Frank was sure he could bounce a coin off those sheets. Only a few decorations were visible, and all were Oriental—a bamboo screen covered with ancient Chinese scenes hung above the bunk, and opposite on the shelf above the roll-top desk, a Buddha sat surveying the scene. The final item, an intricately designed rug, spread out and covered the deck between the rack and the desk.

"Welcome, Mister Ross. Come in, please." Sing began in perfect English, with only a hint of a Chinese accent.

"Thank you, Sing." Frank stepped into the room as the steward stepped aside.

"Red informed me that the captain wants me to assist you in trying to recover your memories of your accident."

"Yes, we're afraid something happened that might be very important to the safety of the ship and her crew."

"Then it is in both our best interests to succeed. Please, have a seat," Sing finished, pointing to the room's sole chair as he closed the door behind them.

"I don't want to take your only chair."

"Please, I will sit on the bed. Besides, it is necessary for the meditation. The pictures," he pointed at the Chinese screens, "will help with the process."

"Very well," Frank sat in the chair, which was placed so that he faced the bulkhead with the pictures. "I don't think we have ever talked much," he continued.

"No, your time aboard has been one of much activity. Your duties and mine seldom cross paths."

"That's hard to believe on such a small ship."

"To the uninformed, maybe." Sing replied, opening a drawer under the bed. "I will prepare the cabin for our session." He pulled a red cloth out of the drawer before closing it. "First, I will subdue the lighting." He draped the fabric over the single bulkhead lamp, and everything in the cabin turned red. Then he moved to the porthole. "It will reduce the circulation, but it is necessary to remove the light." He flipped the clip holding the hatch open, lowered it closed, and secured one of the dogs. Finally, he pulled the blackout drapes across the porthole, sealing off the light from beyond.

Sing then turned off the overhead light, leaving only the red filtered light from the bulkhead fixture. The whole atmosphere changed to one of quiet contemplation.

"That's neat!" Frank whispered.

"Neat. Is that one of your quaint American expressions?"

"Yes, it means cool, nifty."

"Cool? I see nothing cold about it," the Chinese stated.

"Never mind."

"As you wish," Sing responded as he sat on the bed.

"Before we get started, can I ask a personal question?"

Sing nodded, his back straight as a board.

Gesturing around the room, Frank said, "All this, your speech, the books." He pointed to the tomes on the top of the desk. "Shakespeare, Milton, Scott. Where were you born?"

"Hong Kong."

"But—"

"I attended St. Andrews."

"Scotland?"

"Yes, my grandfather on my mother's side was Scottish."

"So, why are you shipping out as a steward on a freighter?"

"We each do our part for the war. I am too old for the army, so I shipped out as a steward like I did as a young man."

"I guess we all make our own choices."

"Yes, it is your choices in life that define you."

Frank stopped, staring at the steward. That was true. It wasn't the lack of opportunities; that was just a cop-out, an easy excuse for not striving for what you wanted. He had come to lament his lack of chances for not living the life he had dreamed of, one full of adventure and romance. But it wasn't a lack of opportunities; it was the choices he had made that put him on the path he followed in life. Like most people, he had remained only vaguely aware that he could have changed his path forever with a single decision.

Once on the path, stepping off would have caused disruptions, ripples in the pond, and that was why most people never try to change their paths. Is that why he didn't? So many people were always counting on him to do the "right" thing, to be there. But in the end, it was he who chose to continue down that path, to be that man instead of the one he wanted to be.

"Are you ready to begin?"

"Yes, I'm ready," Frank replied, a broad smile on his face. He had finally made his choice.

CHAPTER ELEVEN
HARD-A-STARBOARD

The sun was on his back, shining in through the open hatch above. With a flashlight, he was examining the port side bulkhead of number five hold. He had already checked the other four holds and found nothing. If anyone had slipped something aboard during the ship's visit in New York, they had done an excellent job hiding it.

He systematically worked his way down the port side, the beam of light riding over the wall, which consisted of wooden slats, eight inches wide and set four inches apart. He was looking for breaks or deformities in the wood or anything else that seemed out of place.

There! The third board up had been disfigured.

He stepped over to it and shined the light on it. Yes, it looked like someone had pried the nail out with a claw hammer and then replaced it. Whoever had done it had taken their time, working the nail slowly out of the wood to minimize the damage done to the board. Who would do such a thing, and why?

He pulled his knife, which he always wore on his belt, from its sheath, and slid the point in between the two boards. Applying pressure, he slowly began to work the nail out. It gave way and pulled halfway out in an instant. Yes, someone had been messing with it. He continued to work on it, and in short order, the nail pulled free. The board dropped, slightly, revealing a small opening. Moving closer, he could see a tiny void behind the board, the perfect hiding place. He slipped his knife back into the sheath and took hold of the board with both hands. Pulling on the end, he worked it loose until he fully revealed the void behind.

Something was sitting on the crossbeam inside the void. He dropped the board to the deck and pulled the flashlight from his pocket, snapping it on as he did so. Bending down, he moved in to get a better view and found a small package wrapped in brown paper and tied with string hiding within. He moved the flashlight beam around, studying the package and looking for any wires or booby-traps. Satisfied that there were none, he turned the flashlight off and stuck it back into his pocket. Then he slowly reached into the void and oh so carefully picked up the package with both hands.

It was a lot heavier than it looked. What could it be? A bomb, maybe? Or some poor seamen's cache? Gently he set it down on the deck, then propped up his flashlight in a gap between two nearby crates, positioning it so the beam of light shined on the package as it sat on the deck.

Dropping to his knees, he again carefully studied the wrapping and the string. Still no sign of a booby-trap. It could be just one of the crew trying to pad his wallet with a little something extra slipped on board and hidden down here to get it past customs. Any kind of luxury item would do; small, inexpensive here in

America, but unavailable across the pond because of the war. It happened regularly. Seamen could be very enterprising when they wanted to be, like trying to skirt a work detail or making a little extra cash on the side.

Or it could be precisely what he was looking for, what his bosses at Rockefeller Center were scared to death of!

He untied the string and eased the paper away from the package, holding his breath the whole time, but nothing happened. Inside he found a medium-sized tin can, sealed, without a label, and an expensive-looking radio-like device.

He closely examined the can. No label, six inches long, and about four inches around, both ends were factory sealed. He shook it: nothing, no sound. Whatever was inside was dry, a powder maybe.

Putting the can down, he turned his attention to the radio. Again, no labels. It was self-contained, with a single dial on the front and two switches on the side. The dial had random letters instead of numbers. Strange. He tried the switches, but nothing happened. No power, maybe? He noticed two sets of screws on the side, perhaps one for power and the other for an antenna. That would make sense. But what was it for? It was like no radio he had ever seen. He gently set it back on the deck beside the can.

This isn't some seaman's stash. "The captain needs to see this."

Leaving the board as it was, Frank re-wrapped the package, even re-tying the string to hold it all together. He then turned the flashlight off and slipped it into his coat pocket. Then, with the package in his hand, he set off for the captain's quarters. At the foot of the ladder, he stopped and, weighting the package in his hand, silently studied the situation. Finally, he decided it would be too dangerous to climb the ladder with one hand occupied, he didn't want to drop it. He laid the package down on a nearby crate. Then crossed to where the bosun and his crew had left a roll of half-inch manila line on the deck when they knocked off for lunch. They would soon return, but right now, he could use the line.

Picking it up, he returned to the package and tied one end of the rope around the package, then tossed the other end up to the deck above. He waited a few seconds to make sure the line wouldn't fall back down. Then, he hustled up the ladder, two-handed.

At the top, he glanced down at the package just as he stepped off the top rung on to the deck.

Suddenly, a shadow moved, and someone crashed into Frank hard, head down, the point of his shoulder driven into Frank's stomach. The blow caught him by surprise and drove his feet back off the deck and out into mid-air. All his weight came down on his right hand as he swung around, but he somehow maintained his grip on the ladder. Pain lanced up his arm, but he got his left foot back on to the landing. Then his mystery assailant struck again, knocking him off the deck, but this time it was too much for his painfully abused hand, and he lost his grip.

Frank felt himself falling backward, the deck below rushing up toward him. For a second, he saw a figure looking out over the edge above, and then, pain filled his world as his vision exploded into a million pieces before it faded to black.

• • •

Frank jumped to his feet to find himself surrounded by a red mist, which slowly resolved back into Sing's cabin. The cloth was still in place over the light, casting everything in an eerie red glow.

"My God!" He drew a deep breath to steady his nerves and slow his racing heart. Then he dropped back into the chair, his mind reeling from the scene just revealed to him.

"Are you all right, Mister Ross?" Sing asked, staring at him from his perch on the nearby bed.

"It was so real. It was as though I was there, experiencing it as it happened."

"I have never seen anything quite like that before," Sing slowly shook his head. "It was like you weren't here anymore. I even thought you might have stopped breathing for a while."

"It wouldn't surprise me." Frank wondered if he had, in fact, done so.

"I'm sorry, Mister Ross, but I don't think we should try again." Sing's voice was on the verge of cracking. It was clear what he had witnessed had unnerved him.

"It's okay. We don't have to. I've found my answers." Frank climbed to his feet and pulled the door open. "Thank you," he called over his shoulder as he exited, slamming the door behind him.

"The captain needs to hear this," he muttered to himself as he hurried down the passageway toward the forward well deck, passing the mess boy Freddie on the way.

As he emerged into the open air, he pulled up, suddenly becoming aware of his surroundings. In his haste to get to the captain, he had once again forgotten the real Frank's mistake. The same one which had almost cost him his life earlier today. He had to be careful, always aware of his surroundings. The killer, whoever he was, had used that against him, more than once.

That was how he had killed the real Frank. All excited about his discovery, he hadn't been paying attention, didn't look closely enough at the shadows until it was too late—until the killer came crashing out of the darkness.

And he hadn't been paying attention this morning on his way to the bridge. Once again, he hadn't looked close enough at the shadows surrounding him. He hadn't seen that figure lurking there until once more, he burst out of the darkness.

"I can't let it happen again. It could be strike three."

He then noticed the sun shining down on him from an opening in the fog, and the fo'c'sle, nearly a hundred feet away, was a faint outline behind the gray mist. The fog was thinning but was still thick enough that the convoy, arrayed all around him, remained lost in the haze.

He glanced up, and for a moment, he relished the warmth on his upturned face. It wouldn't be long now. The sun would soon burn off the rest of this, leaving a beautiful spring day in its wake. A thought which filled his heart with dread. Perfect weather for the U-boats. Fifty ships, all trailing black smoke, visible for miles, but at least it would make station keeping easier.

He scurried up the ladder to the upper deck and switched back to catch the next one up to the boat deck, where the captain had his cabin. As soon as he stepped out on to the deck, the naval gunner, in his crisp summer whites with a very conspicuous black gun belt wrapped around his middle, snapped to. He was standing watch outside Mac's cabin as ordered by Frank's superiors back in Halifax.

"Any problems?" Frank asked.

"No, sir. That mess boy Freddie wanted to go in and set up the breakfast. Said it was his job. But he gave up after I told him no one goes inside."

Frank nodded as he knocked on the captain's door.

"Enter," a voice commanded from within.

"Carry on," Frank said to the guard as he twisted the knob and pushed the door open.

"Captain," he began stepping into the cabin, "I have the answer." He stopped just inside the doorway. Egan was sitting in front of his roll-top desk, an exact copy of the one in the steward's cabin two decks below, with two crucial differences. This one didn't overwhelm the room, for the captain's cabin was at least twice the size of the stewards, and a mess of paperwork, books, rolled up charts, and several unidentifiable objects, which may have been the remains of earlier meals, covered this one "knee-deep." For such a meticulous man, the desk was a huge surprise to Frank.

"And?" Egan prompted.

"This morning wasn't his first attack."

"I was afraid of that. Do you know who he is now?"

"No, he's very good at hiding in the shadows."

"Then, do you at least know why he's attacking you?"

"Yes. I found what looked like a radio and a canister of something down in number five. It was hidden behind the battens, up against the hull plating."

"Have you gone to checked on it?"

"No, not yet. But I believe it would be a waste of time. If he didn't move it earlier, he certainly did after this morning."

Egan nodded his agreement. "You are probably right, but I still would like it checked out."

"And if it isn't there?" Frank inquired.

"Then you and the bosun need to get very busy searching this ship from stem to stern."

"That will take a while."

"I know. I'm getting used to standing your watches anyhow."

Frank could only shrug his shoulders.

"Well, hop to it, Mister."

• • •

With the number of nooks and crannies on a four hundred and twenty-six foot, six-thousand-ton ship, it wasn't surprising that it took a day and a half for Frank and the bosun to visit each space on board. Frank had guessed from the beginning that it would be a useless exercise. The individual he was competing against was far too intelligent to make such a stupid mistake, twice. And even if he had, the search would take too long. He could easily move the stuff from place to place while they were busy searching someplace else.

With that in mind, they tried to keep the search as low key as possible, even passing it off as a routine survey, but the needs of a ship at sea and the lack of any viable suspect had forced them to leave the crew and all the passengers free to move around at will. In Frank's thinking, the only way the search would work was if they picked the right compartment to start with, for after that first one, it was useless. So, Frank made his best guess and began in the forward 'tween decks, but as he suspected, they found nothing, and he knew the search would be a waste of time from that moment on.

Thus, on Wednesday evening, the third day out, Frank and Bailey emerged from the after house empty-handed.

The fog, which had seemed on the verge of breaking up and burning off some thirty hours earlier had proved to be far more persistent and once more closed in around the convoy as it continued its slow trek east-northeast.

Standing on the after well deck, they couldn't see even as far as the forward edge of the amidships' house.

"I wonder how much longer this fog will hang around?" Frank asked, trying to peer through the gray mist. "This is getting more and more dangerous the longer it hangs around."

"It'll be gone by morning," Bailey answered.

"You get that from above?"

"No, I leave that stuff to the wife. But don't you feel the change?"

Frank stopped, focusing his attention on his surroundings, searching for something different. Yes, something was different. Then he smiled. The ship's movement had changed. The long slow swells of the deep ocean were still there, but now he could make out a chopping motion coming from off the port bow. The seas were changing. He then sensed a slight difference in the wind. It wasn't blowing aft any longer. No, it was off the port quarter now, starting to come around to the northeast.

"A storm's coming," he concluded.

"Yup. It'll blow this fog out of here by morning."

"Not much of an improvement. A pea-soup fog or a nor'easter."

Frank glanced at his watch. The hands glowed in the dark. Sunset had been nearly an hour earlier, and the captain was still waiting.

"Well, I guess I'll go report," Frank said, turning forward.

"Sorry, we didn't find your package, Mister Ross."

"So am—" He stopped in mid-sentence. Movement off the port bow had caught his attention, but the fog was all he could see now. No, there was a shape barely visible hidden deep in the veils of the drifting mist. But nothing should be there, unless . . .

"Sir?" Bailey asked from behind him. "Anything wrong?"

"Something's out there."

Bailey smiled; the man was seeing things again. "Sir, we're at sea . . ." His words died as he, too, glimpsed the growing darkness in the mist.

Then like a curtain, the veils parted for a second to reveal the bow of a tanker, sitting low in the water, her belly full, as she reared high on top a swell headed straight for the *Polites*. Frank intuitively knew it would make contact just forward of where he and the bosun stood. The solid steel prow would cut through the *Polites'* thin side plating into number four hold and open it to the sea.

Ships had two ways to measure how much cargo they could carry—volume and weight. Volume was how much could physically fit inside her holds, and weight was how much that cargo could weigh before it forced her down to her marks, beyond which she would become unstable and dangerous in high seas. Pig Iron, like the load at the bottom of number four, was one of those cargoes that, because of its density, weight was the controlling factor. Thus, number four was only half full, leaving a lot of open space just waiting for thousands of pounds of water to rush in, when that tanker opened her up.

It would take only moments before that extra weight broke the ship's back, and her speed through the water would tear her in two. A few minutes later, the two pieces would be racing each other to the bottom of the ocean, two miles down. It wasn't unheard of for a ship to disappear in less than a minute after a torpedo tore a hole in her side.

And with the speed on that ship, the tanker could even carry on forward through the engine room bulkhead, opening not only number four but also the engine room, another large open space just waiting for the sea to fill.

Frank broke, at a full sprint, for the after ladder to the amidships island, yelling at the top of his lungs. He hoped Captain Egan, who was standing his watch on the bridge, would hear him in time.

"Ship on the port quarter!" he yelled repeatedly.

Behind him, Bailey was just now reaching for the flashlight he had stuck in his back pocket down below. He snapped it on and started flashing it at the dark wraith-like object that once more, was emerging from the fog.

Frank hit the ladder and flew up it, three rungs at a time, still screaming at full volume, "Hard-a-starboard! Collision! Collision!"

"Say, what's all that racket?" finally came a voice from above.

"Tanker, off the port quarter, sir!"

"What?"

"Off the port quarter! Hard-a-starboard!" he yelled as he continued forward on the port side.

Just then, Bailey's flashlight's thin beam reached out to illuminate the ghostly image emerging from the fog.

"Damn!" Egan exclaimed as the situation registered. "Hard-a-starboard," he roared, heading for the wheelhouse door. "Half ahead." He added an engine command to slow the ship allowing the tanker to pull ahead as the *Polites* swung to starboard.

Seconds later, Frank hit the ladder to the bridge deck without slowing down. Just as he did, the ship's horn boomed in the gathering darkness. At the top of the ladder, he spun to take in the scene aft.

"Her heading, Mister?" the captain demanded from within the wheelhouse.

"Thirty degrees starboard of ours," Frank responded with the assurance of a master mariner.

"Steady up on zero-seven-five, Helmsman."

"My rudder is starboard, steading on zero-seven-five, sir," the helmsman replied.

Then the other ship's horn sounded just outside, two short blasts.

"About damn time." Egan stormed as he stepped back on to the bridge wing, glasses already at his eyes. "Lookout, keep an eye out for our starboard neighbor."

"Aye, sir," echoed from the far side of the bridge.

The captain was studying the fast-approaching tanker, but even without glasses, Frank could see the changing aspect on the bow. The two ships were already almost on the same bearing, the tanker slowly gaining on the *Polites* as her speed dropped off.

It was a close shave. He could even make out her name as the gray ghost powered by—the *Cliona*, an Anglo-Saxon Petroleum tanker, eighty-three hundred tons' gross, three million gallons of oil. One hell of a firecracker, he thought as she slid by less than a hundred yards off the port beam.

"Bring her back up to convoy speed, Cadet," the captain ordered over his shoulder, glasses still at his eyes. "That was a close one, Number One," He continued in a voice that only Frank could hear.

Frank smiled in the dark. It was the first time Egan had used that term for a chief officer, a term only used by a captain who trusted his "Number One."

"Aye, sir. Almost too close."

"Bloody tankers act like they are the queen of the ball. Mind you, that oil is important, but that doesn't give them the bloody right of way all the time."

"No, sir." Frank fought to suppress a growing smile.

Egan lowered the glasses, glanced at his mate, and with a wide grin continued, "In this bloody soup, no way to tell who is on the right course. Us or them."

Down on the after well deck, the bosun's flashlight turned off as the tanker pulled ahead.

"Do we follow or lead?" Frank asked.

"Lead, of course. Come left to zero-four-five," Egan commanded, returning to the convoy's base course.

"My rudder is left," the helmsman replied from inside the wheelhouse.

Egan and Frank stood quietly for a moment, waiting for the follow-up.

"Steering course, zero-four-five, sir."

"Steady as you go." Egan finished the sequence. Then he lowered his glasses after completing a final sweep of the horizon. "Over here," he said to Frank with a nod of his head. "Keep your eyes peeled," he said to the lookout as he led the way to an unoccupied corner of the bridge wing.

"Well, are you done with that search yet?"

"Yes."

"And?"

"Nothing. We found nothing." Frank turned to lean on the nearby railing. His eyes lowered to the churning sea below.

"Right. That finishes it."

"No! It doesn't." Frank jerked around to stand eye to eye with the Captain. "It changes nothing. That package is still aboard."

"If it ever was," Egan replied, his jaw set.

"You think it was all in my head?"

"You didn't find it, did you? And you searched the whole damn ship, stem to stern, top to bottom?"

"Yes, but anyone with eyes could see what we were doing. Could have moved it around on us. Probably did. And not just that package."

"What are you talking about?" Egan demanded.

"Hell, Captain. We didn't find any contraband either. That makes this the first time in history an entire crew sneaked nothing illegal aboard. How likely is that? Sailing from the U.S. in the middle of a war? No booze. No stockings. Nothing at all."

"So, if they can hide their contraband?"

"A Nazi spy could easily hide that package." Frank finished the sentence. "I got lucky the first time. He wasn't expecting a search. It was hidden well enough for anything but that."

"So, now what? You continue searching?"

"No, it would be as big a waste of time as the first one unless you lock down the ship until I'm done."

"And how do I run the ship with the crew locked in their quarters?"

"I didn't think so." Frank turned away once more to study the ocean.

"No bright ideas?"

"We could turn back." Frank voiced as his mind filled with images of the people aboard dying in various gruesome ways.

"In case you Yanks missed it, we are fighting a war, and that stuff in those holds is very much needed in Britain right now. Besides, if you are right, turning back will just give our friends more time to prepare a welcoming party the next time we try."

Now the images were all of Helen.

"Then move Mac and his crate to another ship?"

"You're a seaman! Or at least, I think you are. How stupid would that be? Two ships lying dead in the water, trying to transfer people and several tons of cargo. Even if the U-boats left us alone—" He stopped.

Frank looked up, "Then what?"

"We go on. Push through to Liverpool."

"And hope for the best?"

"Yes, afraid that's all we can do, Number One."

Egan placed his hand on Frank's shoulder. "Now, go turn in. I'll finish this watch for you, but you go back on the watch bill in the morning. Zero four hundred." The captain was finished with the cloak and dagger; it was back to the work he understood.

"Aye, aye, sir."

CHAPTER TWELVE

STORM WARNING

As ordered, Frank marched down the two flights past the captain's cabin and on into his own compact compartment. Once there, he stripped off his cap, life jacket, and shoes before lying down. Otherwise, he remained dressed because you never knew when you would need to make a fast exit.

Turning off the light, he laid in the dark, hoping for sleep to claim him, but each time he closed his eyes, his imagination assaulted him with images of passengers and crew—especially Helen—surrounded by flames shooting skyward or worse, drowning in the storm-tossed seas. With each new vision, he heard the real Frank repeating that same line—"And now they all die." Over and over, except this time, it would be his fault, his failure.

The visions proved too much, and he finally gave up. Climbing out of the rack, he stepped back into his shoes, and without even bothering to tying them, jerked open the door and stormed out into the night.

A short while later, he found himself standing at the railing staring at the sea boiling past the solid gray side of the ship, his emotions a mirror of the tempest below. The bosun was right; a storm was coming. The wind had picked up, and the waves were growing stronger as they broke against the hull, not enough yet to affect the ship's motion, but building toward it.

At least the storm would drive the fog away. Already the rising winds had thinned the mist, doubling visibility. He could almost make out the ships beside them. By morning, when he went on watch, the fog would be gone, and he would face a force five—or maybe six— storm blowing in from the northeast. That was almost gale strength. The passengers wouldn't be thrilled; even loaded as she was, the *Polites* would move around quite a bit in a force six squall. He wasn't looking forward to having to keep the ship in position amidst such a blow, but one good thing about it—a tempest like that was sure to drive the U-boats down into the deep. As long as the storm raged, they would remain safe from the Germans—and from the consequences of his failure.

God had given him a chance to do something meaningful. A second opportunity to count—even if it was in Frank's name. It would be his big chance. And what had he done with it? *Nothing.* He cursed under his breath.

No one had asked him what he wanted. *Whose life is this anyway?* he asked himself. *Am I finishing his or continuing mine? And if it's mine, why not take what I want?*

Suddenly, Helen's image wavered before his eyes. Yes, why not her? For a moment, he could almost feel her next to him. But could he do that? Just use her, and then cast her adrift? What about her feelings? Didn't they matter?

Then he realized the truth. *It's not mine or his; it belongs to them, all the people who will die if Mac's baby doesn't make it to England.*

He laughed. God hadn't done him a favor, after all. He hadn't given him a second chance. No. God had given them a second chance, and he was but the instrument. He hadn't been blessed; he had been cursed, and now, he had to find a way to save them.

"Damn it."

"What's wrong?"

He turned around to find Helen stepping off the nearby ladder. She was as breathtaking as she had been in his dreams, but this time, she was real.

"I'm sorry, I didn't mean to startle you. I was just out getting some fresh air."

Frank glanced down at his watch, just past midnight. "It's a little late to be wandering around alone, isn't it?"

"Okay, you caught me. I was little worried about you."

Turning back toward the railing, Frank tried to appear calm and collected. "Nothing to worry about. I've got it all under control."

"Now, we're even," she said, sliding up beside him. The wind enveloped him in her scent. He fought the urge to take her in his arms.

"Even?" he managed, instead.

"Yes, I lied, and now you have."

Smiling, he replied, "Okay, what gave me away?"

"Sometimes, Frank, you're an open book."

"I have to work on that."

"Don't! It's one of your best features," she said in a whisper.

"Probably the reason I suck as a spy though."

"I thought the term was agent."

"Either way, I suck at it."

"I don't know about that. I heard about how you saved us earlier. Running half the length of the ship, screaming all the way."

"That's not secret agent work. That's seamanship, and anyone would have done the same."

"Maybe, but you were the one who did it. Of all the people on this ship, you were the one who saved us from that tanker. Mister Eddy said she would have cut us in half if it hadn't been for you. Is that right?" she asked, her face close to his.

"Probably."

"We all would have died if she had. Right?"

"Most likely," he admitted, already seeing where she was heading, and silently thanked her for it.

"So, as I see it," she continued. "You're not a failure, but a hero. And if God did put you here to save us, you already have. At least once already." She kissed him on the cheek, then turned and disappeared back into the darkness.

"Damn, her. How can you fight that?"

But could she be right?

If the *Cliona* had hit them, a tanker with a flammable cargo, pig iron in number four, the engine room right there, the *Polites* would have gone down in less than a minute, and at that hour, most of the crew and all the passengers were below deck, so few, if any, would have made it off the ship. Any that did would have plunged into churning seas covered with burning oil. Plus, in the fog, it's doubtful the rest of the convoy would even know what happened to them. Everyone would have died. *Could that have been what the real Frank was talking about? If I hadn't been there, on the well deck, at that moment, to see that tanker bearing down on us, they all would have died!*

But what of the Nazi? He was real, no matter what the captain believed. The bastard killed the real Frank and had tried to kill him, too. Oh, yes, he's real! *So, we have a Nazi agent on board, but the real reason I'm here is to save the ship from a collision? Does that sound right? Or am I just grasping at straws?*

No, Helen was wrong. She was simply a nice girl, trying to make him feel better.

He glanced in the direction she had disappeared.

An unbelievably nice girl.

Frank stood still, watching the broiling sea. He couldn't control his thoughts as they jumped from Helen to the Nazi, the ship, his fading memories of another life, and to the image of the real Frank quoting that damned line—"and now they all die.". He finally broached the most troubling question of all.

Why me?

Why did God pick me? Why would God even be interested in me, let alone choose me to handle such a job?

I would like to think it was because I was the best person available. But who in his right mind would think that? Maybe it was the word "available." Perhaps he was the best available the moment the real Frank died. Could God have limits? Did He have mere seconds to pick somebody, or else the opportunity would be lost forever. Maybe only souls just freed of their original bodies could be redirected into Frank's instead of wherever newly released souls usually go. How many were available at that precise instant? A dozen? A hundred? Maybe it was true; he was the best available.

He laughed. *Who are you kidding? You're talking about God, the creator of the Universe. What limits could God have?*

No, it had to be something else.

Perhaps he knew something, something he learned in his other life that was important here. But what? He had had a lifetime of picking up useless little bits and pieces, facts interesting only to him. Maybe cool in a game of Trivial Pursuit, but useless in real life. How many times had people told him that? When would you ever need to know that?

Never, or perhaps, now?

But what? Which fact? Of all the worthless little things he knew, which one could be important here? And with his Swiss-cheese memory, would he even remember it?

Then the *Polites* rose to meet the first crest of the approaching storm. Frank lifted his eyes to the horizon and could just make out the outline of the tanker, low in the water, in the thinning mist. Out where she belonged for once. The fog was fading fast now, and the storm was almost upon them. Tomorrow would be an interesting day.

He would need some sleep to face it. A man can only run so long without rest. So, he took one last glance at the spot where Helen had disappeared into the darkness, and he dragged himself back into his cabin, locking the door behind him. The Nazi was still at large, and a man was defenseless when he was asleep.

● ● ●

A knock in the dark. Frank sat up straight. The surrounding room was pitch black and moving, rolling, really, with a little forward pitching thrown in.

Another knock. "Mister Ross?" a voice called from beyond the door.

"Yes?"

"It's the messenger, sir. Mister Stratton sends his compliments. And reports it is three-thirty, sir."

"Oh! Okay." His wake-up call. He slipped from the rack and opened the door. There stood a seaman in a skull cap and dungarees.

"I'm up, Randolph." The man's name had simply popped into his head. "Please, inform Mister Stratton I'll be up shortly."

"Very well, sir." The man nodded and moved off toward the companionway. No salute. Well, what did he expect? This was the Merchant Navy. Here we say yes, sir and no, sir, but no one messes with the rest of that military stuff like saluting.

Closing the door, Frank switched on the light above the sink and, for a moment, stared at the reflection in the mirror. It still wasn't the right face, but the longer he stayed here, the more familiar it became. "Frank, my old man. You're growing on me." He examined the features—dark brown hair, a dark complexion, clear blue-gray eyes, a strong jaw covered at present with the dark stubble of a day-old beard. It was a good face. He could see why Helen was attracted.

"Won't do to be late. The captain will string me up alive."

A few minutes later, after a quick shave, he pulled back on the few items of clothing he had removed before crawling into his rack and rechecked himself in the mirror. Then with a deep breath, Frank stepped out of the cabin, turning right he quickly emerged onto the weather deck. The fresh breeze on his face finished waking him up. The fog had vanished overnight, just as he thought it would. And instead of the closed-in world of the past few days, he gazed out over a wind-swept expanse just beginning to brighten in the east with the fast-approaching dawn. With their present course, north by north-east, they were now getting high into the northern latitudes. This far up, daylight came early at this time of the year.

Out there, among the wind-tossed waves, he could already make out the dark form of the *Tibia*, a ten-thousand-ton Dutch tanker—the second ship in column four—number forty-two in the convoy; the *Polites* was number thirty-two, the second ship in column three. Ahead of the *Tibia*, another barely visible shape marked the commodore's ship, the *Glenpark*, a five-thousand-ton tramp, leading column four.

Somewhere ahead of her, lost to him in the darkness, was the convoy's lead escort, the old former Canadian Pacific liner the *Montcalm*, now His Majesty's Ship *Wolfe*. She had seven newly installed six-inch low-angle deck guns, which were useless against airplanes. Still, they were safe from those until the convoy got a lot closer to the French coast. Right now, the threat was not from above the water but below it.

He started aft toward the ladder up to the lower bridge deck, his eyes on the chop between the *Tibia* and the *Polites*. It was not quite as strong as he had expected—a force four, maybe pushing five—but it was still growing. They were in for a ride the next couple of days until this storm outran them to the east heading for the coast of Europe and the British Isles.

He reached the starboard wing, two decks above, and with the higher position, he could now make out several more ships to starboard. The horizon to the east was growing lighter by the minute.

He glanced at his watch; he was already a minute late. Not good.

Stepping through the open doorway into the wheelhouse, he was greeted by, "So, good of you to join us," in the captain's posh English cadence. *Damn! I was hoping he would have his head down at this hour.*

"Sorry, sir. Won't happen again. Still getting up to speed."

"No excuses, Number One."

"Right, sir."

Frank took the wheelhouse in with a quick sweep of his eyes. The captain was in his favorite corner, starboard side forward, a sweater under his lifejacket for warmth. This early in the morning, this far north, it could be quite chilly, even in late spring. The helmsman at the wheel was a man Frank knew, but he couldn't put a name to the face. Mister Stratton was near the chart table, probably just finishing up his final entry in the log.

Frank moved over to join him.

"Morning, Number One," the man greeted him without looking up from the logbook as he scribbled the last few words.

"Ralph." Frank used the familiar and saw a flash of white as the man smiled at the use of his Christian name.

Stratton leaned in. "Not standard, Number One, but I like it. Nobody calls me Ralph anymore, just Mister Stratton or plain Stratton," he whispered to Frank.

"Not standard?"

"Oh, no. Not formal enough on the bridge of a British merchantman. Titles only, I'm afraid. Now, down in the saloon, that sort of thing is acceptable. Must keep things and people in their proper places. Not like on an American ship, eh? All democratic like."

"Don't kid yourself. Most American captains are just as—" Frank glanced over his shoulder toward the figure in the starboard corner.

Mister Stratton suppressed a laugh.

"Mister Stratton?" emerged from the corner.

"Yes, sir?"

"Get on with it."

"Yes, sir." Stratton turned to Frank. "Helmsman and lookouts have all been relieved. Captain's standing orders are in the log. We are steering the convoy's baseline of zero-four-eight. Speed is still seven knots, we are turning seventy-three revolutions, but I expect an increase any minute now, what with the fog gone and daylight coming—at least until the storm gets worse. Also, I expect we might start zigzagging soon, though the storm might change that."

"Looks like a force five now," Frank offered.

"Yes, and it's been growing all night."

"I expect a force eight by noon," the captain added from his corner.

"I'd imagine so, sir," Frank agreed.

"If you want, I can let you have some time to read the orders." Stratton continued.

"Anything new since last night?"

"No."

"Then, to bed with you."

Stratton nodded, "I stand relieved."

Frank turned toward the starboard corner, "Captain, I have the watch." Frank finished the standard phrase as Stratton exited stage left without another word.

The captain grunted in response. Why was he even here at this time of the morning? No stars at first light. The fog had vanished to reveal a completely overcast sky.

Frank entered the change of the watch into the logbook and then moved to the port bridge wing. The lookout acknowledged his presence. "Morning, Mister Ross."

"Good morning." Frank looked but again couldn't put a name to the face. "I'm sorry. Since my fall, memory's been like Swiss cheese. Your name is?" he asked over the howl of the growing wind in the standing wires above their heads.

"Reagan, sir. Ordinary Seaman."

"Where you from, Reagan?"

"Belfast, sir."

"Irish, then."

"Four generations. Before that, the Scottish Marches."

"My family started in the same area, Reagan. Only they didn't stop in Ireland, continued on to America just before the War of Independence."

"Aye, I think I heard of that one, sir. Only we have a different name for it."

Frank smiled. "Just a little disagreement in the family."

"Can't keep us apart, sir."

"No. Keep your eyes open, Reagan. We're all depending on you."

"Right, sir."

Frank finished his sweep of the horizon, smiled again at the seaman, and stepped back into the wheelhouse. As he did, the captain chided the helmsman, "Watch your head, Simpson."

"Sorry, sir. The sea is getting a little wilder."

"Can the excuses. Keep her true. No room for your skylarking in these quarters."

"Aye, sir."

Frank had stopped just inside the port door. The captain glanced over at him, then waved him over. Frank quickly crossed the deck.

"Sir?"

In a whisper, the captain said, "Keep an eye on that one. Weakest helmsman aboard. Decent at most times, but with this growing storm, he likes to wander around a bit. No room for that now."

"Right. I'll keep an eye on him, sir."

The captain brought his glasses up to his eyes. Frank got the message; he had been dismissed. So, he continued on out to check on the starboard lookout.

Simpson was at the wheel, Reagan on the port wing, so who was on the starboard?

"Morning, sir," came a familiar voice.

Red, the bosun's favorite. "So, you're on this watch?"

"Aye, Mister Ross. Boats doesn't have enough hands to keep me off the watch bill."

"We must look into that."

"Could you, Mister Ross?" Red inquired, the long glasses still plastered to his eyes.

"One could get the idea that you are a loafer, at heart."

"Now, you wound me, Mister Ross. No one can say old Red doesn't do his fair share of the work. Of course, they are different types of work that need doing, and it is best to use each man to do the types of work that best suit his God-given talents."

"And yours don't include standing watch at four in the morning."

"Amen to that, Mister Ross."

Frank smiled as he raised his glasses to his eyes.

"Signal from the commodore, sir." Red pointed out the flags which had just unfurled on the *Glenpark*'s mast. It was in code; where was that codebook? Frank turned to enter the wheelhouse.

"It's okay, Mister Ross. We have had too many things going on to expect you to have memorized the basic signals yet," the captain declared from the doorway.

"Yes, Captain. I will get that done today."

"See you do. In the meantime, the signal reads: speed ten."

"Right, sir." Frank slipped past the captain into the wheelhouse. *Damn, it! You need to stop acting like a damn amateur! You're supposed to be the chief officer.* "Thank you, sir."

"Check on the cadet, Miller. He should have reported the signal and acknowledged receipt already."

"Right, sir." Frank reversed course, heading back out onto the bridge wing to afford himself a view of the cadet's station on top of the wheelhouse, a position known as monkey island, and the ship's masthead, where the acknowledging reply should be.

"Reply up, sir." Red supplied just as Frank stepped through the doorway. Frank nodded but took a second to confirm it. He had screwed up enough already this morning.

"Done, sir," he relayed to the captain. "Miller, you need to announce any signals from the commodore as soon as you receive them." He shouted up to the boy standing at the railing above his head.

"Aye, sir. Sorry, got wrapped up in the response."

"That's important, son. But first, pass it on. Then respond."

"Yes, sir."

"Be ready to execute. We don't want to be late."

"Right, sir."

Frank made his way to the engine order telegraph, his eyes still on the commodore's flag hoist. Right now, the signal was just a heads up, a warning that the convoy was to increase speed to ten knots, near the maximum that they could expect to maintain with the variety of ships present. As an HX convoy, it was comprised of ships capable of speeds above nine knots. Slower vessels went with the SC convoys, while ones capable of fifteen knots or more, like the *Queen Mary*, were left to fend for themselves, trusting to their speed and the sheer size of the ocean for safety. There simply were not enough escorts to protect everybody.

The commodore would now wait until all ships had acknowledged the order by showing the correct response at their mastheads. Then he would pull his flags down, signaling to execute. All the ships would then increase their speed to ten knots and lower their flag hoists to acknowledge the order.

"There," the captain chimed as the commodore's flags disappeared. Frank grabbed the two handles of the engine order telegraph or EOT and pulled them back. Immediately, he pushed them forward to all ahead full, the internal bells ringing with each change in the setting. Since the *Polites* was a twin screwed vessel with two engines, the EOT had two handles, one on each side, one for each engine. By moving the handles at either end of the telegraph, the bridge, or the engine room would cause the indicator hands on the opposite EOT to advance to match the new position on the first, thus, informing the other of the change in speed. It also rang a set of bells as an audible signal in case the watch at the other end was busy at that moment. Once the other end recognized the change, they would carry out the order and acknowledge it by moving their set of handles to match the first set. That would cause the hands at the other end to move to the new position and would ring the bells again. Frank knew that five decks below, the other EOT was thus mirroring his set of movements, its bells announcing to the duty engineer the change in required speed.

Leaving the handles in the new position, Frank stepped forward, flipped open the engine room voice tube, and whistled into the opening, then stood hunched over the tube waiting for the response.

The duty engineer was on the ball. Behind him, Frank heard the EOT's bells ringing, and a moment later, the call back on the voice tube. "Engine room, aye."

"Make turns for ten knots."

"One hundred revolutions, aye."

Frank closed the tube but knew he would probably need to make several more calls over the next hour or so, adjusting the number of revolutions up or down to get their speed to exactly match the surrounding ships so he could maintain his position in relation to them.

"Very well, Number One," the captain said, pushing himself away from the bulkhead. "Please, note the change in speed in the log and the standing orders. I'm going below for a while."

"Aye, aye, sir."

Frank glanced over his shoulder as the captain disappeared down the inside ladder. It was a promising sign that the captain finally trusted him to be alone on the bridge.

Glancing at the display on the binnacle, Frank noted the heading as zero-four-three instead of the baseline. "Mind your head, Simpson. We don't want a reputation for wandering all over the place."

"Aye, aye, sir," the helmsman replied as he moved the wheel to correct the ship's heading.

CHAPTER THIRTEEN
FORCE EIGHT

The captain was right. The storm had strengthened to force eight by noon, and the once smooth ocean was replaced with one racked by twenty-foot waves, the tops of which were shredded by the forty-mile per hour winds. Wave after wave ran up on the ship from the north-northeast, breaking against the *Polites'* starboard bow, leaving her corkscrewing, the bow rising to meet each new wave. Then the bow would roll to starboard and dive forward as the wave moved down along her port side, and finally, as the wave moved on, her bow would rise, and she would roll back to port just in time to meet the next in the endless line of rollers.

Frank emerged from the fo'c'sle via the starboard side passageway. He had recently finished a quick sweep of the forward holds, numbers one through three. His stated reason was the growing intensity of the storm. This was the first heavy blow since New York, where most of their cargo was loaded and secured. He explained to the passengers the need to check all the straps regularly to see if any were working loose. He then proceeded to describe how dangerous loose cargo could be for any ship in a storm. What with crates weighing upwards of twenty tons, not to mention the pig iron in the bottom of number four, they could easily unbalance a ship so close to her marks, causing her to capsize or rip a hole in her side.

That was all true, but the real reason he was putting so much time and effort into checking the cargo, the one he would admit only to himself, was his nagging fear of what the Nazi would do. He knew he was still out there, somewhere aboard the *Polites*. Waiting, planning something, and simply because the captain believed it was only in his head didn't change that fact. Frank knew the Nazi was real. He had fought him that morning on the weather deck, and he had chased someone onto the fantail. And the real Frank had lost his life to him down in number five. Oh, yes, the bastard was real. And he was up to no good!

He couldn't take sitting in his cabin, waiting and worrying about what the bastard was up to. No, that was way too nerve-racking for him. He had tried catching up on his sleep, with the ship moving as much as it was, all but essential work had been secured for the day. After twenty minutes of rolling around in his rack, his fears had driven him out of bed and down into the holds. That was where the bastard would strike, far from prying eyes.

Maybe if he just wandered about with no rhyme or reason checking spaces as he came upon them, perhaps he could catch the Nazi up to something or see something out of place, just as the real Frank did that first day. Only this time, he would be ready.

Where he presently stood, Frank was protected by the bulk of the fo'c'sle. He heard the wind ripping through the rigging above him on the foredeck as it whipped the sea into a cauldron of seething waves capped by spindrift. He watched as the storm in all its terrible fury unfolded around him. A dozen ships were in view. Each embarked on a wild ride created by the waves, pitching and tossing, each at different angles, different heights, as they met the waves in their individual ways. The larger, heavier ships rose and rolled slowly, more ponderously than the smaller ones, and the escorts, the smallest of all, bobbed around like rubber toys tossed upon a toddler's bathwater.

He glanced at his watch. Five past noon. He was late for dinner. He still had more spaces to search, but he could only do so much. Besides, he had learned long ago that seas like these would quickly nauseate him if he didn't keep some food in his stomach.

Turning aft, he waited for the next wave to lift the bow and ease his passage across the well deck to the amidships house. Then just as the bow soared to its peak, he scurried aft, hand over hand on the lifelines the bosun and his crew had rigged in the forenoon watch. He reached the foot of the companionway just as the ship turned against him, the bow tipping over to ride the flank of the wave down into the trough between it and the next one.

Now, he held on as the *Polites* ran downhill, fighting the pull of gravity, patiently waiting for the inevitable change in the ship's pitch to gain the boat deck and the saloon door beyond.

He heard rather than saw the first breakers hit the well deck behind him. Spinning around, he watched as a wall of water washed aft across the deck, draining into the scuppers as the ship's motion once more drove the bow up the face of the next wave. He stepped up on to the first rung to keep the last of it from engulfing his feet. Then having lost the moment, he had to wait through another wave before the ship's continuing battle with the elements once more helped him on his way up the companionway and across the deck to the saloon door.

"What a ride!" he roared into the wind. The weather was quite exhilarating in its power, a true force eight on the Beaufort scale, which detailed by wind speed the effects of wind and waves. A force eight was a gale or a weak tropical storm, winds between thirty-nine and forty-seven miles per hour. Nothing to worry about but quite a show, nevertheless.

Just then, another wave broke over the fo'c'sle, cascading down onto the well deck, dumping a hundred tons of water on top of number one's hatch and the surrounding deck. He would need to keep an eye on that, for that much weight might beat the cover to pieces, and if it did, a lot of water could pour into the hold below in no time. Loaded as the ship was, it wouldn't take much more weight up forward to drive her bow down, never to surface again.

He pulled the outer door open and stepped into the small vestibule. Most of the time, the watertight exterior doors were kept latched back, open, out of the way, but in heavy seas like these, the bosun's crew would close them to create a little buffer zone between the storm outside and the cabins inside to at least try to keep them dry.

Closing the outer door, Frank pushed through the inner one into the relatively quiet passageway. A moment later, he entered the saloon, where the captain sat at the head of the single fore and aft table set to one side of the compartment. Arrayed along the table were three of the nurses and the third engineer, Sid Russell. Frank removed his foul weather jacket and hung it on the coat rack just inside the door, among several others. Then he moved to the base of the table, pausing beside the chair.

"Captain, may I join you?" he inquired, his right hand on the back of the chair.

"Of course," Egan replied, a smile on his face. "Glad you could pull yourself away from your pressing duties to join us for lunch, as you Yanks call it."

"Sorry I'm late. The time keeps getting away from me," Frank responded as he sat.

Sing, the steward, appeared at his elbow. "So, sorry, Mister Ross, I didn't know you were coming. I have none left," he whispered.

"That's fine, Sing. Just get me anything you can find."

"Yes, Mister Ross. I'll get you something."

He disappeared through the connecting door into the adjoining pantry.

"Did you find anything, Mister Ross?" the captain inquired from the other end of the table. Frank looked up and caught the wink.

"No, sir. Nothing. All the tie-downs are holding up well. The ship's riding the storm high and dry."

"Good, but please continue with your sweeps. It wouldn't do to have anything break loose."

"Yes, sir."

"Now, you will all excuse me," the captain intoned as he stood up. "I'm afraid duty calls." They all acknowledged his departure as he slipped out the door, grabbing one of the foul weather jackets as he left. He headed for the interior companionway to the deck above, most likely on his way to the bridge.

Frank glanced at the three nurses. He wondered where Helen was.

"How are you ladies coping with the weather?"

An older heavy-set brunette, who Frank recognized as Vicky Andrews, the senior nurse, answered. "Most of us are a little worse for the wear, but Rachel is confined to her bed. The poor girl can't keep anything down."

"That's a shame. Have you given her anything for it?"

"Of course," an older blonde named Dolores answered, with a condescending tone in her voice.

"Right. You're nurses. What was I thinking?"

Vicky smiled. "Just a little tired, I would think."

Dolores seemed ready to add something else before she spotted the warning look on Vicky's face. Then changing tack, she instead supplied, "I'm sure that's it."

The third girl, whom Frank had only seen in passing and couldn't put a name to, nodded her agreement.

"How have you found your trip so far, Miss?" He asked.

"It's been a little overwhelming."

"Now, Margaret," the blonde jumped in, "I am sure Mister Ross doesn't want to hear about our little problems."

"But he asked," Margaret whined.

"Yes, I did," Frank came to her aid. She was a pretty little thing with brown hair and a pair of glasses sitting perched low on her button nose. "Truly, I am interested. As chief officer, I am responsible for our cargo, and though it may sound a little strange, passengers are also considered cargo on this ship. So, if any of you have any problems, please feel free to bring them to me. It's part of my job to see you all have a safe, comfortable trip." He finished as Sing reappeared at his elbow, placing a plate full of bangers and a couple of eggs in front of him.

"Should have known."

"It is all I have," the steward said defensively.

"It's okay. I'm growing fond of these little time bombs." He smiled at the women as his fork "popped" open the first one.

• • •

After lunch, Frank made his way up to his cabin, where he crawled into his rack. During the previous hour, the ship's movement had increased, suggesting that the storm was still growing in intensity outside. As he laid there, the rolling left him in constant motion. Back and forth, he rolled from one side of the bed to the other. *If this keeps up, I'll never get any sleep.* But at least the enemy couldn't do much either. Not the worst trade-off.

He braced his body in place, holding himself still in the rack, but as soon as he started to drift off and his body relaxed, the next wave would throw him one way or the other, jerking him awake as he rolled against the bulkhead or the rail along the edge of his rack.

After a while, Frank simply gave up, and he tried reading instead to pass the time until his next watch.

As he tried to sit up, an electric shock raced through his body. He felt his heart jumping within his chest, and he opened his eyes to find himself in a hospital ward. The room stretched off in both directions, two endless rows of hospital beds lined against the two opposing white walls. The ceiling soared high above, and the floor was a dull gray linoleum.

Not again!

Close by, a woman dressed in a white lab coat was adjusting the controls on a huge electrical device sitting on a wheeled cart beside his bed. An extension cord snaked across the floor to a distant wall socket, and several wires ran across from the machine to his bare chest. His white hospital gown had been ripped open down to his waist, and an IV was delivering a clear fluid into his right wrist while a pair of nurses dressed in old-style white starched dresses, chunky shoes, and even a pair of classic nurse's hats sitting high above their massive beehive-type hairdos, stood watching the doctor. The problem was that no one was watching him—the patient.

On the opposite side of the bed, an unfamiliar man and woman stood. No, that wasn't right. The man's features were similar but different somehow from his youngest son's. His hair wasn't right either; it seemed a little too blond. And he was wearing an Army uniform, one of the old World War II olive drab uniforms, complete with an Eisenhower jacket and sergeant's stripes, which wasn't right either. The Army had stopped using that uniform before he was born. The woman was a tall thin blonde, a stranger to him. Who were these people? And why were they here? For that matter, where was here?

He hadn't seen a hospital ward like this one outside of a movie in decades. So, why was he here and not in the private room he had earlier?

"Doctor," the man said, drawing the woman's attention. "He's awake."

"So he is. Great," she said, moving to the edge of the bed. "We weren't sure we could bring you around again, Sergeant." She took hold of his wrist and started checking his pulse. For a moment, all was silent as she counted his heart rate. "Good. Blood pressure, please?" she asked one of the nurses.

"Can you understand me," she asked, while behind her, the nurse pulled out a black rubber cuff and ball with a gauge attached.

He nodded; it was all he could manage.

"Great," she said as she stepped aside and let the nurse get to him with the blood pressure device. *What's with all the old school stuff?*

"Where am I?" he croaked through vocal cords grown rusty with disuse.

"You're in the military ward of the MacArthur General Hospital. You're here thanks to your son's status. It's a good thing, too. I know you wouldn't have made it without this." She patted the machine. "Civilian wards don't have access to equipment like this."

"Son's status?" he managed. His voice sounded a little clearer this time.

"Yes, front line combat. We are enormously proud of our soldiers. Risking their lives as they do. You never know when the Germans and the Soviets will have another one of their regular dust-ups in the Urals."

He, of course, was back in his real body again, but this didn't seem right to him. Everything was different. The Germans and the Soviets at each other's throats in the Urals? The Germans never got close to the Urals. Stalingrad was as far as they went. But it wasn't just that; it was the uniforms, the medical equipment, the hospital still using wards. He had been in a private room, and while the man was a close facsimile of his son, he was sure he wasn't. Besides, his son was in the Air Force, not the Army.

Then, he noticed a mirror sitting on the nearby table. As he realized the face in the glass wasn't his or Frank's, the pain came back with a vengeance, another elephant standing on his chest. He had forgotten how bad it was. His vision narrowed and faded, plunging him back into darkness. Was he really dying this time? Had he failed? His second chance gone. Had God given up on him?

Please, God, don't!

CHAPTER FOURTEEN
CALL OF PASSION

The knock sounded loud in the small cabin.

"Mister Ross?" a voice called through the wooden door.

Frank opened his eyes to find himself curled up in a ball and wedged under the desk across from his rack. The overturned chair was pushed up hard against his back.

"Mister Ross, are you in there, sir?" the voice called again.

"Yes," Frank moaned, pushing the chair away with an arm that felt frozen and stiff, as though rigor mortis had set in.

"Do you need anything, sir?"

"No, just a little hard to get moving," Frank replied. He had to concentrate to get his body to move, his muscles to respond. It was like he had to relearn how his body worked. Slowly, he liberated himself from under the desk, a difficult task with limbs that felt like dead weight. He was done with being jerked back and forth between this life and the other. First, here, and then there. *Please, God, one or the other. Right now, I don't care which, 1941 or . . . when was the other?* He couldn't remember, and although he was sure he had been back in his real body once more, it wasn't the future he remembered. Something had happened to change it completely. But what?

"But sir, Mr. Stratton . . ."

Damn! How could he be expected to keep track of time with all this crap going on? "Okay, it's late, and I'm due on the bridge. Anything else?"

"Well, yes, sir. Mister Eddy and Mister Stratton are betting on whether or not you will be on time."

"They're what?"

"Betting on whether you will be on time or not."

"And why are you telling me this?"

"Well . . ."

Crap! "Let me guess. You're in on it?"

"Well, yes, sir."

"Tell them I'll be there," he roared, tired of all this bullshit. "Now, go away!" he ordered as he, at last, managed to drag himself to his feet.

Leaning back against the wardrobe for support, he flexed his arms and legs, slowly and painfully beating life back into them. How had he become such a joke? He was certain if they knew what was going on . . . To hell with it!

He had no time for self-pity now.

Instead, he pushed himself away from the wardrobe and managed to stand up straight, for a moment, before his legs gave out and he fell backward, landing on top of the desk. He grabbed the wooden top for support and succeeded in keeping himself upright, safe for the time being. Forcing air into his lungs, he could feel his body gradually starting to warm up, the chill receding. Was he returning from the dead? How long had he been gone this time? He gazed around the cabin. It was a mess. The storm must have thrown him from the bed, and his lifeless body had rolled around down there on the deck, flopping from side to side, knocking the chair over, rolling every which way until finally wedging itself up under the desk. He could feel the aches and pains all over his body, and he knew he was going to pay for it.

Reaching out with an unsteady hand, he grabbed the nearby sink and dragged himself across to it. Rising once more, he set his legs apart, creating a more stable base, and began to roll with the ship's constant motion.

Yes, it seemed Frank's body had been rolling around for quite some time. Every inch of it looked black and blue. He checked out several of the most painful areas before giving it up as a lost cause. He could see the scene, his body rolling around and bouncing into every corner and sharp edge in the compartment. And now it seemed the warmer he got, the more it hurt, which was probably the nerves waking up and screaming at the abuse they had endured.

He caught sight of his reflection in the mirror and smiled. At least, he was back to Frank's face, and though it was still strange, it had grown familiar to him over the last few days, besides, it was getting harder and harder to remember what his real face looked like.

"Mister Ross, you have five minutes," Sing's voice announced from the corridor.

"Thank you." The steward was looking out for him—or was he in on the bet, too?

He forced himself to start moving. No time for this now. He had to get to the bridge, he had duties to perform. Grabbing his coat and binoculars, he was out the door, almost running down the steward, who was still waiting in front of the door.

"Sorry," Frank called over his shoulder as he pushed past the steward and headed toward the companionway, trying hard to ignore all the pain moving caused him.

• • •

The next four hours were, for Frank, a struggle, fighting to maintain the *Polites'* position—row two column three, eight hundred yards aft of the *Loch Ranza* in row one, and a thousand yards off *Cliona*, now back in her rightful place, to port in column two, and *Tibia* to starboard in column four. At the same time, the *Scottish Trader* battled to maintain her position eight hundred yards astern. His job was greatly complicated by the winds blowing in from the port quarter at forty knots and the twenty-foot waves those winds were pushing across the wide-open expanse of the North Atlantic.

The convoy had lost three ships to the fog, ships which just disappeared in the soup, gone without a trace. Hopefully, they had turned back to Halifax or maybe detoured to St. John's. But the fog had been easy with the ships slowed to six knots and the wind and seas calm. Now, it was different with each ship on its own wild ride, up, down, left, and right, as the winds and the waves worked pushing and pulling on every square inch of each ship both above and below the waterline. The results were uneven, as each wave was different. One would hit from twenty degrees abaft the beam and the next from thirty. One was twenty feet tall, the following only ten, and a third twenty-five. First, the winds would whip around and push in the same direction as the waves, and a moment later, they would shift and move the other way.

Each ship was different, in size and shape, with varying amounts of rigging. Some had large superstructures, and others had little, if any. Some were blunt-nosed with a straight up and down prow. One which had to be driven through the waves with brute force, while others were of the new style, curved, angled, flaring out at the sides, designed to glide through the water. The ships also had endless combinations of engines and propellers—there were diesels, like the *Polites*, and old fashion steam engines, but even those had their differences. Most were of the triple-expansion type, but some had the new high-speed turbines. Most had a single propeller, others had two, and the old *Wolfe* had four. There were also differences in the rudders and hull shapes under the waterline.

All these factors worked against the convoy, trying to pull it apart at the seams, driving some ships faster while it slowed down others. Some it pushed to port, and a few were even drifting to starboard. It was Frank's job—and that of every other officer of the deck in the convoy— to use their combination of engines, rudders, and propellers to fight the wind and waves in order to maintain their station, a thousand yards apart, and eight hundred yards behind.

Two turns up on the engines, down one, up three, watch your head. Orders were given fast and furious to the helmsman and the engine room below. He and his lookouts had their glasses always at the ready, as he slid back and forth, to port and then to starboard, always watching the *Cliona* and the *Tibia* as they fought the storm, doing his best to keep the *Polites* dead center between them while following the *Loch Ranza's* stern as it rose and fell with each wave. He was always watching the distances. Was the *Polites* gaining on her or falling back? He even used the *Cliona* and the *Tibia* by keeping them abreast on the port and starboard wings. If they were maintaining their proper positions, he couldn't help but be in the right place. Of course, the *Tibia* was following the *Glenpark,* the commodore's ship, the convoy's guide. All the ships were supposed to line up off of it, but the formation was only as good as the various ships. If they screwed up, all bets were off.

Mister Stratton lost his bet, when by the skin of his teeth, Frank arrived on time, earning him an atta-boy from the captain, and making Stratton's wallet ten pounds lighter. If Frank could just repeat it, he might start to change his reputation.

During the entire watch, Egan stood, silent and brooding in the starboard corner, taking in everything. At the end of the watch, after the third mate, Eddy had relieved him at twenty hundred hours, and Frank was making his way off the bridge, the captain murmured, "Impressive, Number One."

"Sir?" Frank stopped dead in his tracks.

"Your performance this watch. Quite impressive." Egan turned back to the window, finished with the conversation.

"Thank you, sir."

Frank left the bridge. Another compliment from the captain. It seemed he was on a roll, and since Egan wasn't a man given to gushing over his subordinates, any praise was special.

It was so unexpected that the other issues didn't work their way back into his mind until he was alone in his cabin with the door closed behind him.

Was that vision of the future real? Or was it just another dream?

He turned to look in the mirror.

He had to admit he had started to doubt himself, to believe the others might be right about him, that it was really all in his head. He was beginning to believe that he was Frank Ross, Chief Officer of the *Polites*. He was just a regular guy who had slipped and fell in the bottom of number five, injuring his head, scrambling his memories, and all these visions of the future, of his "other life," were just the result of his mind playing with him while trying to fix itself. After all, who did he think he was? Handpicked by God to fix history? Really!

But could it really be only a dream! It had felt so real, like he had lived it. Like he had been that other man, the one who wasted all his time wishing and dreaming for something different, something like this. Maybe that was the reason everything back there felt like a dream now. He had been sleepwalking his way through life, always dreaming of adventure and romance but never reaching for it.

No! It wasn't a dream; he wasn't the real Frank. He had met the real one out there, in the clouds. He had talked to him. The real Frank had failed. *It wasn't me down there in number five!* The real Frank had fought and lost, and now they were all going to die because of it. It was so critical that he succeed that without it, even history would change.

That's it! The different future. It's what happens if I fail. It's why I was sent here. Yes, saving the people is important, but Mac's baby is the real mission. It must get through.

He shook his head and smiled at himself. He had started to doubt, to give in and believe them, so God had allowed him to see the other future, the one that would happen if he failed, a future where Germany and the Soviet Union were still fighting each other, and America was caught between them, always on the edge of total war.

But that's not what's supposed to happen. God wants the old timeline restored, and He put me here to fix it. Frank pounded on his chest. *But what do I do? How can I change it?*

A knock sounded at the door.

He spun around and jerked the door open. Helen stood there with her hand raised to knock again.

"Oh," she said, retreating a step. "You're here." She smiled.

"I just came off watch." He held out his binoculars for some unknown reason.

"I took a chance. You looked so lost at dinner."

"You were there?"

"See?" She glanced up and down the passageway. "Can I come in?"

"It's frowned on."

"Really? After what we have been through?" She reached out, her hand resting on his forearm.

He stared down at it, the warmth soaking into his skin, flowing through him, filling him. He nodded, stepping back out of the way.

She slipped into the cabin and pushed the door closed behind her. Frank stood still, his eyes locked on the back of the door, too afraid to risk meeting her eyes and losing himself in their green depths. He listened to her as she moved farther into the compartment and felt the warmth in his arm fading away.

"Something's happened," she sensed.

"Yes." His eyes remained on the door.

She waited a moment for him to continue and then prompted in a whisper, "What?" He couldn't concentrate as her scent, clean and fresh, filled the cabin with a hint of perfume. He closed his eyes. Even without looking, he could see those green pools, the brown hair surrounding her pale face, and those bright red lips.

"I was back there again. In my real life, only it wasn't." He stopped, unable to go on.

"Damn it. Frank, look at me," she pleaded.

With a shiver, he did as she asked. Turning around, he opened his eyes, and they met hers. She could tell he was deeply troubled by what he believed he had seen. It was all she could do not to pull him into her arms and comfort him. She had to look away to save herself.

"What wasn't?" she managed in a low whisper.

"My life." He jerked the chair out from under the desk and collapsed into it, burying his face in his hands. She waited, standing beside the bed, her eyes on his broad back. She tried studying the material in his shirt to keep from losing control.

"It wasn't the same," he finally mumbled through his hands.

"What wasn't the same?" She asked, happy to have something else to think about.

He twisted the chair around and lifted his face to hers. "Everything was different. The people, the places, the details, even me! It was all changed."

She started to reach out her hand to brush his face but pulled up just short of touching him. Then as she began to pull her hand away, he reached up and grabbed it. His grip was steel, as if he was holding on for dear life. She could see unshed tears shimmering in his eyes and suddenly realized her cheeks were wet as well.

She sat down on the bed, mostly because her knees were about to fail.

"How was it different?" was all she could offer.

"This war was still going on. The Allies hadn't won because the United States hadn't entered the war. And the Germans and the Russians were still at each other's throats. My son was there, but he wasn't the same. His face, it was all different, but somehow, I still knew he was my son. He was in the Army. I don't have a son in the Army. And that hospital, the equipment, the wards, it was all wrong." He dropped his head back into his hands.

She silently stroked his hair.

"You don't believe me, do you?" he inquired, his head still down.

"I don't know what to think," she replied. "You go on and on about the future, but it makes little sense to me."

Looking up, he asked, "Like what?"

"I don't know. Well, like you just said, the Germans and the Russians were still at each other's throats. But the Germans and the Russians signed a peace treaty in thirty-nine."

"Right, they did, but the Germans broke it, they invaded Russia in... that's right! They invaded Russia in June of forty-one. This month!"

"Now, why would they do that? They're still at war with England."

"Right. It was the beginning of the end. First, they didn't finish off England. Then they attacked Russia, and finally, after Pearl Harbor, they declared war on the United States. It was all too much for them to handle."

"There you go again. What does Pearl Harbor have to do with it?"

"After the Japanese attacked Pearl Harbor, Roosevelt declared war on them, and Germany honored the treaty they had with the Japanese."

"So, Hitler took on all three—England, Russia, and America—all at once? Only a nut would do that."

"Right, he was a nut and drugged out of his mind. He believed he was still winning the war right up to the moment the Red Army entered Berlin. Then he—" Frank stopped in mid-sentence and jumped to his feet.

"Don't you see? It was all different because I failed!"

"No, you didn't fail. You've already saved us all. Remember?"

"But that doesn't matter. I mean, that wasn't what they sent me here to do."

"Then what are you supposed to do?"

"I don't know, but I know who might."

He jerked the door open and bolted out of the cabin. Up the nearby companionway to the lower bridge deck, around the corner, and he pulled up in front of the guard outside Mac's cabin.

Of all people, Red had the watch. "What are you doing here? I thought the Navy guys were standing guard."

"Right, they were. But we don't have enough of them to stand guard both up here and down in the hold. So, the captain added a few of us to the watch bill," Red replied, the frustration clear in his voice.

"How upsetting."

"Right!"

"So, anything happening?" Frank inquired.

"No, nothing. Worthless duty, if you ask me, standing outside this cabin. What do they think will happen? We're on a ship in the middle of the Atlantic. Not like we don't have enough work to do without this bullshit. Excuse my French, Mister Ross. But this is the third time I've had to stand this watch so far, and you're the first person to even come by."

"Good. Maybe I can do something about that."

"How?"

"Have to talk with him first." Frank pointed at the cabin door behind Red. "Can I go in?"

"No skin off my nose."

Frank knocked on the door. A voice from within answered, "Who is it?"

"Frank Ross, the chief officer. May I see you for a moment?"

The door swung opened, the light snapping off as it did. "Come in, come in, I'm going nuts in here, all alone." He clapped his hand on Frank's back as he led him into the dark compartment.

"Can you close the door?" Frank asked. "We need to talk."

"Of course." Mac pushed the door shut, and Frank heard the latch catch, just as the light snapped on. Frank glanced around the room, the so-called owner's suite, and realized it was as spacious as the Captain's cabin next door.

"Sit down." Frank pointed toward one of the chairs. "I have some questions to ask you."

"Fire away, but you know I can't answer anything about the stuff down in the hold, what it does, or where it's going. It's all top secret and hush-hush. You know. Not even my wife knows anything."

"Do you know who I am?" Frank started.

"Yes. That British commander told me; you work for British Intelligence. But it still doesn't matter. I can't tell you anything."

"That's okay. I don't care what it is. It's just that my job is to see both you and it get to England. I have reasons, good reasons, to believe the Nazis have an agent aboard this ship. Maybe more than one. Why would they be so interested in you?"

"I understand; it might even make it easier if you knew," Mac began as he sat down, "but my orders don't allow me any options."

"Even to save your life?"

"Yes, even to save my life. That equipment must get through. No matter what."

"I see. Thank you," Frank nodded as he turned to leave.

"That's it?"

Frank stopped at the door. "Yes, sometimes you need to be reassured what you're doing is important. And the higher the cost, the more important it needs to be."

"Well, believe me, this is important."

"And believe me, the costs are higher than you will ever know."

Frank exited before Mac could respond.

"Well, Mister Ross?" Red asked outside.

"What?"

"Can we stop these useless watches? Like you said."

"Oh, no. Believe me, Red. They're far from useless. That man," he pointed at the door, "must get to England alive."

Frank then walked away deep in thought.

• • •

A few minutes later, Frank opened the door to his cabin and found Helen still sitting on the bed where he had left her.

"You're still here?"

"No, I'm back in my cabin."

"Funny," he said, closing the door. "Why?"

"We didn't finish our conversation before you ran off."

"We didn't?"

"One would hope men will someday be a little less clueless."

"No, men are men. And we will never measure up on that count," he said as he dropped back into the chair.

"Really, Frank. This is all beyond me. I'm not sure what to make of it. It's just too hard to believe."

"I understand. If I were in your place, I probably wouldn't either. I even lost myself for a while there, but now I'm sure I am right. If I fail, everything changes, and changes for the worst. The bottom line is, do you trust me?"

"It's not that easy."

"I think it is. Either you believe in me, or you don't? Which is it?"

She stared at him, sitting there with hope in his eyes.

"I do. God help me, but I do."

"Then that's all that matters."

"What about us?" she asked.

He stared back, his emotions at war behind his eyes.

She slipped off the bed and down to her knees before him.

"Why are you fighting? I know you feel it, just like I do."

"But this isn't my life."

"Whose is it, then? Even if what you are saying is true, the real Frank Ross is dead. This is your life now. Not his."

"But for how long? A day, a week?"

"I don't care. I've told you before, none of us have a guarantee. Every one of us can die at any moment. You, me, everyone. All we can do is live what life we have to the fullest, with every breath we take."

She rose. Cupping his face in her hands, she turned it toward her and softly kissed him. She then pulled back, looking at him and watching for his reaction. Frank closed his eyes. Every part of him screamed for him to give in, to accept her offer.

Helen waited a moment longer, and then her need drove her on. She sat down in his lap, pulling his face to hers, her lips pressed hard against his. Frank felt the warmth of her body, tasted the sweetness of her kiss. And at that moment, he knew she had won. It was beyond him to deny her any longer.

"You know there is no going back?" he whispered into her ear. She answered him with another kiss.

His arms slipped around her, pulling her tight, her breasts crushed against him. She moved, pulling him along with her up on to the bed, her arms entwined around his shoulders, her body molded to his. His tongue pushed her lips apart and slipped into her mouth, touching hers as it rose to meet him.

His body responded to her presence. They were working on pure instinct now, but still, his mind refused to give in, to submit to the urge.

This is not your body, not your time! He was here for a reason, and this wasn't it.

But God, she felt so good. Never had a kiss affected him so profoundly. His breath was gone in an instant, stolen by his soaring passions.

You can't do this!

God, I want her!

It's not fair to her.

Frank pulled away. Helen stopped, her eyes glazed over with passion, her lipstick smeared across her face.

She knows.

But does she believe? Truly?

He sat up.

"What's wrong?"

"This! I can't." He slipped off the bed and crossed to the chair. "Please, go." He almost succeeded in driving the passion from his voice.

She smiled. "Come here." She held her arms out toward him.

"No, it's not right. Please, go," he said as he turned his back on her.

Tears filled her eyes as it finally registered in her lust-addled mind. "You can't mean that."

"I do."

Frank moved toward the door, but she reached it first, throwing her body hard against it.

"You don't mean that. I know what you are doing, and it isn't necessary. You don't have to protect me. My eyes are wide open. I know we may only have tonight. That's why I won't let you do this." She stared up at him.

He could see the promise, the truth of her love. How had this happened? Why now? He had looked for love all his life and to find it now. Here! In someone else's body and time.

"Frank?"

"That's not my name."

"Then what is your name? I'll call you anything you want me to."

"I don't know my name!" He turned away, pounding his fist against the nearby wardrobe.

"Then I'll call you darling, sweetheart, or lover! It doesn't matter. I love you. Please don't send me away. Tonight, might be our only chance. You said God had given you this chance at a great adventure. Maybe it's a great romance too?" She pulled him back against her, her arms wrapping tight around him. She leaned her face against his back.

"Doesn't it mean anything to you that I love you?"

"It means everything," he whispered.

"Then show me. Make love to me. Forget all the rest. Just take this time and love me. Show me what I mean to you."

He took her hand in his and brought it to his lips. He was a man hanging on for dear life—this life, not the other. The other was gone, done. Old, empty, lifeless, and dull. No adventure, no love. He had just been biding his time waiting to die, a total waste of God's gift.

But here, in this place, at this time, he was alive! And she loved him!

He could feel his heart pounding away in his chest, not the real Frank Ross, his chest, for now, he was the real Frank Ross. This was his chest and his heart, his body that pressed hard against hers, warm and willing. It was him who she wanted. How many times must she throw herself at him before he realized that this moment, this very moment, was the one he had been dreaming of for all his life? This was his great romance and the love of his life.

Giving in, he swept her up into his arms. Crushing her against him, he gazed into those green pools, but this time he willingly lost himself in their depths. He could lose himself there for the rest of eternity for all he cared. For the first time in his life, he saw love in a woman's eyes for him and no one else. He had thought there was another man in the room, the other Frank, but now he knew it was just the two of them, Helen and him, the real Frank Ross.

"I love you, too."

And she rewarded him with the most beautiful sight he had ever seen, his woman smiling at him with nothing but love in her eyes.

Their lips touched, softly at first, as he carried her across the tiny compartment and laid her on the bed. She turned toward him spreading her legs around him, forcing her skirt to ride up high up on her thighs. He dropped to his knees before her. She reached out and pulled him in close, crushing her breasts against him. He nibbled on her ear. She giggled.

"You're ticklish."

"A little," she whispered against his cheek, the sweet scent of her breath blowing across his face.

His kisses slowly moved down her neck and across to the other side, where they began to work their way back up to the other ear. Again, she giggled, her hands exploring the expanse of skin across his back. Somehow, they had found their way under his shirt on their own, for her mind was too messed up to be of any help.

Then his lips pressed against hers, and in an instant, their tongues tangled together within first her mouth and then his as she met his passion with her own.

She began unbuttoning his shirt from the top down until she ran out of buttons, and her hands found a whole new virgin territory to explore as her fingers spread across his bare chest. Frank pulled away and glanced down. He looked up into her face, and she smiled, a mischievous little grin turned up the corners of her mouth.

"How did that happen?" she asked.

"Don't know. I was busy elsewhere," he whispered back, watching her fingers dance across his chest.

"Doesn't seem fair," she said, presenting her own chest to his eyes. She then pointedly glanced down at her blouse and back into his eyes. "Well? Do I have to do my own too? Or will you do the honors?"

He smiled, shook his head, and whispered, "I think I've created a monster." Then, his fingers began to work on her first button.

PART THREE

ADRIFT

CHAPTER FIFTEEN
THE HOURS TICK AWAY

Frank stepped into the wheelhouse from the port bridge wing with the ship's sextant in his right hand. His eyes were fixed on the set of figures he had just scribbled down during his sightings, lines of bearing to the North Star, Polaris, Mars, and Antares. After a few minutes with the Nautical Almanac and the sight reduction tables and presto—he had the *Polites'* current position.

"And the answer is?" Captain Egan asked as he joined Frank at the chart table in the small alcove set behind and to the right of the ship's wheel.

"Sir?"

"Our position, Number One?"

"Oh, fifty-three degrees, twenty-eight minutes north, by forty-three degrees, forty-seven minutes west."

"And that puts us?"

"Let's see." Frank pushed the books out of the way, exposing the chart below. Picking up a set of dividers, he plotted the position using the latitude and longitude markings along the edge of the chart and then, with the dividers set to the chart's scale, counted aloud, "Three hundred . . . eighty nautical miles south, south-east of the tip of Greenland, sir."

Egan moved in closer, double-checking the chart. "We're drifting a little southwest," he observed, comparing the new position to the old DR, or dead-reckoning line, which was an educated guess based on the current heading, speed, and an estimate of the ship's drift due to wind and tide. Based on the computed position, they were drifting a little more than the old estimate toward the southwest, probably because of the northeast winds which were still pushing hard against the port side of the ship which acted like a set of sails, steadily pushing her off in the opposite direction.

"A couple of miles a day," Frank computed.

"Right. Please, have Mister Stratton take that into consideration on his new DR."

"Aye, sir."

Egan then drifted back to his corner as Frank finished up the morning sighting and recorded the results.

"Are you planning on searching the holds again today?" the captain inquired as Frank joined him at the front of the wheelhouse, to once more check on the distance to the *Loch Ranza*.

"Yes." He saw no reason to lie.

"I thought you would. How long are you going to keep it up?"

Frank turned toward the captain. "Until we reach Liverpool, sir. Unless you order me to stand down."

"Good answer."

"Captain?"

The two stood staring at each other for a moment, "As long as you continue to perform your other duties adequately, I don't care how you spend your free time. Within reason, of course. Just . . . make sure you're getting enough rest. I don't want you falling asleep on watch. Wouldn't be good to have to shoot you for dereliction of duty. Might cause an international incident, what with you being a Yank and all. Could even cause you bloody Colonials to fall in with the Boche this time around."

With a slight upturn in the corners of his mouth, Frank ventured, "Aye, sir. I wouldn't want to put you out any."

"Mighty nice of you." The captain finished the exchange.

Frank slowly crossed the deck to the opposite corner, his mind awhirl. What did he mean by "within reason?" Did he know about last night? Frank tried to remember how much noise they had made. He had stopped a couple of times; certain she was getting too loud. What they were doing wasn't technically illegal—they were both consenting adults—but it was definitely frowned upon by the traditions of the sea and by most societies as well. Was the captain trying to give him a warning? Stop screwing around with the passengers.

He continued staring straight ahead, but his mind was two decks below in his cozy little cabin, reliving his last goodbye, bending over the half-naked girl as she laid tangled in the damp sheets, half asleep, for one last kiss.

"Number One, I think we are a little too close to the next ahead," the captain called from across the wheelhouse.

"Aye, sir." He pulled his mind away from the intoxicating memory to focus on the *Loch Ranza*. The captain's comment and the bedeviling visions it dredged up had driven all thought of his duties from his mind.

Refocusing his attention, he took a quick glance at the distance and, stepping to the voice tube, whistled into it. "Engine room, down two turns, please."

"Down two turns, aye," came the immediate reply.

He capped the tube and strolled out onto the port wing, as much to get away from Egan as to check on the *Cliona*. He needed distance right now. And a little fresh air. *Damn it, Frank. Keep your mind on the job. Too much is at stake.* And with a lot of effort and a little help from the stiff breeze, he mostly did just that for the rest of the watch. Egan, for his part, remained in his corner, quiet, always watching. On a couple of occasions, Frank was sure he heard a faint snore or two drift from that part of the wheelhouse as he walked past, moving from side to side, checking on the positions of the other ships, and keeping the lookouts on their toes. He even occasionally glanced aft to check on his tail. It wasn't necessarily his job; the *Scottish Trader's* chief officer was responsible for maintaining her position on him, but still, you didn't want to be taken by surprise if the ship behind tried to climb up your backside.

For the last four days, he had followed the same routine. Up at half-past three, on the bridge till eight, a quick bite in the saloon, and then the rest of the morning creeping through the holds and the lower decks, torn between the hope of finding the package again and dread if he did. For as long as he didn't, there was still the small possibility he was wrong. That it was just a waste of time, like Helen said, that no one was planning on destroying the ship, other than the U-boats, and the Luftwaffe, as if that wasn't enough. But the minute he found something, it all became real, and he would have to deal with it—how, he had no idea.

He moved his glasses over to the commodore's ship, the *Glenpark*, checking the yardarms, where any new orders would first appear. It was just visible in the early morning light, the sun still a degree or two below the horizon. They were in the time of day known as civil twilight, the last six degrees or twenty-four minutes before sunrise. The sky was lightening in the east, revealing another beautiful day, just like the last two since the storm blew itself out late on the twentieth.

That was when they had got their first good look at the convoy's escorts, a destroyer, and three corvettes of the Royal Canadian Navy. The *Ottawa*, the flagship, named for the nation's capital, was an old British destroyer recently transferred to the Canadians because the Brits were having trouble crewing all their new ships. So, they would pull the men off some of their old ones and turn them over to the Canadians, the Aussies, and the other Commonwealth nations to man and use in their part of the war. Thanks to this policy, the Canadian Navy was quickly adding ships and developing into one of the largest in the world.

The corvettes, on the other hand, were new construction, two hundred and five feet long with a single four-inch gun on the fo'c'sle and a simple triple-expansion engine in the belly, making them only a couple of knots faster than their current charges and, in most cases, slower than the U-boats they were guarding against. In a slugging match, it would be the *Ottawa* and the old *Wolfe* that would go toe to toe with the U-boats. The corvettes would be useful only if they could keep a lid on the situation and force the submarines to remain submerged; for then, it limited the enemy to five or six knots maximum, and only for a few hours at most on their batteries. Meanwhile, the convoy would continue on at its current speed of eleven knots, slowly moving out of range. Still, the real problem was that the corvettes could sit on top of the U-boats for only so long.

With only a five-knot advantage over the convoy's rate of advance, it would take three hours to catch up for each hour the warship fell behind. So, as soon as the corvette broke off contact, the U-boat could surface and cruise along just outside of the range of that useless four-inch gun, letting the little ship lead it right back to the convoy. Then, the submarine would make a fast run around the outer edge of the formation, and it would submerge and wait for another chance as the convoy came on at a steady eleven knots.

Sometimes, the sub could even beat the corvette back to the convoy; if some of its comrades remained in contact with the merchantmen, they would lead it straight back. But something was better than nothing, and everybody aboard was visibly more relaxed since the Canadians had joined up with them. Also, in seven days, they would meet up with a new British escort group whose job it would be to take them on into Liverpool. The Canadians would then turn back, taking over the westbound ships the Brits had escorted out to that point. The British group would be far larger and more heavily armed than the present one, ready to fight its way in, if necessary.

After lunch, he would spend a couple more hours in the bowels of the *Polites* looking for things he hoped he would never find and then grab a quick nap—an hour or so—before his evening watch from 1600 to 2000 hours. The sun would just be setting around the time he got off watch. This far north and so close to the summer solstice translated into an incredibly long day, over seventeen hours of daylight, which wasn't such a bad thing. The night was the worst, the time of the tin fish. For it was then that the U-boats were free to do anything they wanted. They had only seven hours of darkness now, ten o'clock to about five in the morning.

In December, it would be the other way around, seven hours of daylight and seventeen of darkness. *God, help us poor sods then.*

After his evening watch and another quick bite (the steward was very helpful, always ready with a warm plate of food when he needed it), he would push off for one last session in the holds, staying until around midnight before turning in for the night. He would then spend a few uncomfortable hours trying to sleep because you never knew when or if the U-boats would attack. Therefore, you slept with most of your clothes on and your life jacket close by to speed up your escape to the boats or your battle station if it should happen while you were asleep. He and Helen had taken on more than merely the risk of discovery last night.

Each day, they were getting closer to the English coast. So far, they had seen no sign of the U-boats beyond fragments of meaningless radio messages that "Sparks," the radio officer, caught at odd hours of the day, but everyone knew what they were—the Wolfpacks. Some seemed to be from behind them, picket boats maybe, strung out across the sea routes searching for the next eastbound convoy. Had any of them sighted the *Polites*? Perhaps one of those bits of gibberish was the convoy's course and speed, but most were from in front, U-boats waiting for the ships to get close enough to attack. It was only a matter of time.

● ● ●

The sun was up, and the sky was pale blue and almost empty.

Frank opened the voice tube and whistled. A moment later, a disembodied voice answered. "Yes."

"Up a turn, please."

"Up a turn, aye."

Frank capped the tube and once more lifted his glasses to his eyes. Yes, that should do it, right at eight hundred yards.

He glanced at his watch. Eddy should be here any minute now. The helmsman had already relieved at a quarter till, and he and the lookouts were more than ready for their reliefs.

The captain had slipped below just after first light to grab something to eat and then a few winks of sleep before the noonday sightings. He unquestionably deserved it. For the last couple of days, the captain had spent more time on the bridge than off, and once the convoy reached the hunting grounds, he would probably never leave.

"There you are," Eddy called from the wheelhouse door.

Frank took a final glance around from port, where the *Cliona* was in position, to the *Loch Ranza* dead ahead, then *Glenpark* to starboard leading column four, followed by *Tibia* and *Everleigh*, and then the *Scottish Trader*, dead astern.

"You checked the logbook?" he asked, joining the third mate in the wheelhouse entrance.

"Anything new?"

"No, but did you check it?"

"Yes, sir. I checked the logbook. Course is zero-seven-four, speed eleven, zig-zag pattern alpha."

"Right, the helmsman has been relieved, and the lookouts are relieving now."

"Right. Anything else?"

"No. Captain's below. I think he's got his head down. You stay on your toes. I'll be in the saloon or my cabin for the next thirty minutes if you need me."

"Right, then. I've got it."

"I stand relieved. Helmsman, Mister Eddy has the conn."

"Aye, aye, sir."

The two officers separated, Eddy stepping forward to the windows to begin his first sweep of the surrounding convoy, and Frank, feeling it far too beautiful a day to go below too quickly, exited the wheelhouse via the port door. There he stopped, standing at the after railing taking in the scene around him. Though he had "checked" this view a dozen times in the last couple of hours, it had been in the line of duty, when the sole purpose was to monitor the other ships and their distances from the *Polites*. Now, he was on his time. He was the passenger, taking in the beauty of the sea, the wonder of the world around him.

And what a scene! It was a shame that the only time you got to see such a sight was in the middle of a damn war. Within his line of sight were at least a dozen ships; two dozen more were faintly visible out on the horizon, too far to see clearly without assistance. Yes, even with the individual ships blurred in the distance, the view was quite impressive.

Never had he seen so many ships underway in formation, traveling at eleven knots under a cloudless sky and spread out on a carpet of deep blue. Even in their war paint, it was a sight to see; one that his duties had left him little time to enjoy until this moment. He had been way too busy searching for that damn package he knew was somewhere on board. He should be on his way right now to the saloon to grab a bite and then head on down into the bowels to renew that endless search. Maybe today would be his day.

But why today? And not yesterday? Or even the day before? Undoubtedly, the purpose of the bomb was to sink this ship. Hadn't the real Frank told him as much? *And because of me, they all die.* What else could it mean but that the ship was going to be sunk with all hands? But if your purpose was to sink this ship, to stop Mac's machine, whatever it was, from reaching England, you would want to wait until you were well out to sea, away from land and any safety it could provide. But we reached that point days ago. If it had been him, he would have pulled the trigger sometime during the storm; that would have been the ideal time to do it. The ship would have just disappeared in the middle of the night. The other vessels might even chalk her loss up to the storm itself. Something broke, she took on water, and down she went. Also, you would have had the added power of the storm's fury to guarantee the ship's demise.

So, why didn't they?

Some movement caught his eye, aft on the boat deck. Freddie, the young mess boy, was leaving the radio shack with an empty tray in his hands. Sparks, the radio operator, must be too busy to go to the saloon for breakfast; for unlike himself and the other watch officers, poor Sparks had no one to relieve him.

Though it pained him to pull his eyes away from the view, it was time to head down.

Frank stopped by his cabin first to drop off his glasses and his windbreaker. But if he were honest with himself, it was also because a part of him hoped Helen would still be there, in his bed, waiting for him to return.

Alas, the cabin was empty when he opened the door, though her scent still filled the compartment. He took a deep breath, and then with one glance at the bed, his cheeks flushed bright red. It seemed they both were in too much of a hurry to notice the state of the room, and especially the bed. One look and it was obvious what had happened there. He even found her bra tucked into a corner as he quickly straightened the room up. "I hope no one has been in here while I was on watch," he said to himself as he slipped the garment into a drawer. He would have to find a way to discreetly return it to Helen later.

He headed down to the saloon. Sing would have his breakfast ready, the standard two eggs, toast, and a couple of bangers waiting in the oven for him.

He reached for the saloon door; someone on the inside beat him to it. The knob turned, and the door jerked open. He stopped, and his eyes were once again lost in those green pools.

Helen was with her usual companions, and her attention was on Potts, who was the first to see Frank in the passageway. She stopped in mid-sentence, staring at him. Helen turned her head to see what had caught Potts' attention, and the moment she caught sight of him, her smile froze, and the color rose in her cheeks.

"Mister Ross," she acknowledged as her voice broke. "Did you hear the news?"

"No, Miss. I just came off watch," he said, trying to seem aloof and failing miserably. He hadn't been prepared to see her yet.

"Sparks caught the morning news broadcast from London. It seems the Germans have invaded Russia."

"Yes, they seem to have caught them napping, and the Reds are in full retreat all along the border," offered Potts.

"Quite a shock, wouldn't you say, Mister Ross?" Helen finished with a smile and a wink. "Who would have thought it possible?"

She forced herself past him. That scent of Chanel registered for just an instant as she continued down the corridor, followed by her two companions. *What did that smile mean?*

From the corner of his eyes, Frank caught Sparks exiting the saloon through the opposite door. He would have liked to talk to him about the news. Did he have any additional information? *I'll have to swing past the radio shack on my way below.*

Sing stood in the pantry door as Frank entered. "Ah. Mister Ross, you are a little late this morning. But I will have your food out quickly."

"Thank you, Sing," Frank replied as he took his place at the foot of the table. He found himself alone in the saloon, the largest public space on the ship. It was decorated in a modern manner, with linoleum tiles on the deck and wood paneling on the bulkheads. The single large table used by the officers and passengers for dining ran fore and aft next to the pantry, and in the opposite corner was a sitting area with a couple of upholstered couches and several lounging chairs. A wooden bookcase bolted to the deck was used to separate the two areas. The bookcase held the *Polites'* limited library, which was composed of a small array of books and magazines provided by the ship's owners at her commissioning twenty years earlier and added to over the years with additional volumes left behind by various officers and passengers.

Sing set the plate of eggs and bangers on the table before Frank. "Coffee?" he asked.

"Yes, please. I need something to keep me going. Too bad we don't have any Red Bull."

"Red Bull?" Sing looked puzzled. "What does a male cow have to do with staying awake?"

Frank tried to suppress his laugh but couldn't. "Sorry, Sing. Inside joke. You wouldn't understand it."

"You would be surprised."

"Yes, I know. But it's American humor. It would take way too long to explain." *Not to mention, it would prove I've lost my mind.* "The coffee, please."

Sing stepped to the serving counter. "Black, two sugars?"

"Right."

Something seemed wrong, out of place. But what? Staring at his plate, Frank let his mind drift for a moment. Maybe it would come to him.

Sing turned back with the coffee. "Is something wrong with the food?"

"No, I've just got a lot on my mind today." Frank smiled up at the steward as he picked up his fork and knife and dug into his breakfast, the problem forgotten for the moment.

A few minutes later, he pushed the last bite of toast into his mouth and washed it down with a final gulp of coffee.

"Great, as usual," he announced as he stood up, brushing the crumbs off his clothes.

From the pantry where he was busy cleaning up after breakfast, Sing acknowledged the compliment.

Frank picked up his cap and set it on his head. It finally fit right since his head wound had finally healed, and just as important, it no longer hurt every time he touched it.

"I'll see you later," he called to the steward as he left the compartment.

Where to start today? Yesterday, he had started aft and worked his way forward. Let's do it the other way around today. He stepped out the hatch onto the weather deck and greeted the beautiful day again. A strong breeze blew in his face. He gazed out across the open sea, noting in his mind's eye the positions of each of the surrounding ships. A couple of them were a little out of place. One was a little too far forward, crowding the next ahead. Another was a little too close to port. What was that ship's name? The *Everleigh*, another tanker, nine thousand tons, full of that crucial liquid, black gold, the Texans called it, and they should know. How many of them had made a fortune off that stuff?

And there, maybe a mile beyond the tanker was one of the tiny corvettes, its prow rising and plunging with each new wave. *Rough riding, they were very wet ships as I remember. How much good were she and her sisters doing them? I guess they are better than nothing.*

He headed forward along the port side and ran head-first into Helen, who suddenly appeared from behind a vent in a planned ambush. "Helen," he exclaimed.

"Frank," she replied.

"Do you need something?"

"This," she said, glancing up and down the promenade along the port side, then she reached up and kissed him.

"What was that for?" he asked as his heart raced in his chest.

"I love you, and I believe you." Then, she scampered forward toward the saloon before he could say another word.

He stood there for a long moment, with a huge smile on his lips. Then whistling, he continued down the ladder to the well deck and on forward toward the fo'c'sle head. It felt good to have someone who believed in you.

• • •

Three hours later, Frank entered the engineering spaces through a watertight hatch on the 'tween decks. Below him, the ship's heart—the twin diesels—purred away, driving the twin shafts at better than one hundred revolutions per minute. They had been built by the Anglo-Danish firm Burmeister & Wain, the same company that supplied the engines for the world's first ocean-going motor ship, the *Selandia,* back in 1911. The two engines below him had been improved by a dozen years of practical experience before the Bolt Line ordered the *Polites*, their first motor ship. They were not known for experimenting; tried and true was the only way to go.

Each engine was a five-cylinder, four-stroke marine diesel producing fifteen hundred horsepower at six hundred revolutions per minute, which was then reduced through a set of double reduction gears to the maximum shaft speed of a hundred and twenty revolutions. The three-foot-thick shafts then ran aft via the shaft alleys (two long dark tunnels) to turn the bronze five-bladed propellers that drove the *Polites* smoothly through the water.

As he stood there, wave after wave of heat rising off the diesels floated by on a constant breeze flowing through the space driven by the roaring air handlers. They pulled fresh air down through the goose-necked vents standing in rows on the weather decks above and dumped it via a series of outlets down into the lower levels of the engineering spaces. Then, as the air picked up the heat radiating from the engines and the other equipment, the breeze carried it up through the fiddley and out the open skylights above. Meanwhile, some of the incoming air was bled off to feed the diesels, which needed enormous amounts for proper combustion.

Frank noticed Angus Brown at the control panel mounted on the forward bulkhead between the massive diesels. Surely, it wasn't that late already! He glanced at his watch; it was five minutes till noon. *Damn, time sure flies when you are having fun.*

He stepped through the forward hatch into the starboard alleyway, and there at the aft companionway, Freddie, the mess boy, was handing Lynch, one of the mechanics, a Thermos. Freddie caught sight of Frank and smiled. "Mister Ross."

Lynch, his back to Frank, stiffened, then half turning around, he forced a smile onto his face. "Mister Ross," he mouthed.

"Men."

"Just picking up a little java for the watch section," the mechanic stated in a heavy cockney accent Frank found almost too much to believe.

"Fine. But shouldn't you be getting back?" Frank inquired.

"Right you are." With the Thermos and its precious contents in hand, Lynch pushed by Frank and through the hatch into the engine room.

Frank's attention turned to the mess boy. There was something about him that was bothering Frank, something he couldn't quite put his finger on.

The boy thereupon bobbed his head and said, "Excuse me, Mister Ross, if you don't need me. I should be getting back to the galley." He scurried up the companionway without even waiting for an answer.

Strange? What was it about Freddie? He couldn't remember. Well, he was sure it would eventually come to him. His stomach then made itself heard with a loud grumble. He suddenly realized it was lunchtime, and he was famished. So, taking a clue from Freddie, he beat his way up the ladder toward the saloon.

This time, he didn't run into Helen or her friends, but three other nurses at the table kept sneaking glances at him all through the fifteen minutes he sat eating the thick mulligan stew Sing served for lunch. Frank sat there the whole time with a fake smile plastered on his face and wished them all a good day as he wiped his mouth and brushed the crumbs off before leaving the compartment. Women. It didn't matter where you were. They never changed, always butting their pretty little noses in where they didn't belong. It was obvious they thought something was up. Had he said or done something? Or had they overheard Helen and him last night? Either way there wasn't anything he could do about it, and besides, he had work to do.

Down in number four, he continued with his search as he tried to put that sinking feeling behind him. He swept number four and number five, and once more, he found the vent screen hanging loose on the port exhaust in number five's 'tween deck, one of several he had seen throughout the ship. One was just fifteen feet away from Mac's crate, practically right on top of the guard the captain had posted to watch it during the voyage. He had raised the matter with the bosun again this morning. It was a security problem, and even though the bosun believed it near impossible to gain access to the holds via those exhaust vents, he couldn't guarantee it. But the bosun was the captain's man. The two were almost like a married couple, knowing what the other wanted or needed before either asked for it. So, until the captain got involved, things usually didn't get done. He made a mental note to bring it up, this time with the captain.

Then he made his way forward to the engine room and down the companionway to the second platform, the lowest deck in the ship. He crossed the steel grates that served as decking in engineering. The grates were far easier to remove than deck plates, thus, allowing better access to the multitude of machines that were crammed into every available space. They also served to increase visibility and thus relieved the claustrophobia one usually felt in this crowded compartment.

Passing the engines, he slipped into the starboard alleyway that ran from the rear of the engine room to the stern glands where the propeller shaft passed through the hull and out to the screw beyond.

Frank wasn't spending any time on the engineering spaces because those compartments were always manned when underway. No one could hide anything in there without being seen. They even logged his visits to and from the alleyways into the engineer's logbook. It simply wasn't a place someone would try to hide anything, not with all the other unmanned compartments available.

The shaft alleys were different. Fifty-foot-long tunnels, dimly lit, with a three-foot-thick shaft spinning at a hundred revolutions a minute, they were dark, noisy, hot, and very tight—the perfect place to hide something. Since the engineers only ventured into the alleys a couple of times each watch to check the bearings for signs of overheating, it would be easy to slip in and out without being seen, for the alleyways each had several entrances, only one of which was in the engine room.

Frank waved to Angus, still at the control panel, as he passed through toward the alleyway. Angus shook his head and said something, unheard by Frank, to the motorman Lynch standing beside him.

He couldn't help but smile to himself. *They think I'm a fool.*

The alleyways were as they had been the day before and the day before that, just as Frank imagined they had been every day since the day the *Polites* got underway for the very first time, nearly twenty years ago. And exactly like every day before, he found nothing.

Finishing his quick search, he exited the alleyway via the escape tunnel instead of walking back through the engine room. The tunnel was a narrow up and down ladder leading straight up from the alleyway to the fantail, three decks above. It was barely large enough for one good-sized man at a time to climb the bare steel rungs running up the starboard side of the shaft. It offered a quick way up and out of the engineering spaces should anything happen—like a torpedo through the side of the hull—and a convenient way for Frank to avoid having to face Angus and Lynch again.

As he climbed out of the tunnel and on to the fantail, he once more ran into the mess boy, Freddie. This time, the boy was leaning against the upper rail of the lifelines, staring aft. Beside him sat a garbage pail he had recently emptied over the side. He was lost in thought, and it wasn't until he heard Frank's boots on the deck that he jerked around in a flash. For an instant, Frank saw fear in the young man's eyes. Then it vanished, and the happy-go-lucky boy returned.

"Oh, it's you, Mister Ross."

"Who were you expecting?" Frank asked.

"Oh, no one in particular."

"No, you were afraid of something," Frank insisted, crossing the deck to stand towering over the boy.

"It's just . . . with this being my first voyage, some of the others have been picking on me."

"Oh," Frank said, relaxing. "Hazing, you mean. Some of that always goes on, but it's mostly only in fun. If you tell me who they are, I will talk with them. Get them to leave you alone."

"No, Mister Ross. That would make things worse. I'll handle it myself. Besides, we're only a couple of weeks away from home now. It'll be over then. Next time, I won't be the new boy."

"Well, if you think so. But anytime you want to talk, my door is always open."

"Sure thing, Mister Ross. Thank you."

Freddie turned back to watching the rooster tails the twin screws were churning up in the water below. Frank stood still watching the boy. Something was still eating at him.

"Is there something you wanted, Mister Ross?" the boy asked over his shoulder.

"No, just a little tired. It's a nice view, but I need to get some sleep before my watch."

The boy nodded as Frank headed forward. A huge smile spread across his face as he glanced up at the four-inch gun soaring above his head.

CHAPTER SIXTEEN
THE SERPENT STRIKES

Frank awoke with a jerk. He sat up in bed. Something was different. His mind searched for the source. Whatever it was, it had reached into his dream, filling him with fear, leaving his heart racing as he fought to . . . what? He couldn't remember; the dream had vanished like vapor through his fingers.

He sat still, his body taut, surrounded by the silence, ready to explode, as his heartbeat gradually slowed to normal. His mind fought its way back to reality from whatever hell had filled his dreams. The fog slowly cleared.

He all at once realized the silence *was* the problem. The only sound he heard was the creaking and moaning of the ship as she slowly rocked at the mercy of the waves. The diesels had stopped! The*y* were dead in the water.

He jerked around, throwing his legs off the side of the bed and sliding his feet into the shoes he had left beside his rack. He had gone to bed fully dressed, as usual.

With an economy of movement, he tied the shoes and was up and out the door into the passageway in mere moments. He flew out the weather door aft toward the fiddley, and he ran into the steward heading forward.

"Sing, what's going on?"

"Something's wrong with the engines," was all he could provide.

"How long?" Frank asked. Remembering the convoy, he spun around to look out at the empty sea.

"Almost an hour."

"Damn it!" he roared as he sprinted for the hatchway to the engine room. How had he slept for an hour? No wonder his dreams were overflowing with threats! It was his unconscious mind trying to warn him. He had failed, again. He had driven himself to the point of total exhaustion and had spent last night with Helen instead of catching up on his sleep. It was the last straw; his body had refused to respond to his mind's call of danger.

He jerked the engine room door open, and a blast of warm air hit him—not the fiery furnace he was used to—more confirmation of how long the engines had been down. The engine room was almost pleasant. He practically slid down the ladder toward the lower platform, his hands moving so fast they almost didn't touch the rungs. He stopped several steps short because the area below him was packed; it seemed like the whole engineering department had turned out. The chief engineer was on top of the starboard engine, working with one of the motormen on the first cylinder head. Both men were fighting with a huge socket wrench, trying to remove a series of bolts set around the top of the cylinder.

Frank saw the third engineer Sid Russell standing in front of the control panel.

"Hey, Sid!" he yelled, attempting to be heard above the noise of a dozen men talking all at once and the few pieces of equipment still running. Although the ship couldn't move, she wasn't completely dead yet, as the auxiliaries were still providing electricity, water, and steam.

"Sid!" he yelled again. This time the engineer heard and jerked his head up, his eyes searching for the source until they found Frank hanging from the ladder.

"What's up?" Frank continued.

Sid stepped over to the ladder, and Frank leaned down closer to listen.

"We started losing compression on the starboard engine a couple of hours ago. I covered it at first by throttling up a tad. Then it started on the port engine too. Chief decided to play it safe and shut them both down before it did any more damage."

"What's causing it?"

"Won't know until they get it open."

Just then, the chief engineer jumped down off the starboard engine. "Damn it. What is this shit?" he bellowed. His words were clear as everyone else instantly shut up, leaving only the hum of the auxiliaries in the background. He stormed past the two men beside the ladder. Sid glanced at Frank for a second and then followed the chief without another word. Frank slid down the last rungs to the deck and quickly caught up with them. He saw the chief's hands were coated with black crude oil, which he was working back and forth between his fingers. Looking closer, Frank saw what looked like sand mixed in with the oil.

The chief stopped beside a large tank labeled 'Fuel Oil Settling Tank.' Frank knew this was used to clean the fuel by letting it sit for a few hours during which most of the particulate in the fuel would settle to the bottom, which allowed the pumps to pull clean fuel from the top through a set of heavy screens. Thus, any junk that could damage the engines would remain in the bottom of the settling tank. But from the look of that oil on the chief's hands, something was very wrong.

The chief wiped his hands clean on a rag tucked into his belt. "Let's take a look."

He stepped up on a platform grate beside the tank, unscrewed a couple of retaining bolts, and lifted the access plate off. He reached in with his left hand and pulled out a handful of the oil, which he let run back into the tank between his fingers until it left him with a thin layer of the same sandy substance in his palm. The oil in the tank was full of whatever it was.

"Where did that come from?" asked Sid.

"The hell if I know, son," the chief replied.

"Sabotage," Frank whispered. Both the engineers glared at him.

"What?" the chief demanded.

"It's sabotage. What a damn fool I've been. He didn't want to sink us. He wanted to stop us." Frank stared at the overhead as the pieces of the puzzle finally dropped into place.

"Shit!" he yelled, heading for the ladder, leaving the two engineers standing dumbstruck. He scurried up the ladder and bolted out the hatch onto the weather deck. Turning, he scanned the horizon to the north-east, the direction the convoy was sailing. Nothing. The sea was empty. They were alone!

He sprinted forward, past a group of blue and white-clad nurses, not even taking time to check for her, but he thought he caught a hint of Chanel. He ran up the companionway to the upper deck and around the corner, then on up to the starboard bridge wing. He burst into the wheelhouse without stopping. He attacked the chart table, searching for a loose set of glasses, which he found in the second drawer down. He rushed through the door and out onto the wing. Behind him, Captain Egan, in his usual place, and Second Officer Stratton, standing beside him, glanced at each other as Egan voiced their mutual opinion. "What is that crazy Yank up to now?"

Outside, Frank slowly and deliberately scanned the horizon from two points to port all the way around to a point aft of the starboard beam. Nothing, not even a puff of smoke. The convoy had moved on and was already out of visual range. If it was after dark, maybe the Aldis lamp might still get a signal through, but in daylight, they had no chance of visually contacting the convoy.

Frank glanced up at the sun, slowly sinking in the west, but still hours away from the horizon. *Eleven knots, they'll be fifty miles away by then, even with them zigzagging.*

The radio! It was their only hope.

Frank turned to head aft to the radio shack and came face to face with the captain.

"Okay, what's going on, Number One?" he demanded.

"The engines. It was sabotage, sir." Frank didn't have time to waste words. The color drained from the old man's face. "Someone put something in the settling tanks. Both engines are a mess."

"You were right."

"Hell no, I wasn't. It never dawned on me. For the last three days, I've been wandering around in the dark at the bottom of those damn holds, searching for a stupid package. I was afraid whoever it was would blow a hole in the side of the ship when all we had to do was watch the damn engines. I've been asking myself over and over, why is he waiting? Why hasn't he already sunk us? Once we got out into deep water, we were too far from shore for help to reach us in time. So, why was he waiting? Now I know. He was waiting for us to bring him to his friends. He was waiting for us to get here."

"His friends?"

"Don't you see? They don't want to stop Mac and his baby. They want them! That idea never crossed my mind, but it only makes sense. If it is so important for the Allies to have it, it would be just as important to the Nazis.

"And now," Frank threw his hands wide, pointing out toward the empty seas beyond, "here we sit, all alone, going nowhere, almost defenseless, just waiting for them to swoop in and claim the prize."

"Damn."

"May I use the radio, sir?"

"The radio? Why the radio?" Egan was still reeling from the shock.

"Maybe the convoy can send someone back for us."

"Yes, yes. It's worth a try."

"Thank you, sir." Frank handed the glasses to Egan and sprinted down the companionway, two decks down to the boat deck, then back past the nurses, who were still standing in the same spot as before, still watching the show unfolding before them. His expression as he ran by stopped any attempt to start a conversion, and instead, they all stared with growing apprehension at his rapidly shrinking back.

At the after house, Frank took the steps up to the upper deck, where the radio shack sat perched like a bird's nest, two at a time, and then burst through the door without knocking.

"Sparks, I need to send a message to the commodore," he announced to the speechless operator within. "Now. It's a matter of life and death," he continued.

"We are under strict orders to maintain radio silence," Sparks began.

"I know that, but we must contact the convoy. Our engines were sabotaged. They stopped us *here* on purpose."

As that sank into Sparks' brain, the smile faded from his face. "My God."

He quickly reached over, rising half out of his chair, and snapped the main switch on the front of the transmitter, breaking the clay seal the authorities had applied just before they left Halifax. He sat back down and pushed his chair to the left, centering himself in front of the machine. His right hand reached out and patted the heavy sending key, which was bolted to the tabletop, but nothing happened.

He looked up at the transmitter's dials and needles, a puzzled look on his face. His hands went to the dials, and he spun several of them around. Frank watched the meters, but nothing changed. They all remained fixed at zero.

"What the hell?" Sparks mumbled.

He stood up, his legs pushing the chair back away from the table. He jerked open a desk drawer and started digging through the pile of junk inside until he finally found a screwdriver and started to loosen one of the screws on the face of the metal cabinet, but the screw was already loose. "Damn." He dropped the screwdriver and, with both hands, pulled on the front of the transmitter. It swung open on a set of hinges along the bottom of the faceplate. Sparks stared at the total mess inside the cabinet, a mess hidden behind the cover.

Frank instantly realized the saboteur had struck again.

"It can't be," Sparks declared. "I checked it yesterday, and it was fine."

"The emergency set?" Frank suggested with little hope.

"Of course!"

Sparks jumped across the room to a second table set against the port bulkhead. He broke the seal on the second transmitter's power switch and snapped it on. But again, nothing happened; the meters all remained motionless.

Sparks pulled on the faceplate; the screws were loose, just like the other transmitter. Frank closed his eyes as the mess inside registered. He took a deep breath.

"Can you fix them?"

"Sure, with a new transmitter."

Frank turned and stepped out onto the weather deck. *Twice! He's beaten me twice now.*

He glanced up. The nurses were still there, at the rail. She was with them. His eyes were drawn to her image, standing toward the back of the group. He had failed her. After all he had done, he had failed her, failed them all. Exactly like the real Frank, except he had to stand here and see the fear as he told them about how he had failed. *The real Frank had gotten off easy. Sure, he had died, but it had been quick. The fall ended with his head busted open, and it was all over . . . for him. Then He dumped the whole damn mess on me. Now, I have failed too. Only I get to hang around and watch as she realizes I failed her.*

He knew then he loved her, really loved her. He had from that first day. He wanted so much to be able to save her, and everybody else on board, but especially her. He needed to be the hero, at least in her eyes.

Finally, he pulled his attention away. He couldn't stand that look on her face any longer.

Then he noticed two decks above the nurses, Captain Egan standing with Stratton. They were staring at him, too. They knew he had failed. "And now they all die," he whispered to himself. All of it was for nothing.

"Damn it!"

Sparks exited the compartment behind him. "It had to be this morning."

"What?" he asked, pulling his mind back to the present.

"The transmitters. It had to be this morning. It was the only time I was away. I went down for a bite to eat. The first time in days."

CHAPTER SEVENTEEN
FIGHTING BACK

A series of images flooded into Frank's head: Freddie emerging from the radio shack with a tray in his hands, Sparks leaving the saloon a few minutes later, Freddie handing Lynch a Thermos bottle as he went on watch in the engine room, and finally, Freddie on the fantail standing beside the four-inch gun.

"Good God, no!"

As fear filled his face, Frank bolted past Sparks, down the ladder aft to the well deck, past the hatches for numbers four and five, then up the companionway to the fantail, and there he hauled up short in front of the massive naval gun sitting with its single barrel pointing skyward.

How would he have done it? Frank wondered. He was already sure Freddie had done his dirty deed here, just as he had fixed the engines and the radios. He could see the whole plan now. First, he stopped us dead in the water, knowing the convoy would continue on without us. They had no choice; it was the standing procedure. You don't stop for anything, not casualties and especially not stragglers. So, with Lynch's help, he killed the engines. An hour later, we're out of sight of the convoy, hull down, beyond the horizon. Then he slipped into the radio shack when Sparks came down for breakfast. With a screwdriver, he opened the transmitters and smashed everything inside. Presto, we have no way to call for help. And last, he would have to fix the four-inch gun, our only hope of defending ourselves. A Hitler youth, that's what Freddie had to be. He was too young to be anything else, a pint-sized fanatic for the Nazi regime, trained from childhood, willing to do anything for the Fatherland, for the Fuhrer.

Suddenly, Frank knew how he would have done it. He glanced around and found the sponge, used in cleaning out the barrel, stowed against the nearby blast shield. Grabbing it, he flung open the breech and carefully ran it up the barrel. It slid in smoothly for the first three feet and then smacked up against something. He pulled the sponge back a foot and rammed it hard against whatever was in the barrel once, twice, to no avail. He couldn't force it to budge, not even an inch.

He slid the sponge out, dropping it on the deck. Bending down, he looked up the bore and couldn't see any light at all. "The dirty little bastard," he muttered to himself. "Just far enough up so it wouldn't have interfered with loading the gun, and since they don't use the sponge on the first shot. The crew wouldn't have known it was there, until . . . it blew the gun to pieces when they fired it. The little bastard would have killed or injured everybody standing nearby."

He had no doubt now that he was right. In vain, he once more searched the empty horizon. Dead in the water, unable to call for help, and now completely defenseless. "Some master spy you are!"

He had played right into Freddie's hands, so fixated on the idea of the Germans trying to stop the stuff from getting through that he couldn't see anything else. He wasted all that time searching the holds, running around in circles while the little bastard was laughing his ass off. *I couldn't let the Nazis stop us. No, we had to get through. Not once did I think maybe they wanted us to get through. Where they could just swope in and grab...*

"The stuff!" Suddenly, he knew where Freddie was. He raced forward.

Back past the nurses, who were still watching his antics, but this time, he slowed down long enough to warn them. "Ladies! Get in your cabins now! And stay there." His eyes met hers for a moment, and he saw a slight nod before he continued forward.

He ran up the ladder to the bridge and into the wheelhouse.

"So, you're finished running around like a mad man?" Egan asked from behind him.

Embarrassed, Frank spun around to face the captain. "Sorry, sir. It was necessary."

"Could you please fill me in on what *it* was all about?"

"Could we speak *privately*?" he motioned toward the far corner. Egan nodded and headed that way. Frank moved up close beside him.

"Captain, the engines were sabotaged, as were the transmitters, and the four-inch gun. And it was all Freddie, the mess boy. He's the spy. Him and Lynch, one of the motormen."

"Freddie! That skinny little runt from the Saloon? I find that a little hard to believe."

Frank interrupted him, "Captain, I know how you feel. I could kick myself. It was staring me in the face all day, and I missed it every time. I saw him come out of the radio shack with a tray, thought he was picking up Sparks' breakfast plates, only I saw Sparks leaving the saloon a few minutes later. Then, I watched him deliver a thermos to Lynch down in the engine room. A thermos that was just about the same size as that can I found. And finally, I found Freddie out on the fantail, right beside that damn gun."

"I still find it hard to believe. If you are right, then it was Freddie who attacked you in number five and on the deck a few days ago."

"Yes. Or maybe he used Lynch for his dirty work. Either way, the little bastard got the jump on me. Don't you see it all makes sense, Captain? He sabotaged the engines with something like sand, probably poured into the settling tank from the top, where it was sure to be fed to the engines. Lynch had plenty of time to pour the contents into the tank when no one was looking. And the only time Sparks was out of the radio shack today was at breakfast, the same time I saw that little bastard coming out of there."

"And the gun?"

"Well, he was acting weird when I ran into him on the fantail. Maybe with me always running into him, he thought I was on to him. But like the fool I am, I had no idea what he was up to. He made up some story about him being bullied, and I bought it hook, line, and sinker."

Egan had stopped talking. His mind occupied with digesting the facts Frank had just provided him. Frank lapsed into silence as he swayed from side to side with the ship's motion. Waiting for the captain to reach the same conclusions he had. Finally, Egan glanced over and said, "It makes sense, Number One."

"Damn, I was afraid you would say that." Frank turned away.

"Afraid I would agree with you?" Egan asked, puzzled.

"Yes, it means it isn't just my mind running away with me. It's true."

"But you forgot one thing. The radio. The one you found with that package, that first day. What's it for?" Egan asked.

"That's the worst part of it. They want Mac's baby for themselves. So, I would guess the radio is to call in the cavalry when we're all trussed up and ready for delivery."

"That's just great. But there must be something we can do?" the Captain inquired.

"We can try to stop them."

"Again, how?"

"The stuff. They want it. So that's where they will go."

"Right." Egan started for the ladder. "Mister Stratton, please have the word passed for the bosun to meet me in my cabin."

"Aye, aye, sir."

Egan was already halfway down the ladder. "Number One, are you coming?"

"Yes, sir." Frank jumped and caught up with the captain just as he entered his cabin. The older man went straight to a safe mounted on the bulkhead above his roll-top desk. Pulling a large set of keys from his right pocket, he flipped through them one at a time, checking each one in the light streaming in through the nearby window until he found the right one.

Using the key, he opened the safe. Leaving the key in the lock, Egan dragged a couple of ledgers and several large packs of multi-colored money from the safe, dropping them on the desk below. Then he produced a long-barreled .38 caliber revolver from within the safe. He checked the gun. All six chambers were full. He closed the cylinder and handed it to Frank.

"One for you. One for me," he said, pulling a second gun from the safe. "How are you, old girl?" he asked the dark blue Webley MK VI service revolver. He glanced at Frank. "Had the old girl since the first war." He checked its load and pushed it into his belt under his coat.

"Let's see here." He reached into the safe again, and this time, produced two boxes of ammo. "This one's for you," he said as he tossed one box toward Frank. The other one went into an inside pocket of his jacket.

A knock sounded at the open door behind them.

"You wanted me, sir?" Bailey asked.

"Yes, Bosun. Come in."

Bailey entered, and at first sight of the gun in Frank's hand, said, "Trouble, sir?"

"The Huns are afoot. It seems they think they have us right where they want us."

"That so, sir?" he replied as he took a third weapon, a cool automatic, from the captain. "Are we planning to fight the U-boat with sidearms?"

"Afraid not. These are for the ones already aboard."

Bailey glanced at Frank., "So, Mister Ross has found his shadow?"

"Shadows, it seems. Little Freddie and Motorman Lynch."

"The mess boy?" Bailey inquired in disbelief.

The captain shrugged his shoulders and handed the bosun a box of ammo for the automatic. "Grab a few men and meet us in number four."

"Aye, aye, sir." The bosun disappeared out the door.

"You ready, Number One?"

Frank nodded. The captain returned the papers to the safe and closed it with a turn of the key, pocketing it afterward.

"Let's go, then."

The two men exited the cabin, Frank slamming the door behind them. Down the ladder, they went. Frank had to run to keep up with the older man.

As they reached the main deck, Frank noticed the nurses had taken his suggestion and cleared the weather decks. Whether they had returned to their cabins or just the saloon, he could only guess.

He continued trailing along behind the captain as he stormed aft, past the engineer's cabins, then down to the well deck, where they turned forward into the amidships structure and then down another ladder to the 'tween deck.

The captain stopped at the closed hatch at the bottom of the ladder. "Here we go," he said.

Egan threw the dogs and jerked the hatch open, stepped over the knee-knocker, and entered the space beyond. Frank followed right on his heels. Then, all hell broke loose, as they were greeted with a volley of bullets. Frank instantly threw himself to the deck. Bullets bounced around him, ricocheting off the bulkheads in all directions. He heard several of them zip by his head and braced for the sharp pain that would signal one had found its mark, but it never came.

After what seemed an eternity but could have only been a few seconds, the shooting stopped, and the sound of the ricochets died away.

Frank remained still, listening for any movement. He picked out someone laboring to breathe off to his left, but nothing else moved. So, he slowly dragged himself, staying as low as possible, behind a nearby crate. Once behind it, he levered himself up into a kneeling position, fighting to catch his breath as he waited for his heart to slow down.

His movements had failed to draw any more fire from the assailants, so he crossed his fingers and took a deep breath before he poked his head out around the crate to study the situation. He needed more information. The hatch to number four was closed, the dogs in place. The captain was lying on his side, his back to Frank, his gun still in his outstretched hand, but he wasn't moving.

"A pair of damn fools," Frank whispered under his breath. He couldn't see any other way to do this. With another deep breath, he slipped silently along the deck to the captain's side. Kneeling behind him, Frank slowly rolled him over onto his back. The older man's eyes opened, the pain plain in their watery depths. Frank heard himself sigh in relief.

"Walked right into that, didn't we?" the captain managed after a moment. Then a sharp jab of pain hit him, and he closed his eyes again.

"Sorry, sir."

"Sorry, what for? My own damn fault. I'm afraid I didn't quite believe you."

"Then why?"

"Had to make sure, didn't I? Wouldn't be much of a captain if I didn't."

Frank heard a noise and jumped to the side, trying to drag the .38 out of his pocket, hoping he would manage not to shoot himself, as he did so. Throwing himself to the deck, with the gun in hand, he stopped just short of pulling the trigger when he saw Bailey and Red looking through the open hatchway.

"Bosun, in here fast," he called, crawling back over to the captain. "The old man's shot."

"Bloody hell," Bailey roared as he and Red burst into the compartment. "We heard the shooting, got here as fast as we could." The two men joined Frank kneeling beside the captain.

Shots rang out again, and they all hit the deck.

Frank glanced around the crate just as Lynch jumped back through the open hatch into number four and the steel door slammed shut. Then one by one, he watched the dogs clinched up, locking the hatch up good and tight.

Standing up, Frank said, "Just to show us they're in charge." He looked down at Red and Bailey. "We would be fools to charge that door."

The captain coughed. Frank was instantly at his side, "How are you, sir?"

Through pain-filled eyes, Egan glanced up at him. "How do you think I am? I've been shot. It hurts like hell." And he collapsed into a coughing fit.

"Red, get him to the nurses, as fast as you can. And then get back here with the armed guard."

"Aye, aye." Red slipped his hands under the captain's arms. "Here we go, sir." He picked up the older man, his right arm going around Egan, holding him tight to his side. Then, mostly carrying him, Red started forward, the captain hanging loose in his arms.

"Wait a minute," Egan whispered as he dug into his pocket. Producing his set of keys, he held them out toward Frank. "You might need these."

Frank glanced down and nodding took them without a word, unable to speak.

Red then helped the captain through the hatchway, and they disappeared forward.

Bailey rose and stood beside Frank. "You're right about being fools, but we can't let those bastards have that thing, whatever it is."

"No, we can't."

"So, do you have a plan?"

"Me?"

"Afraid so, sir. With the captain down, you're in charge now, Mister Ross."

Frank moaned and looked up at the overhead; his vision focused far beyond the gray metal. "Are you happy now?" he asked. "I'm in charge."

Bailey glanced at the overhead, "Who are you talking to?"

"Nobody, Bosun. I was just hoping for some divine inspiration," he said.

"You in good with Him?" Bailey asked. "We could sure use some help." The bosun was grasping at straws. The man he had ignored since the day he came aboard, the one he and all the others believed a nut, had just been proven right and was now their only hope.

"Based on the last few days, I doubt it." Then an idea came to him. Would it work? There was only one way to find out. "Okay, I've got one. You stay here. Keep an eye on that hatch. Keep making some noise, too. I need them to be watching you. But please, don't do anything to get yourself killed. Wouldn't look good on my record. And keep Red with you when he gets back." Frank reached down and picked up the captain's discarded weapon. He felt the weight of the gun in his hand. No wonder the captain liked it; it felt solid, a weapon worthy of betting your life on. He put it in his belt on the side opposite from the .38. "You'll have to manage with just the one gun. I will need both of these." He started for the hatchway.

"What have you got in mind, sir?" Bailey asked.

"No time to explain, but when I make my move, I'll need you to come running. Fast."

"How will I know when that is?"

"Believe me, you'll know."

Frank exited the hold and flew up the ladder to the main deck. He could still see that vent screen hanging loose in his mind. He had pointed it out to the bosun, telling him to get it secured, but this morning's rounds had revealed it untouched. Just one more example of the fact the bosun was Egan's man. Let the old man merely point at something he didn't like, and Bailey had half the deck force turned to in less than five minutes, but let someone else tell him something, and all you got was a long list of reasons it would be a while before he got to it.

It was all part of Frank's struggle. He needed the crew to get the work done, but with what was going on, you really couldn't blame them for questioning his authority or even his fitness for the job.

But now that "problem" had presented him with a chance to get the drop on Freddie and his henchman. "Thank you, Bailey," he whispered to himself.

The loose screen was on the port side exhaust vent. Good thing it was on an exhaust vent and not a supply one because it would have been hell getting pass the fan that force a continuous flow of air down through the hold.

He stepped out on to the after well deck. He could see the port exhaust hood, a squat metal cover set on top of the round vent rising out of the deck next to the aft mast set amidships between the hatch covers for numbers four and five. He would have to remove that hood first and quietly so as not to arouse any suspicion from below.

But first things first. He would need a little more help. He glanced around and spotted Sparks taking a smoke break a couple of decks above him beside the radio shack. Forcing a smile onto his face, he started up the companionway toward the radio operator.

"Sparks, just the man I was looking for," he said as he approached him.

Sparks turned and removed the cigarette from his mouth. "What can I do for you?"

Frank slid up close beside the man and whispered, "Freddie, the mess boy, is our spy, and right now he's holed up in number four, right below us. He and Lynch, the motorman, are armed to the teeth. They just shot the captain, and I need your help."

Sparks' eyes shot open, bulging with surprise. He brought his hand up to his face and yelped in pain as he burned himself with the forgotten cigarette. He threw the offensive item over the railing, his mouth now working, but no words emerged for several heartbeats as he struggled to grasp what he had just heard. He smiled as a new thought hit him. "You're kidding, right?"

Frank shook his head as he continued staring at the radio operator, waiting for him to accept the sudden change.

"My God!" Sparks exhaled. Slowly shaking his head, he stepped to the rail, staring down into the dark, foreboding sea.

Frank felt for him but didn't have time to go easy. He glanced at his watch; time was flying by. How much did he have before Freddie's comrades made their appearance? Not much. Not enough for Sparks to pull himself together.

"I'm sorry, Sparks. I know it is a lot to comprehend all at once, but I need your help. And I'm afraid there is some real risk involved."

Sparks turned back. "What do you need me to do?" he said, an eager smile on his lips.

Frank paused for a moment. Sparks might be a little too eager, might prove to be more trouble than helpful, but he had no one else to turn to, and time was running out fast. That U-boat could show up at any moment.

He pulled the .38 out of his belt and held it out, "Take this."

Sparks locked his eyes on the pistol. Swallowing hard, he reached out for the gun. "What you want me to do with this? I've never fired a gun in my life."

"That's okay. If everything goes right, you won't have to fire this one, either. You are just going to give me some backup." Frank pulled his jacket open enough to reveal the captain's gun tucked into his belt.

They exchanged glances, and Sparks carefully took the .38 from Frank. He felt its weight and then smiled.

"Careful with that. It's loaded. All you have to do is snap off the safety and pull the trigger."

"I aim first, right?" the radio operator joked.

"I hope so." Frank smiled before he moved on. "Do you know where the bosun's stores are?"

"Yes, I think so."

"Fantail, port hatch, down the ladder, first door on the left."

"Right." Sparks was frowning with the effort of following the plan.

Frank unclipped the huge ring of keys from his pants. He held out the correct key. "Take this. Get inside the storeroom. Pass through number five and wait beside the forward hatch that opens into number four."

"That's where Freddie is?"

"Yup. Don't make any noise. Just sit there and wait. When you hear me yell, come through that hatch as fast as you can. I might need your help. Now, get going."

Sparks lumbered aft and down the ladder as he tucked the gun into his belt.

"Oh," Frank called after him. "When you come through that hatch, the bosun and Red will be coming in through the forward hatch. Try not to shoot either of them—or me, for that matter."

"I will do my best," Sparks said as he hurried aft and disappeared into the fantail housing.

Frank took another look at the sea surrounding the ship. There was still no sign of the enemy. Then he glanced over the side where Sparks' cigarette had vanished. "This is the one time I wish I smoked." It always seemed to calm down John Wayne before the big battle.

"Mister Ross."

Frank turned to see the messenger approach.

"I've been looking for you, sir. Mister Stratton wishes to—"

"Yes, yes, I know. It's time for me to take the watch. Do you have paper and a pencil?"

"Yes, sir." The messenger, an ordinary seaman named . . . what was his name . . . nope, no idea . . . produced a pad of paper and a stub of a pencil.

Frank took them, and placing the pad against the bulkhead, wrote out a quick note to Stratton informing him of the current situation and instructing him to hold the watch and to stand by. He also ordered him to keep an eye out for any ships on the horizon. He was to sound the ship's horn the minute he saw one. Frank figured even in the exhaust duct; he could hear that.

Handing the pad and pencil back to the messenger, Frank said, "Get this to Mister Stratton, now."

"Aye, sir." The man turned and headed forward.

Time to go to work.

Scrambling down the ladder, Frank reminded himself to be careful. With the engines down, the *Polites* was eerily quiet. Even with the bosun making noise amidships, it would be easy to alert Freddie and Lynch to his presence right above them. And if he did that, he was sure to receive a very warm reception, one not at all to his liking.

After making sure he firmly set the gun in his waist-band—he didn't want to lose it—he grabbed the bottom rim of the vent cover and began working it up and off the duct, pulling first with his left and then with his right. At first, the cover refused to budge, but as he continued working it back and forth, it gradually began inching its way up the neck. Frank prayed it wouldn't give way all at once with a loud screech.

The prayer must have worked, or at least his luck held out, and the cover continued inching its way up the duct until it finally popped loose into his hands.

Frank closed his eyes, and he mouthed a quick thank you just in case it was the prayer. He set the cover down on the deck beside the now open vent.

Leaning forward, he took a glance down the duct. The smooth steel sides faded into the gloom of the darkness several feet below. The open screen, at least he hoped it was still open, wasn't visible from this height.

Well, here goes nothing.

He climbed up and over the edge of the open duct and sat balanced on the lip, his legs dangling down inside the vent. It was about three feet in diameter and made of metal rings about the same height. Stacked one on top of the next, they were then attached by screws drilled into the metal from outside with the pointed ends sticking into the duct. The same method was used to attach the ends of each of the rings themselves, thus creating a lot of very sharp points just waiting to snag him or his clothes on the way down. *This is going to be fun.*

He struggled out of his jacket, tossing it onto the deck at the foot of the cowling. At least he could reduce the chances of snagging his clothes.

Pushing off the edge, he slid down into the dark reaches of the vent, using his feet and hands to stop his progress by pushing out with all four appendages. He found he could hold himself in place without too much trouble because of the tight confines. He then allowed himself to slide several more feet lower. His head was now below the top of the duct, and his feet were lost in the darkness below. Looking up, he could see only a small patch of blue sky, a single white cloud drifting across it driven on by the light breeze. *Say hi to England for me. I don't think I'll make it after all.*

Frank could feel the panic well up inside him. His heart was racing again; it seemed it would soon burst from his chest. He could hear the blood coursing through his veins, and his stomach threatened to return the remnants of his lunch.

He closed his eyes and centered his mind, willing his heart to slow. "Breathe deep," he whispered to himself. "Don't lose it now."

Gradually, his heart slowed, the rushing sound faded from his ears, and his stomach stopped churning.

His hands began to cramp, and as he repositioned them, he slid a couple more feet downward. His heart raced off again, his calming work gone in a flash. Pushing the fear away, he redoubled his efforts, and this time, the calming exercise was easier. A moment, he was ready to continue his descent.

The screws proved to be the tricky part, but somehow, he worked his way past the first row with only one scratch, and that thanks to a sneak attack from the rear.

Then, quietly, he worked his way down another three feet to the next row of screws. This time, he wasn't as graceful as the first. He was beginning to get tired. One screw ripped his left pant leg open and left a three-inch-long jagged line of blood on the skin underneath.

How many more rows? It couldn't be too many. It was an exhaust vent; the intake was in the overhead, which was right below the well deck where he started. So, perhaps three rings, he hoped. Three rings, and he had worked past two already.

He looked down through his legs; yes, he could just make out details from the deck below. He couldn't hear any sounds, but he could feel the warm air lifting past him toward the opening on the deck above.

"I hope this works," he whispered as second thoughts assailed his confidence. "How did I ever get myself into this? Oh, that's right, I didn't!" He glanced up at the patch of blue sky above. "Did I?"

Taking hold of the gun—he wanted to be ready as soon as he hit the deck—he counted to three and praying the others were prepared and in position, he let go. His weight carried him down past the open vent into the dark interior of the 'tween decks.

He braced himself just as he hit the top of a wooden crate. He lost his balance and fell backward onto another, the wooden sides of which gave way in a loud crash, spilling Frank and the contents onto the steel deck.

He kicked at the debris entangling his feet, fighting to get to his knees while trying to jerk the big gun from his belt. But something had caught the barrel, and the weapon refused to come out. *God just don't let me shoot myself*, he prayed. Afraid to lower his gaze and lose sight of the enemy, he blindly kept jerking on the handle, hoping it would somehow come loose before they recovered from the initial shock of his entrance.

Freddie was over near the hatch to number three, the one he had withdrawn through after shooting the captain. He had a nasty looking machine gun in his hands. *How had he got that aboard?*

"That's far enough," a voice boomed from behind Frank. *Lynch!* Freddie's assistant stood a few feet away, his feet spread wide, and another of those machine guns tucked in tight against his stomach, the short barrel pointing right at Frank's chest. He had no chance. He had lost again. His hand fell away from the still-trapped handgun. *Where the hell were the others?*

Then, the hatch to number three flew open, and the bosun and Red burst through a moment before Lynch peppered it with a hail of bullets. He missed the fast-moving seamen as they threw themselves in opposite directions.

As he hit the deck, Bailey pulled the trigger on the big black automatic. Frank heard two bullets as they screamed past him.

At that moment, Sparks emerged through the hatch from number five, the .38 in his hand, ready to play his part, but he was a second too late, and that second cost him dearly. Unlike Bailey and Red, who beat Lynch's burst of fire, Sparks ran straight into Freddie's. The line of bullets cut a bright red stripe across his chest and hurdled the small man back hard against the bulkhead. There, he collapsed into a pile, as though someone had thrown a rag doll away. His finger twitched, launching a single shot. The bullet ricocheted off the deck in front of him and spent itself somewhere in the overhead.

But Sparks had bought Frank time. And before Freddie could bring his gun to bear, Frank took advantage of it and dove behind a nearby crate just as another volley of bullets rang out, adding to the already deafening roar in the compartment. Freddie's eyes locked on where Frank, his constant nemesis, disappeared. How many times had he tried to kill that damned American?

Freddie peppered the crate with another burst of fire, but this time the gun clicked on empty afterward.

As Freddie's vision cleared, he watched Lynch collapse into a pile across the way. He had had the poor luck to be standing behind Frank, and the young Nazi's stream of lead had neatly cut him in half. The boy stared at the dead man for a moment before realizing his gun was empty and turned his attention to reloading. Popping the empty magazine from the gun, he started to reach for the extra one on his belt. But Bailey was faster, as he emerged from his hiding place with the big black automatic pointed at the center of the boy's chest. "Stop!" he roared. Frank rose to his feet and added the captain's weapon to the mix, having finally freed it from his pants.

Accepting his reversal in fortune, Freddie dropped the empty weapon to the deck, the new magazine still in his hand as he slowly raised his arms above his head. "I surrender. You won. This time."

CHAPTER EIGHTEEN
COMMAND DECISION

Red pounced, snatching up the weapon before Freddie could change his mind. He also relieved the former mess boy of the magazine and quickly patted him down for any other weapons, finding several knives and a handgun.

"My, my," Red whispered.

Frank stuffed his gun back in his belt. *I'll have to find a better place to carry it if I am going to play "John Wayne" anymore,* he thought as he crossed over to where Sparks laid unmoving. A cursory glance was all it took to verify the man was dead. Bailey checked on Lynch and found him in the same condition.

"One each," Red said. "It's what you get when you have a bunch of bastards spraying a compartment full of bullets."

"Yes, but where's the guard?" Frank asked, picking up the .38 from where Sparks had dropped it. Pointing it at the German, he demanded, "Where is he?"

Freddie smiled, "Over there." With a flick of his head, he indicated the far corner.

"Bailey," Frank ordered with his teeth clenched and the .38 pointed in the German's direction.

Nodding, Bailey reluctantly crossed to the far corner and looked down at the guard, a bright red spot in the center of his chest. "He's here," was all Bailey said as he forced down a sudden urge to take a few swings at the mess boy.

Sensing the change in the bosun's mood, Frank turned to Red. "Get him out of here," he ordered, pointing at the German.

"What you want me to do with him?"

"I don't care. You can push him over the side as far as I'm concerned. Just get him the hell out of my face."

"Put him in the chain locker," Bailey offered.

"That sounds good," Frank agreed. "And maybe when his friends come calling, we can forget where we put him."

"It doesn't matter what you do to me. I've already won. That will soon be in the right hands." Freddie nodded toward the crate towering above them in the middle of the compartment.

"Get him out of here before I do something I'll regret!" Frank roared.

"Come on, maggot. You're upsetting the man," Red said as he grabbed the helpless boy and pushed him forward through the open hatch.

Frank stood, staring at the overhead for a minute after Red and his captive left. Kneeling, he slowly searched Sparks body for his set of keys. He would probably need them later. He tried not to think about the dead man but couldn't stop himself. It was all his fault. He might as well have killed Sparks himself, not to mention the guard. No, he hadn't pulled the trigger, but if not for him, they would still be alive. *I got them killed.* It seemed he could feel the man's dead eyes boring into him. How was he ever going to live with this?

Once more, that eerie voice rang out in his head. "And now they all die."

"So, what?" he whispered to himself. *Just because they're all going to die, I should be all right with these two deaths. No. But maybe, thanks to their sacrifice, I can save the rest.*

Finding the keys, Frank stood up as he pushed them into his pocket.

"Bosun," he began, "it's only a matter of time before he's right. Those friends of his are on their way. And that," he pointed at the crate marked with the war office seals, "can't fall into their bloody hands. Way too much is at stake."

"Aye, sir. But what can we do about it?"

"Get that hatch open," He pointed up. "We'll drop it over the side. Let the sea swallow it."

"You can't do that!" a new voice declared from the hatchway.

Turning, Frank found Mac standing just inside the compartment.

"It's too important. It would take years to replace."

"I know, but I can't let the Germans get ahold of it."

"But do you know . . ." The words trailed off as Mac walked up to the crate. He placed his hand on the wooden container as if he were drawing strength from his creation like Frankenstein and his monster. Then he spun, a gun clasped in his hand. He pointed it directly at Frank.

"Your job is to get me and this to England. And I demand you do it!"

Bailey shook his head, "Bloody hell, it looks like I need to talk with the damn quartermasters about what they allow on board. Everybody seems to have a gun."

"You will deliver us or else."

"Listen." Frank stared at the small round hole at the end of the gun. "It's too late for that. The engines are dead. It will take days to fix them, if ever."

"Then get another ship."

"They destroyed the transmitters too. And killed the only man who could have fixed them." Frank motioned toward the body near the door.

"I don't care how you do it. That's your problem. Just do it!" Mac screeched.

Frank spread his hands in a sign of surrender, his eyes locked on that little black hole, which seemed to be growing larger by the minute, as it began to wave back and forth. Mac was using it to emphasize his words.

"I can't. The Germans..."

Mac cut him off. "You locked up the only German on board."

Just then, a noise caused Mac to spin around.

Helen burst through the opening at a full gallop, fear in her eyes and short of breath. She had run the whole way aft. She had known instantly Frank was in the middle of it the moment she had seen the captain and heard the news. He seemed to have a knack for finding trouble. She was out of the saloon and down the passageway before any of the others could react. She heard Potts yelling for her to come back but had no intention of doing so. Frank had survived his little encounters so far, but she knew he wasn't indestructible, and she could just see him lying on the floor, a bullet hole in his chest.

She had reached the weather deck with fear still clouding her mind, and without a thought for her own safety, she flew down the ladder to the main deck, jumped over the damn knee-knocker and entered the amidships structure, she turned left, and scurried down another ladder, emerging into the 'tween decks space for number three. It was amazing how much you could learn about a ship in a short time when you were in love with a seaman. Pulling up, she stopped just inside the space, momentarily disoriented. Well, maybe she had a little more to learn. Which way now? Then, she heard angry voices in the next compartment aft, and at a full sprint, she darted through the open hatchway into number four, her eyes searching for his face, unaware of anything else until the gun discharged just inches in front of her.

Bailey and Frank both took advantage of the distraction and charged. Meeting in the middle, they sandwiched Mac between them, just an instant after the gun exploded. The three men went down in a pile of tangled arms and legs—all three fighting for the weapon. First one, then the other, had it. It fired again, the bullet thudding into the wooden hatch cover above.

Then Frank saw his chance and batted the gun out of Mac's hand. It slid across the deck, ending up wedged under a crate in the far corner, the dead guard's boot just beyond it.

With the gun gone, Bailey used his strength to manhandle the far smaller man to his feet, the back of his shirt knotted in a ball wrapped tightly around the bosun's fist, leaving his arms hanging useless at his sides. Mac tried kicking with his feet instead, attempting to catch Bailey in the groin. That resulted in Bailey, in a fit of rage, lifting Mac off his feet and tossing him across the compartment where he slammed up hard against the unyielding steel of the starboard bulkhead. Mac then landed sprawled on the deck. After a moment, he tried to climb to his feet using the bulkhead for support but only managed to get a few inches off the deck before collapsing back down into an unconscious pile.

Frank shot across the compartment to Helen, who had stopped dead in her tracks at the sound of the gunshot. "Are you hit?" he demanded, his eyes searching for any sign of a bullet hole or blood oozing from her body. Then suddenly, she was in his arms, her mouth locked to his. Her body pressed hard against him, and for a moment, Frank forgot himself. He was aware of nothing beyond them as the rest of the universe ceased to exist. Everything went quiet. His vision narrowed to her face, and the rest of the compartment faded from view. All he felt was her arms around him, her body pressed against his, and her lips, warm and sweet, covering his mouth with kiss after kiss.

In the background, Bailey couldn't help but stare at them; he had to give to the Yank. The girl was a looker. Finally, he turned away and glanced down at the deck, studying the pattern worn in the gray paint.

"I heard the news and thought—" she whispered. The words were muffled as her lips continued to cover his face with kisses.

"Are you hurt?" he asked again, breathlessly.

"No," she replied as she pulled away to get a better look at him. Her face was lit up with the brightest smile he had ever seen. For a second, he couldn't breathe as he looked at her. She was so beautiful. It was as if he was seeing her for the first time. How was it possible for anyone to look so perfect? He could think of no better fate than to drown in those green pools. They kissed again. She buried her face against his shoulder, and he was for the moment satisfied just to hold her.

"I heard about the shooting," she began again. Then, she looked up into his eyes with tears streaming down her cheeks. "And I had to know." She buried her face again, and a tremor ran through her as she pressed hard against him.

Frank took her chin in his hand and gently lifted her face so he could look into her eyes. "I'm glad, but you could have gotten yourself killed running in here like that."

"Mister Ross?" Bailey began, his hand tapped Frank's shoulder. "I hate to bother you two. But—" He left the rest unsaid.

Frank closed his eyes, gave Helen another squeeze, and pulled away. "Right." He walked across to where Mac's gun had ended up, using the time to gather his wits. *God, she felt good!* He fought for control. Everything in him screamed for him to run away with her, but he had work to do and people to save. Maybe there would be time, later.

He squatted down beside the crate and wiggled the gun out from under it. Standing back up, he pointed at Mac. "Get him back to his cabin."

Frank turned to face Helen, forcing the urges down as he did so. "The captain?"

She shook her head. "A doctor might save him, but the only thing we can do is make him comfortable," she said, glancing at the deck, unable to face the pain in his eyes.

"Bloody hell," Bailey rumbled. Mac hung limply over his shoulder, fireman-style. "The captain was a damn good man. Best captain I ever had. He certainly deserved better." He started for the hatch.

"When you have him secured," Frank said, "get to work on that hatch cover."

"Aye, aye, sir."

Frank glanced at Helen. He needed time alone with her, but there was no time for that, not now and maybe not ever. "I feel like a boat on a cross-sea, pulled in two directions at once."

She reached out toward him, longing in her eyes. "It's okay, Frank. I believe you."

"You said that before."

"Don't you understand? The Germans attacked Russia." She waited a moment, then smiled as she caressed his face. "Just like you said they would several days ago."

"Oh!" He smiled. "I see. You believe it all now."

"Yes."

"But I'm afraid, I still have work to do," he said, his voice breaking on the last word. Her hand dropped to her side. "Here." He held out the gun he had picked up. "Just in case. The Germans are on their way."

Her eyes widened before they shifted to the crate behind him. "That?" she asked.

"Yes. It can change the course of the war. If they get it, we're done for."

"Then do what you have to." She took the gun, stuffed it in a pocket, and vanished back through the hatch without another word.

Frank felt his heart going with her. How long he stood there staring at a rust spot on the deck, he wasn't sure. It felt like an eternity, but it couldn't have been more than a few minutes before he heard that line echo in his head again. "And now they—"

"I know, I know. But God, please take care of her."

A shaft of light broke into the space from above as the first boards from the hatch cover were removed. Bailey was already hard at work while he was just wasting time.

Kicking himself into gear, Frank moved forward toward the engine room access and stepped out on to the upper platform. Below, he could see some of the black gang still pulling the engines apart, while others were busy cleaning parts already removed. And right in the middle of it all was the chief.

"Chief!" Frank shouted down at him. With the engines secured, his voice carried well, and the chief engineer looked up at once. With a nod, the chief said something to the second engineer standing beside him and started up the ladder.

"We were lucky," he announced as he got closer. "The generators pull their fuel from a separate settling tank. So, we won't lose the lights, but the mains are shot. We have to replace all the seals." He stepped off the ladder onto the upper platform beside Frank. "It'll take a day at least. The good news is we have enough material aboard to do it."

"No easy way to put this, Chief, but the captain's dying."

The chief's face went pale, the slight smile he had been wearing gone. "Dying? How?"

"The mess boy, Freddie, and your man Lynch were German spies. They did your engines in, destroyed the transmitters, and spiked the four-inch. We were on our way to check on that special cargo in number four when they shot him."

"Bastards! Lynch! I'd like a few minutes alone with him."

"Freddie got him, too."

"His own man? The idiot."

"You won't get an argument from me."

They stood silent as the work continued below.

"What are your orders?" the chief asked.

"My orders?"

"Yes, with the captain down, you're the Master now."

"Damn, that's right." The real Frank had a master's ticket. *God, what are you doing to me? It was bad enough as second in command but as master?* He glanced up at the overhead. *Someday I'd like to know what you were thinking.*

"Well?"

"We don't have a day. Even if I am wrong about the raider."

"Raider?" the chief asked, his voice sliding up an octave.

"That bastard didn't sink us for a reason. He sabotaged those engines right here on purpose. The Germans want that crate."

"Damn. Hadn't thought of that. So, what are we going to do?"

"We're going to drop it over the side."

"That's too bad. Sure, could have used it, whatever it is, but you're probably right. We can't let the Huns have it."

"No. We can't." Frank stopped, a new thought dawning on him. "Chief, you keep working on the mains. Concentrate on one at a time. That might get us moving faster."

"That's an idea." He started back down the ladder.

"And Chief?" The engineer looked up. "Be ready to abandon ship when the word is passed."

The chief nodded as he continued down the ladder.

Frank exited the engine room and hurried forward to the nearest companionway, where he climbed the ladder to the main deck and then headed forward. On the well deck, he stopped to scan the horizon. Still no sign of the Germans. *Good!*

He continued up the companionway to the boat deck and then on to the cabin deck. He paused at the captain's door. It was standing open, and he could see several of the nurses, their backs to him, whispering among themselves. Next door, George was standing guard, a black automatic stuffed in his belt.

"The bosun put you here?"

"Aye, sir."

Frank reached for the doorknob.

"It's locked, sir."

"Okay." Frank dug into his front pants pocket and produced the huge set of keys he had recovered from Sparks' body. He flipped through them, trying not to remember those dead eyes. Then one at a time, he tried the keys in the lock and with the third one, the door swung open. "There we go."

Frank stepped into the dark cabin. Bailey had left the curtains drawn and the lights off. Frank found the switch, and the overheads snapped on.

Mac was still out cold, lying on a bunk set against the forward bulkhead, blood crusted in his brown hair from the wound on his head.

"Now, where would he have put them?" Frank asked himself out loud.

"Put what, sir?" George inquired from the doorway.

"Just talking to myself." Frank glanced around the compartment. Not too many places to look; it was maybe twice the size of his cabin, a washbasin with a medicine cabinet on one side, a wardrobe, and a dresser on the other. The cabin's lone chair was pushed up under the dresser, and a motionless fan was mounted on the bulkhead above the dresser.

Frank started on the wardrobe first. Jerking the door open, he found several suits on hangers swaying back and forth with the motion of the ship. Two extra pairs of shoes were set side by side on the floor of the cabinet. He rifled through the suits, glanced in the shoes, and moved on to the drawer beneath them—nothing but undergarments there.

Finished with the wardrobe, Frank moved on to the dresser. The top was clear; Mac was an immaculate man, everything in its place and a place for everything. The left drawer held toiletries, a watch, some cuff links. The center one held writing materials—pen, pencils, paper, and envelopes. In the right drawer, he hit pay dirt.

"There you are."

A leather-bound briefcase, locked, was the only thing in the drawer, Mac's name—Mackenzie Smith—was boldly printed on the attached label. So that's who he was. Mac's plans, blueprints of the device, whatever it was, would be inside. He had to destroy them, as well as the crate in number four. The Germans, engineering wizards that they were, would have little trouble replacing everything they threw overboard if he were to let these plans fall into their greedy little hands.

Frank glanced again at the limp body on the bed. He felt for the man, Mac had put a lot of time and effort into this, but it was too important and too dangerous to risk the Nazis' getting a hold of this stuff.

He grabbed the briefcase, closed the drawer, and exited the cabin.

"Go ahead and lock it back up," he ordered as he exited. The inside ladder would be the quickest way up to the bridge, his next destination, but he would have to pass the captain's door again and maybe run into Helen. He wasn't ready for that, not after that scene down in number four. So, he reversed course and backtracked out onto the weather deck.

Once he was outside, he swung onto the ladder up to the port bridge wing. Running up the ladder, two rungs at a time, he was on the wing before the lookout turned to greet him.

"Any sign of the Germans?" he asked.

Stratton, now over an hour past the end of his regular watch, turned to face him from the far corner.

"No, sir. Nothing."

Frank continued across to stand near Stratton. "I'm sure someone will be coming along soon. This stuff is too valuable to let sit out here." Frank lifted the briefcase and set it on the windowsill.

"What's that?"

"Mac's blueprints."

The two men lapsed into silence as they slowly swayed with the *Polites* as she rode the mid-Atlantic swells, entirely at the mercy of the sea.

"Any word on the engines?" Stratton asked.

"A day, at least."

"I was afraid of that."

"No hope from that quarter."

They lapsed back into silence.

"Here, you take this," Frank indicated the briefcase, "I need to go check on the bosun. See if he is ready to dump that damn crate over the side."

"What do you want me to do with this?"

"Have the messenger weight it and drop it over the side the minute you sight a German ship."

"And if we get lucky?"

"One of ours? Won't be. Not out here."

Frank exited the wheelhouse and started down the ladder, watching the activity on the after well deck as he went. He could see Bailey had the hatch open, and Red had the boom rigged with a set of lines already lowered down into the hold.

"Good man, Bailey."

The ship's horn sounded, loud and long.

Frank turned to look back at the bridge. Stratton was on the starboard wing, pointing south. Looking in that direction, Frank quickly saw what he was pointing at, a large freighter, dark and low in the water, almost bow on to the *Polites*, maybe five miles out. And from the bone in her teeth, she was making at least twelve knots.

He quickly did the math. Twelve knots, two thousand yards each multiplied by twelve, seventy-two thousand feet per hour, or twelve hundred per minute five miles, ten thousand feet, out. They would be on the *Polites* in fewer than ten minutes.

Glancing back at the bridge, Frank watched as Stratton made a show of dropping the briefcase over the side. That meant it was a German ship, one of their raiders, or maybe a supply ship like the *Altmark*. Frank waved at him and scurried down the ladder to the well deck.

Over the coaming of number four hatch, he looked down on the scene below. Bailey and a couple of deck-hands were busy connecting straps on the crate.

"Bailey!" Frank yelled down at the bosun.

Bailey stepped back as he glanced up.

"We're out of time. Jerry's here. You ready with that?" Frank pointed at the crate.

"Another minute, sir."

"Make it quick. We don't have much more than that left."

Bailey waved acknowledgment and quickly returned to work. As he circled the crate, he pointed out several adjustments to the straps, then stepped back, watching as the deckhands made the corrections. A final once over, and Bailey looked up and signaled his readiness.

Frank looked over toward Red, standing ready beside the winch. "Lift away," he ordered.

Red moved one lever forward, and the steam-powered winch whirled to life. Then he eased the other back toward his body, his eyes locked on the lines running from the hook at the end of the boom, high above their heads, down into the open hatchway. The boom lifted, the angle to the mast increasing, slowly taking the slack out of the lines.

Frank glanced over his shoulder at the fast-approaching German vessel. It had closed the distance to less than two miles, easily within range of those twin six-inch guns mounted on her bow. *Why hadn't they used them yet?* The *Polites* wasn't going anywhere. Maybe they were simply waiting until they were inside small arms range. There was far less danger of doing any damage to the prize that way.

As he watched, he could see the angle on the bow beginning to change. They had put the rudder over to port, which would bring her up starboard side to the *Polites*—not much time left.

Turning back, Frank saw the lines were taut. Glancing down, he watched the crate, safely settled in a cargo net, several feet off the deck, smoothly gliding up toward the open air.

He continued to give the up signal to Red, who couldn't from his position at the winch see down into the hold. Blind, he was relying on Frank to guide him until the crate emerged from the hold below.

Frank tried mentally willing the crate up faster; they were rapidly running out of time. He could feel the German ship behind him. The top of the container finally cleared the coaming. Just a little more, and they could swing it out and drop it into Davy Jones' lap.

Then, from across the way, a machine gun opened up, followed almost immediately by a second and a third. They were sweeping the *Polites'* weather decks. *They are trying to stop us,* Frank thought, as he threw himself to the deck against the warm steel of the coaming.

The three streams of bullets swept back and forth across the weather decks from bow to stern. Someone screamed nearby. Frank glanced up to see the crate hanging motionless above the coaming. He looked over at the winch. Red had vanished, and the lever was in the stop position. This was his last chance. *The Germans will keep shooting to keep our heads down until they get men across to us, and then it will be too late.* A raider like that would have two or three hundred men; he had forty and a half dozen guns. Once they were across, they would quickly overwhelm his crew.

He started for the winch, staying as low to the deck as possible. Bullets continued whizzing by him. The machine guns were now, after the initial sweeps, taking turns at blasting away at the helpless freighter. But somehow, none of them hit Frank.

"Halfway there," he whispered to himself. He felt something tug at his right sleeve. A glance confirmed a neat round hole just below the elbow. "A man could get killed," he said to nobody. Then he laughed. What did it matter? The real Frank was already dead. And what of him? This wasn't his life. He knew that, at best, he was here only for a short time. So, why worry? He had a job to do.

He rose to his knees and crawled toward the winch. As he came around the big machine, he stopped dead in his tracks. He fought to keep his lunch down as he took in the scene. Red had caught the full force of the first blast. His chest was torn open; the flesh ripped into a bloody mess. And even worse, his face was gone. If Frank hadn't already known who it was, he would never know from the remains.

Frank had seen death before, but this was far beyond anything he had ever imagined. The metallic taste of blood filled the air. It was spattered everywhere and running across the deck to pool at the base of the winch. How could anyone do this to another human being?

But they couldn't see what their bullets were doing. They were too far away for that. To them, we were merely the faceless enemy, disembodied creatures who must be destroyed, actors set on a stage performing a play written by men thousands of miles away—men who likely would never know what happened here, on this spot in the middle of the Atlantic Ocean. To see a man who he knew, had spoken to, had eaten with, now a useless hunk of meat, to watch his blood, still bright red with oxygen, running across the decks heading for the scuppers, was just too much.

Frank's courage vanished. He threw himself hard against the bulk of the winch, pressing as close to the machine as possible, shielding himself from the hail of bullets sweeping across the deck. Closing his eyes, he tried to calm himself, wishing he could drive that image of Red from his mind.

He could still hear bullets bouncing all around. The air was alive with the nasty little insects. He glanced up at the sky. "God," he began. Then, he caught sight of the lever; it was covered with something wet and bright red slowly inching its way down the gray metal. "My God!" He looked over at the crate, still swinging with the ship's gentle roll. "Help me! Please!"

Just then, someone opened up with the .30 caliber machine gun on the bridge wing. They swept the raider as she sat riding the waves two hundred yards to port. For a moment, all firing from the Germans ceased, but only for a moment, before one of the guns resumed shooting. But they were now concentrating on the bridge and not the well deck where Frank was hiding.

His mind clicked into gear, and he jumped to his feet in front of the winch. Grabbing the bloody handle, he suppressed his repulsion to the goo he felt under his fingers, and he pulled it back. The motor engaged, and the crate started up again. In a few seconds, it cleared the coaming, and Frank pushed the handle forward, disengaging the clutch. Then he threw the second handle to the other setting and reengaged the clutch. The crate swung smoothly across the deck and over the bulwark, out over the sea.

One of the German gunners noticed the movement and redirected his fire toward Frank. The *Polites* lone gun had now gone silent. Frank dropped to the deck behind the solid bulk of the winch as bullets once more whizzed all around him. He was now their sole target! How they all missed him, only God could answer.

He glanced around the corner of the machine and verified that the net with the crate was now swaying back and forth as it hung over the side twenty feet above the choppy waves of the North Atlantic.

The Germans were too late. They had lost! Frank held his breath, waiting for a break in the fire from the raider. The Germans noticed some movement back aft on the *Polites* and, for a moment, redirected their fire toward the new target. In doing so, they gave Frank the break he was waiting for. He rose to his knees, reached over the winch, and grabbed the release. The motor whirled to a stop, the clutch opened, and the line played out, running down the boom and through the padeye at the end. Faster and faster, pulled by the weight of the crate in the sling. It hit the water with a huge splash that lifted high in the air and then rained down across both ships.

When the water cleared, the crate was gone, on its way to the bottom of the ocean, almost a thousand fathoms deep. The German guns fell silent. As Frank rose to his feet, the only sound he could hear was the high-pitched whine of a motorboat engine.

CHAPTER NINETEEN
A PRICE TOO HIGH?

Why was he still here?

An hour had passed since the Germans boarded the *Polites* and took control. There was no reason to fight back; the only thing that would have accomplished was getting people needlessly killed. As soon as they reached him, they jerked the captain's gun from his belt as he stood with his hands in the air, surrounded by the German sailors, all armed with submachine guns.

Once disarmed, one of the Germans herded him forward toward the saloon, where an officer, a Naval Lieutenant, was already busy interviewing the crew and the nurses in perfect English. Even the German accent was missing.

"Ah, you are the chief officer?" the German began.

"Yes, Franklin Ross."

"You are an American?" he inquired.

"Yes."

"And yet you serve on an English ship?"

"I go where the work is," Frank responded, looking out one of the open portholes.

"You Yankees, so high and mighty. Above the rest of us, but in the end, all that matters to you is money."

"A man has to eat, doesn't he?" Frank continued with the simple answers.

"Your captain is dead." Frank closed his eyes. It was hard to hear, though he had known the captain probably wouldn't survive.

"You didn't know?" the German asked. Frank shook his head. "Too busy, eh?" Frank didn't answer. "We know who you are, Mister Ross."

"Sure, you do. Thanks to your spies, I'm master of this ship." He looked at the German. "Would you please leave?"

"Jokes won't help you, Captain Ross. As a spy, you are subject to summary execution."

"No!" a female voice cried out from across the room. Frank forced himself not to look at her.

"I don't have any idea what you're talking about." He continued to play the game.

"As I stated, we already know you are a member of British SIS and are also secretly working for your own government. A dangerous gambit. One that you have now lost."

Frank couldn't stop himself from staring at the German. "How would you know that? Even if it were true."

"Because I told them," Mac said as he walked into the compartment through the pantry door. "Yes, I told them all about the great Franklin Ross, one of Donovan's thugs."

Frank stared at Mac, lost for a moment, and then it dawned on him. "You're with them."

"My real name is Mackenzie Schmidt. My father was an officer in the Imperial German Army. He died in the trenches at Verdun. When my mother and I moved to America, she thought it would be easier if we anglicized our family name."

"Then, why go back to the Germans?"

"Money, of course. FDR's minions have no idea what's important and the damn Brits; it's all king and country. I'm German-born and American-raised, for God's sake. What do I care about Georgie's spare? The Nazis were the only ones willing to pay my price."

"You were using us."

"That is the first intelligent thing I've heard you say, Mister Ross," Freddie said, entering the compartment. "And here I was beginning to doubt you had any intelligence at all. Though it was entertaining, watching you search the ship over and over. I lost count of how many times you looked right at that package. And never once—"

"I'm glad someone enjoyed themselves. Too bad about Lynch."

"How much longer?" Freddie asked the lieutenant, ignoring Frank's comment.

"A few minutes. I'm still investigating if it is worthwhile to save any of them."

"Other than Mister Ross here, I doubt it."

"I tend to agree, but I have my orders." The lieutenant signaled the guards to bring the next candidate over.

"Just remember, every minute we waste endangers the mission."

"Your mission is already a failure," Frank smiled. "The crate and the blueprints are at the bottom of the ocean."

"You mean these blueprints?" Mac asked, holding up a briefcase identical to the one Stratton had thrown overboard.

"But—"

"A dummy set. I hid the real ones where you would never have found them. Why take chances?"

"Like with a certain package," Freddie said.

So, that was why he was still here. The Germans had the plans and Mac. History still was going to change. He hadn't won after all. But it wasn't over yet; he was still here. Which meant there had to be at least one more chance for him to win. One more chance to fix it.

He glanced around the room. The lieutenant was at the table, talking to one of the nurses, telling her that since she was neutral, she had nothing to worry about; they were only at war with the British. Freddie and Mac had moved off to the service table, having a quiet conversation as they each fixed themselves a cup of coffee. Two guards, with submachine guns at the ready, covered the two doors out of the saloon. How could he possibly stop them? He didn't know, but he had to destroy those blueprints, somehow. Mac had put the case down on the deck, against the cabinet, at his feet. Too far. Frank wouldn't even get halfway there before Mac would reclaim the case. Not to mention the guards, the lieutenant, and Freddie, all of whom were armed and ready.

There was nothing he could do now, but there was going to be an opening. All he had to do was wait and keep his eyes peeled. *Be ready. Don't miss it. Just keep watching. It will come.*

The lieutenant said something in German to one of the guards, who glanced over at Frank. He knew they were talking about him.

The guard snapped to and rendered the classic Nazi salute, "Heil, Hitler!" and started across the compartment toward Frank. "Move." He motioned toward the door with the barrel of his weapon.

Frank forced a smile as he stood up and turned toward the door.

"Have fun," Mac said with a smirk on his face.

"Loads," Frank replied as he passed by them and out the door. He could sense Helen's eyes following him every step of the way.

Outside, the guard lost all pretense, jamming the gun barrel to the small of Frank's back to speed him up. "Faster," the guard growled. Frank stumbled forward, using the time to survey the situation. He quickly decided now wasn't the time, either. "Down," the guard directed, pointing toward the after well deck, where the rest of the crew was quietly milling around after their interviews, awaiting whatever fate held.

"Okay, okay!" Frank said, trying to appease the brute. "I'm going." The German smiled as the English officer with the three stripes cowered in front of him and his gun, just like all the rest.

As Frank made his way down onto the well deck, the guard pointed toward him as he addressed another guard standing nearby, delivering a set of instructions before pivoting about and strutting back toward the saloon.

Frank glanced over at the still bloody winch and then up at the empty boom above, slowly swaying in the light breeze with the slight roll of the ship. He felt uncomfortable standing so close. The image of Red sprawled across the deck, blood everywhere, was still vivid in his mind. He drifted as far away as he could before the guard barked a warning in broken English.

His pulse gradually began to slow, and he forced himself to relax. *Just keep your eyes open,* he told himself. *It will come.*

He slowly studied the layout. Six German sailors were posted around the well deck, and like the guards in the saloon, they were well-armed. Two were on the fantail, towering above the crew, one to port, the other to starboard. No chance there. A second pair, including the one the brute had spoken to, was on the upper deck just forward of the well. Again, no chance there. Too far to go. The final two were together at the foot of the port companionway, in place to control the prisoners, but they could quickly step back out of the way to provide the others a free field of fire if they needed to. They were his best chance, but how?

Then, the brute returned with more prisoners. This time it was Helen and her two friends, Potts and Marion.

Frank watched as the women started down the ladder at the guard's insistence. He was just as forceful with them as he had been with Frank, his gun once more jabbing the prisoners' backs. It didn't matter to him if they were women. It was all the same. What a perfect little Nazi he was! Frank began to push his way through the crowd toward them, driven by his sense of decency. But as he did, Helen caught his attention and silently shook her head, willing him not to push it. He stopped, forcing down his anger. She was right. As much as it pained him to stand by as the bastard abused her, he couldn't afford to risk everything because a guard had gotten a little rough with Helen.

The three nurses reached the well deck with no further trouble from the guard and began to work their way into the crowd. They suddenly found themselves face to face with Frank. After a long awkward pause, with Helen and Frank staring at each other, the other two nurses quietly moved off toward the far side of the hatch, where the rest of the nurses waited. Helen finally managed a sad little smile and then trailed off after her friends. *Good*, he thought. It was probably for the best. The farther away she stayed from him, the safer she would be, though he couldn't help but let his eyes follow her.

Bailey and George moved up beside him. "Looks like Jerry's got us in a pickle here, sir," Bailey said.

"Yes," Frank replied absentmindedly, his eyes still watching Helen.

"What are we going to do, sir?" Bailey continued.

"I don't know. Yet." Frank said, forcing his attention away from her. Looking at her with puppy-dog eyes wasn't going to save anyone, least of all her.

His eyes searched the area. There must be some way. It couldn't be over. He was here to change this, so there must be something he could do. But no matter where he looked, he couldn't see any way out of this. He was stuck down here with six submachine guns aimed at him, and he couldn't see any way to stop the Germans.

But somehow, he had to!

Bailey tried again. "Any idea what they have planned?"

Frank turned and stared at Bailey. His mind shifting gears as he did so. What did they have planned? He ran back over the conversation in the saloon. It was clear they were nervous. Time was at a premium. It was also clear that the fewer people who knew about this, the better. Why else attack the transmitters? Everyone knew the escorts would never leave the convoy to save us, a lone ship, no matter how important we were. It was against their standing orders. Besides, even if they did send a corvette back for us, it wouldn't have stood a chance against that raider. He remembered one of the German raiders would even succeed in sinking an Australian cruiser later in the war. He glanced over at the ominous shape floating a little ways off their starboard side. One little four-inch gun against the four six-inch guns he could see from here. It would have been hopeless.

No, they destroyed the transmitters to shut us up. They want us simply to disappear. We dropped out of the convoy with engine trouble and just vanished. The British wouldn't know what had happened until the Germans started using whatever it was Mac had sold them. Then, it would be too late.

So, what did all that add up to? He looked up at the Germans on the boat deck, fear suddenly eating at his heart. He glanced across the crowd, his eyes searching for Helen. It meant they were all going to die! The Germans weren't going to leave any eyewitnesses.

He was overwhelmed by a sense of complete failure. After everything he had done, they were all going to die, here in the middle of nowhere, mowed down by those four submachine guns, or maybe they just planned to leave the crew aboard while the raider poured six-inch shells into the *Polites*. They would all vanish with her into the silent depths of the Atlantic, the secret forever buried with them.

He couldn't help himself from gazing out across the deep blue expanse beyond the bulwarks. Maybe someone was out there.

The bosun saw the glance and the growing fear in his eyes. He leaned in close, "Steady yourself, Captain. Won't do to have you falling apart. Might scare the passengers. Not to mention me."

Frank glanced at the bosun. He called me . . . Captain.

"I came to the same conclusions, sir," Bailey continued, ignoring the change in Frank's expression. "Don't mind saying it left me a mite wobbly in the knees."

Frank nodded, regaining control of himself. "You're a good man, Boats." Using Egan's nickname for Bailey seemed natural, but the one thing Bailey didn't understand was that it wasn't for himself that he was afraid. He had known from the beginning he wasn't getting out of here alive. It was Helen he was afraid for. He had come to realize she was the woman of his dreams, the one he had spent a lifetime looking for, the love of his life. No wonder he hadn't found her. He glanced up at the clear blue sky above. *You put us a half-century apart.*

"Excuse me," he said to the bosun. "I have something I have to do."

He pushed his way through the crowd toward her. Halfway there, she noticed him, and the determination written on his face. She stood still, suddenly, afraid of what he was going to do.

Potts immediately noticed the change in her. "What's wrong?" she whispered into Helen's ear.

Helen didn't answer; she just continued watching Frank's approach. Following Helen's line of sight, Potts glanced in Frank's direction. "Him again. Do you want me to handle it?"

"No." She moved forward to meet him.

Frank wasted no time pulling her into his arms, tight against him. He kissed her cheek. "I'm so sorry," he whispered in her ear. "I didn't know."

Her arms seemed to move on their own, wrapping themselves around him, holding him tight. "It's not important."

"But it is!" He held her back at arm's length. "I thought it would be easier for you to go on without me."

"It was too late for that."

"I know that now. I wasted so much time. Time, I could have—" He couldn't go on.

"How were you to know?" she managed, tears coursing down her cheeks.

Damn, Freddie is right. I'm as stupid as dirt! The last one to figure it all out.

He continued to study her face, gazing into her eyes. Through the tears, it was finally plain to him. He had loved her from that first moment.

But there was still hope!

He was still here. God had sent him here to fix this, and as long as he was here, there had to be a way. One last act to fix it all. And he now knew, not just hoped, but knew like he knew the sun would rise tomorrow no matter what else happened, that moment would come. All he had to do was stay alert, watching, ready to act when it did. The Germans, in their arrogance and stupidity, would make a mistake and give him one last chance. But for now, he was happy just to hold her and to feel her warmth against him. He would have loved to have held her for a lifetime, to drift off to sleep each evening beside her, to watch their children grow, and to be that little old couple holding hands as they walked into the sunset together. But this—if it was all they had, it was enough to have known her and felt her love.

Thank you, God. His life now had meaning. He counted. In the end, God had given him his greatest wish, to be a hero in her eyes.

She reached up and pulled his face down into a kiss. Their lips touched, and he felt her warmth as he tasted her sweetness.

"So, touching," came the mocking voice from the deck above.

Frank pulled away, pushing her behind him as he turned to face Freddie, who stood there with Mac and the German lieutenant.

The interviews were finished; all the crew and passengers were now on the well deck. It was time to go.

"Tell the little whore goodbye, Mister Ross," Freddie continued.

Frank turned toward her and took her hands in his. He leaned forward and kissed her lightly on the lips. He mouthed, "I love you," for his voice was suddenly absent. With tears coursing down her cheeks, Helen squeezed his hands and found her voice, too, was gone. They embraced, their arms wrapping around each other one last time.

He felt the cold metal of the gun pressed against his side. He glanced down. She opened her hand enough for him to see. It was Mac's gun, the one he had given her down in number four. The Germans had failed to search her; she was only a nurse after all. He looked up. She smiled. They didn't need words; he could see it in her eyes. He took the gun as they slowly parted.

"Parting is such sweet sorrow," Freddie mocked them.

Frank took one last look at her and turned to his final task. He felt the weight of the revolver as he slipped it into his pocket. Mac's gun, it was fitting, somehow.

At the foot of the ladder, a German sailor met him with another of those submachine guns. With the barrel, he indicated Frank was to continue up the ladder to join his enemies above.

He glanced over toward Bailey. He smiled, and Bailey nodded farewell. Frank climbed the ladder, both hands on the railing; otherwise, everyone might see the trembling that he suddenly couldn't stop.

At the top, he willed his hands to stay away from his pocket, lest he give away his plan.

The Lieutenant addressed him. "We have decided that you might know something of value to the Reich. Thus, I am afraid you will have to accompany us."

Behind him, Freddie grinned. "Though, in the end, you might wish you died here with the little bitch."

"Enough," the lieutenant commanded.

Freddie continued smiling.

"The boat is waiting."

Frank stood still at the railing as the lieutenant stepped back to let Mac and Freddie move past him toward the boat waiting for them at the port side accommodation ladder.

Freddie passed Frank first, the grin still in place. He was enjoying himself, believing he had won.

Then, Mac went by, the briefcase tucked under his arm. He had no intention of letting it out of his sight. It was just as Frank knew it would be. Too bad simply destroying the plans wouldn't be enough.

The lieutenant started to turn to follow Mac; for a split second, only the guard had eyes on Frank. He kept his vision centered on Mac's back as the guard tapped him with that gun barrel again, nodding for him to follow the others.

As he waited for the lieutenant to begin moving, Frank's hand slid into his pocket. His fingers slowly closed around the butt of the gun, his index finger curling over the trigger.

Everything rested on these next few moments, but nothing would stop him now.

He quickly drew the gun out of his pocket. The guard saw it emerging from under the jacket and tried to react, but it was much too late for that. It happened too fast. The gun was there in Frank's hand. His finger tightened, and the revolver exploded, a fraction of a second before the submachine gun did.

The bullet tore through the center of Mac's back and exploded out the front of his chest, taking a chunk of his heart with it. Mac spun around in space and saw the line of bullets rip across Frank's chest, but Frank was already moving. Momentum would finish the job.

He fell headfirst into Mac, throwing the dying man over the rail into the blue water below. Mac hit with a huge splash and instantly disappeared, as Frank hoped, taking the briefcase with him.

Frank came up hard against the railing and just barely stopped himself from following Mac over the side. His strength was all but gone. His legs collapsed under him, and he sat down at the railing, turning back toward the Germans. He heard a scream somewhere far away. He glanced down at his chest. "What a mess," he managed before looking up at Freddie.

Freddie was redder than anybody Frank had ever seen before, and he casually wondered how long it would be before that vein across Freddie's forehead exploded.

The former mess boy stared down at the dying man, the fool he had led around in circles for days but who in the end had beaten him. Mac, the plans, and the machine were all gone. Frank had won, and Freddie's anger raged within. The bastard was too far gone to hurt. He wouldn't feel it. But there was a way to strike at him even now.

He realized his gun was already in his hand. He must hurry before the bastard died.

There she was, doing the work for him. Helen burst onto the boat deck, her face one of rage. Freddie pulled the trigger.

A bright red spot suddenly appeared in the center of her blue and white uniform. She stopped dead in her tracks.

Freddie glanced down at Frank to see if—

"You animal." The lieutenant swore as he pulled his trigger.

Freddie felt the bullet for an instant as it tore into his skull, and then he was tumbling into darkness.

Everyone stood still as Frank, his chest gaping open from a half dozen bullets, fought to his knees and caught Helen as she collapsed.

His strength was gone just as suddenly as it had appeared, and he fell back against the railing. Helen ended up in his lap. She smiled up at him. "You didn't think I would let you go on alone?" she whispered.

"No." He couldn't hold his head up any longer. It slid over against an upright, and he found himself staring up toward Helen, though he could still feel her body in his lap. She stood there in unblemished white, her hand stretched out for him, her green eyes beckoning him on as a white light enveloped them both.

EPILOGUE

It was hard. Hard to believe he was gone. Twelve days he had hung on, even rallied a couple of times or at least seemed to, but in the end, the damage was too significant, and the old man had passed away, still deep in the coma caused by his heart attack. They had been with him at the time. It was something they had feared; he had been in poor health for the last several years, but you're never really ready for it when it happens.

EMS had responded quickly. She thanked God for that. She was also glad Bill was there. She couldn't have gone through it alone. Even though he was Bill's father, they had grown close in the years since she married Bill.

She glanced over at her husband, so much like the old man, who was silently surfing through the dozens of books stacked on the two bookcases here in the small room he had used as an office. Bill had taken his father's death extremely hard; he was the youngest and had always been very close to his father. They were always doing things together, arguing over the issues of the day, so much alike they reinforced each other's points. She wasn't sure how Bill was going to handle this loss.

Maybe the act of going through the old man's stuff, sorting and packing it up, was helping to bring back memories of the good times they had shared. It always seemed to help her, and Bill was looking better today.

She pulled open the next drawer on the desk. It contained several hanging files, most with loose papers in them. Pushing them back, she read through the pages in the first folder. They were copies of old bills. She pulled one out, a water bill three, no four years old. *Why in the hell did he still have these? Why was he even still getting hard copies? I guess habits are hard to break.*

She wiped away another tear that had somehow escaped. How many did that make?

She was about to close the drawer when she noticed the last folder, all the way in the back. The pages weren't loose. No, it was a binder, a thick one, held together by a pair of silver rings.

She pulled it out of the folder. The blue cover was blank, but she went ahead and started to flip through the pages. It was a story, typed, double spaced, clean.

"What's this?" she asked, holding up the binder.

Bill glanced over his shoulder, "What?"

"This." She handed it to him.

He began flipping through it. "Oh, he wrote it out."

"Wrote what out?"

"Grandma's story."

She continued to register a blank. Her face a mirror as she waited for more information, but he just continued to skim the pages. "Well?" she prompted.

"Oh, back in the war, World War II, Grandma was a Red Cross nurse. Well, they sent her to England the summer before Pearl Harbor, I think. One of the nurses had an affair with one of the officers on the ship. They didn't make it to England. Somewhere in the middle of the ocean, the Germans sunk the ship. Grandma ended up spending ten days in an open lifeboat, but her friend and the guy were both killed during the sinking." He lapsed into silence, reading.

"That sounds so sad."

"It was. There were even rumors that the officer was a spy and that someone sabotaged the ship. Supposedly, the Germans searched the ship before sinking it, looking for something. Anyway, several people ended up dead, including Grandma Phyllis's friend."

He put the binder down on the desk, "Father always said it would make a great story. Talked about writing it up someday." He glanced down at the binder. "I guess he finally did."

THE END

AFTERWORD

Of course, *A Hero's Passage* is foremost a work of fiction, but to lend realism to it, I have based it on and included elements from real life. The *Polites* never really sailed the seven seas, but in most details, she is remarkably like thousands of other ships that did in the years before and after the Second World War. And like most of those ships, her crew is a cosmopolitan group from most of the major maritime countries of the world.

In this case, the *Polites* has stepped in for a real ship, a Norwegian freighter called the *Vigrid* that sailed with convoy HX-133 from Halifax in June 1941. She was carrying a group of ten American Red Cross nurses traveling to England. They were going to assist the English people, the non-combatants, who were suffering at the time under the lash of the German Blitz. Like the *Polites*, she suffered engine trouble (though probably not caused by a German spy) and lagged behind the convoy, where U-371 found and sunk her with the help of two

German made torpedoes. All the passengers and crew, forty-seven souls, safely abandoned the ship in her four lifeboats. Two headed north toward Greenland and the other two east toward Iceland (both destinations were about the same distance away). The two little groups tried to stay together, but the wind, the sea, and the lack of sleep eventually drove the four boats apart. An American destroyer found one of the northbound lifeboats eleven days after the sinking, and a British warship found one of the eastbound boats eight days after that. The other two lifeboats with twenty-six people, including four of the nurses, were never seen again. As for Mac and his secret crate, they are my Maguffin, borrowing a term from another creator of fiction, one far greater than I.

Off the ship, Commander Ian Fleming, of James Bond fame, part of British Intelligence at the time, did, in fact, visit the United States and Canada in June 1941, though not to meet Frank Ross and Colonel "Wild Bill" Donavan in Halifax. However, he may have met Wild Bill, President Roosevelt's emissary to the British in Washington. But if he had got to Halifax, he could have, like Frank and Helen, had lunch at the Green Lantern and taken in a movie at the Orpheus or Capital theaters downtown, maybe even watched *Blood and Sand*.

Finally, as for my anonymous hero, he too is a creation of my imagination, and though there is some of me in his makeup, most writers write to experience life through someone else's eyes, to walk in someone else's shoes. Then again, don't we all enjoy a good daydream now and then?

GLOSSARY OF TERMS

ABLE SEAMAN: a fully qualified member of the deck department.

ACCOMMODATION LADDER: a portable flight of steps down a ship's side.

AFT: toward the stern or rear of a vessel.

AIREDALES: a naval term for aviators.

ALDIS LAMP: a signal lamp used for optical communication between ships at sea.

THE ANDREW: traditional slang term for the Royal Navy.

ATHWARTSHIPS: at right angles to the fore and aft or centerline of a ship.

AUXILIARIES: machinery other than the main engines, such as generators and pumps.

AYE, AYE: a reply to an order or command to indicate that it, firstly, is heard, and, secondly, is understood and will be carried out.

BATTEN: any thin strip of material, especially wood.

BEAUFORT SCALE: a scale describing wind speed devised in 1808.

BEAM: the width of a vessel at its widest point, or a point alongside the ship at the midpoint of its length.

BINNACLE: the stand on which the ship's compass is mounted.

BITT: a post or pair of posts mounted on the ship's bow for fastening ropes.

BOATS: traditional slang name for the Bosun.

BONE IN HER TEETH: a slang term for a prominent bow wave as a result of high speed.

BOOM: a spar attached to the mast used to lift and lower cargo in and out of the holds.

BOSUN: a non-commissioned officer who is the senior member and supervisor of the deck department.

BOW: the front of a vessel.

BRIDGE: a structure above the weather deck, which houses the command center of the ship.

BRIDGE WING: a narrow walkway extending outward from the bridge or pilothouse.

BSC: British Security Co-ordination: a covert organization in New York City to investigate enemy activity in the Americas during World War II.

BULKHEAD: an upright wall within the hull of a ship.

BULWARK: the extension of a ship's side above the level of the weather deck.

CABLE LENGTH: a measure of length or distance equivalent to 600 feet in the U.S.

CANUCK: a slang term for a Canadian.

CANVAS: a durable fabric used for making sails, tents, etc.

CHAIN LOCKER: a space in the forward part of a ship that contains the anchor chain when the anchor is secured for sea.

CHANDLER: a dealer in supplies or equipment for ships.

CHANNEL: nautical term to indicate a marked lane of safe travel with a guaranteed depth across its width.

CHOCK: an opening in a ship's bulwark designed to allow mooring lines to be fastened to bits mounted on the ship's deck.

COAMING: the raised edge of a hatch, designed to help keep out water.

COMBER: a long curving wave.

COMMODORE: a civilian put in charge of the good order of the merchant ships in a convoy.

COMPANIONWAY: a hatchway in a ship's deck with a ladder leading below.

COMPARTMENT: a portion of the space within a ship defined vertically between decks and horizontally between bulkheads.

CONVOY: a group of ships traveling together for protection.

CROSS-SEA: a sea state with nonparallel wave systems.

DAVY JONES: a slang name for the spirit of the sea or the sea itself, as in Davy Jones' locker.

DEADEYE: a device used to guide and control a line usually round with three holes in it.

DECK: any of the structures forming the horizontal surfaces in the ship's general structure.

DODGER: a hood or structure used to protect the crew from wind and spray.

DOGS: a handle used to secure a hatch or door through a watertight bulkhead, usually used in groups.

ENSIGN: the principal flag flown by a ship to indicate her nationality.

EOT: engine order telegraph: a communications device used between the pilot and engine room to order the desired speed.

FANTAIL: the aft end of a ship.

FATHOM: a unit of length equal to 6 feet.

FIDDLEY: the uppermost part of the stokehole of a steamship.

FORE: toward the bow of a vessel.

FOREPEAK: the part of the hold at the bow of a ship.

FOULED ANCHOR: is an anchor with a chain wrapped around it used as an emblem of rank or specialty in the U.S. Navy and Merchant Marine.

GUNWALE: the upper edge of the hull, the top timber on the rail around the outer perimeter of the deck.

HARDBOARDS: hard shoulder boards worn with a uniform to indicate an officer's rank.

HATCHWAY: a covered opening in a ship's deck through which cargo can be loaded or access made to a lower deck, the cover of which is called a hatch.

HAWSEPIPE: the shaft or hole in the side of a vessel's bow through which the anchor chain passes.

HELMSMAN: the member of the crew who is responsible for steering the ship.

HOLD: the lower part of the interior of a ship's hull, especially when considered as storage space for cargo; in merchant vessels, it extended up to the underside of the weather deck.

JACK TAR: a term used to refer to seamen of the Merchant or Royal Navy.

JACOB'S LADDER: a flexible hanging ladder consisting of vertical ropes supporting horizontal rungs used to allow access over the side of a ship.

JERRY: a nickname used by Allied soldiers for German soldiers used in World War II.

KEEL: the principal structural member of a hull, positioned at or close to the lowest point of the ship.

KNEE-KNOCKER: the bottom portion of a watertight door's frame.

LIGHTSHIP: a permanently anchored vessel performing the functions of a lighthouse, typically in a location where construction of a lighthouse is impractical.

LIMEY: a slang term for Royal Navy sailors, originally due to the Royal Navy's practice of adding lime juice to the sailor's daily ration of grog (watered down rum) to fight scurvy.

MAIN DECK: the uppermost continuous deck extending from bow to stern.

MARKS: also called plimsoll line: a special marking, positioned amidships, that indicate the draft of the vessel and the legal limit to which the vessel may be loaded.

MAST: a vertical pole on a ship that supports sails or rigging.

MONKEY ISLAND: a high platform above the wheelhouse offering better visibility.

OFFICER OF THE DECK: an officer stationed on the bridge who is in charge of the navigation and safety of the ship during the watch.

OILSKIN: a type of cloth used for foul weather gear and to protect documents from the sea.

ORDINARY SEAMAN: a rating for entry-level personnel in the deck department.

OVERHEAD: the ceiling of any enclosed space below decks in a vessel.

PASSAGEWAY: an interior corridor or hallway on a ship.

PILOT: a specially trained person qualified to navigate a vessel through difficult waters.

POINT: a unit of bearing equal to 11.25 degrees or one thirty-second of a circle.

PORT: the left side of a ship or vessel.

PROW: an alternative poetic term for the bow of a vessel.

QUARTER: either side of the stern or rear of a ship.

RED DUSTER: a slang term for the naval ensign of the British Merchant Navy, a red flag with the Union Jack in the upper left corner.

RIGGING: the system of masts and lines on ships and other sailing vessels.

ROOSTER TAIL: the disturbance created by a ship's passage through the water.

RUDDER: a steering device that is placed aft, externally relative to the keel.

SAD SACK: a slang term for an inept person.

SCAPA FLOW: a body of water in the Orkney Islands used by the Royal Navy as their chief naval base during both World Wars.

SCREW: a propeller.

SCUPPERS: a series of openings in the bulwarks for draining water overboard.

SCUTTLE: a small opening, or lid thereof, in a ship's deck or hull.

SIS: Secret Intelligence Service: British intelligence agency also known as MI6.

SQUALL: a sudden sharp increase in wind speed associated with a storm.

STANDING WIRES: rigging that supports masts and spars in contrast with running rigging.

STARBOARD: the right side of a ship or vessel.

STEM: an extension of the keel at the forward end of a ship.

STERN: the rear part of a ship.

STOKEHOLD: the boiler room of a ship.

SUPERSTRUCTURE: the parts of a ship that project above the main deck not including the masts.

TILLER: a lever used for steering, attached to the top of the rudder.

TRAMP STEAMER: a steamship engaged in the spot market with no fixed schedule or itinerary, will take any cargo available to any port it can reach.

TRAWLER: a fishing boat that uses a net to catch fish.

'TWEEN DECK: any deck on a cargo ship located between the main deck and the hold.

UNION JACK: the national flag of the United Kingdom of Great Britain and Northern Ireland.

WEATHER DECK: any deck exposed to the weather, usually the main deck and above.

WEATHER DOOR: any door which opens on to an exposed deck or weather deck.

WELL DECK: a weather deck lower than the decks fore and aft of it with bulwarks or railings outboard.

WHEELHOUSE: structure on a ship where the wheel is located, also called the pilothouse or bridge.